I filled a syringe with morphine.

Could innocent blood ever be washed away?

Would my hands ever be clean again if I continued on this course? The gas would make them choke, gasping for breath as life was strangled to nothingness. Morphine would make them euphoric, and an overdose would put them to sleep, peacefully, with no pain. A sleep from which they would not wake, but they would be safe from the evil that awaited them otherwise.

I filled the second syringe. I thought of each child as I punctured the rubber stopper, the needle sucking up the lethal fluid filling the tube. *Little Wilhelm.* My treasured leader of the pack. The braces on his legs never stopped his imagination from soaring. *Lara.* An artist's soul expressed with the one good hand she had. Art reflective of the beauty living in her heart. *The twins.* Isn't intelligence measured with creativity? I would sorely miss their energy.

My hand slipped, and the needle grazed the knuckle of my thumb. I swore and bit my lip. *Perfect. I'll kill myself before I get a chance to euthanize my children. Then, after I enter Heaven's gates, if He lets me inside them, God can tell me I am an idiot and a murderer.*

I rubbed my shoulders. They hunched with an invisible weight that made my back ache.

Kindertransport

by

Jennifer Childers

Kindertransport

COPYRIGHT © 2008 by Jennifer Childers

Cover Art by *Nicola Martinez*

The Wild Rose Press
PO Box 706
Adams Basin, NY 14410-0706
Visit us at www.thewildrosepress.com

Publishing History
First Vintage Rose Edition, 2009
Print ISBN 1-60154-522-3

Published in the United States of America

Dedication

To the heroes, saints and martyrs
whose names we will never know.

Prologue

My tiny patient lay in her bassinette. A protective tent covered it, feeding her oxygen and keeping her isolated. Hollow eyes rimmed with blue circles looked at me with complete trust. Her feet, purple from lack of circulation, wiggled slightly, working their way out of her white receiving blanket. It was against the rules, but when she cried, I picked her up and cuddled her in the rocking chair, humming, soothing her back to sleep.

"I'm sorry, angel." I wished there were more I could do.

I angled the baby so her head was higher than her feet, helping her to breathe more easily. As she nestled her head against me, I held the swaddled infant close, keeping her warm, breathing in the soft scent which graced every newborn. She would be in Heaven soon. I wondered what she could accomplish in such a short time on earth, but I do truly believe God has a purpose for everything. Still, it hurt to know this precious package would be gone so soon.

Her condition was incurable. Tetralogy of Fallot was a death sentence. Regardless of the diagnosis, comforting her in her last days was more important than hospital policy. I could get fired for breaking the rules, but I couldn't leave her to die alone. With my armload of treasure, I hummed and rocked and hoped she would die knowing someone loved her.

Blue babies were never expected to live long. The heart beating within the tiny chest did not pump the blood into the pulmonary artery to be oxygenated, leaving her cyanotic, hence the name 'blue baby.' Sometimes death comes in a week, sometimes a month. Her face would live in my heart always.

"She is sweet, isn't she?" Gretchen spoke. She leaned in at the doorway and smiled at us, pausing to peer along the hallway to make sure no one neared the room. I held my breath. Courage is always easier to come by when the risk of being caught is small. "It's clear. The other girls must be on supper break."

I exhaled. The little package snuggled closer to me. I could swear she sensed my feelings. "Good. I'm sorry, but I just feel if she is going to die anyway, rocking her can't hurt."

"I won't tell," she promised.

That moment cemented my friendship with Gretchen.

When death was imminent, I notified the parents and called a priest to issue the last rites. Gretchen and I prayed with the family, lending support in every way we could. The hardest thing I ever had to do was talk to the parents. I wanted to ease the pain, but no words could erase the loss or bring the baby back.

Gretchen put an arm around me. We watched the service and participated when appropriate. She didn't believe in infant baptism, but as a nurse she had agreed to care for the whole family. An emergency baptism was performed, and the baby died at peace.

On Christmas Eve, I gave the baby post mortem care. My heart ached, and tears fell in a damp path down my cheeks. She would never see her first Christmas, I realized, as I said goodbye.

A funeral would be held in three days, according to tradition. I cried, and prayed, and kept the faith. And that was as it should be.

Chapter 1

On Christmas morning, 1938, Germany celebrated the strengthening of a nation, a growing economy, and the resurgence of national pride. The Reich had promised respect, a new world order, and justice after the unfairness of the Versailles treaty. Jobs were available in factories like Porsche. The creation of an affordable car, the Volkswagen, would put a car in every garage. The economy was growing again, and most people were happy.

The Reich had kept its promise. Germany rose above the losses of the last war, as well as the deprivation of the fruits of our labor. The cost for this national strength was paid for with loss of personal liberty.

With this in mind, I made my way to Gretchen's house with the intent of inviting her to church with me. Her own religion had been outlawed. My faith meant a lot to me, and I was determined Gretchen should be allowed to worship with me, even though Catholics, while free to practice, were looked on with distrust. This suspicion went back to the Versailles Treaty, signed by a Catholic and a Social Democrat. Both groups were now viewed as potential enemies of the state.

Wishing we had time for a hot cup of coffee before we left, I felt the brisk morning air lay chilled fingers across my cheeks, while snow crunched under my feet, covering the landscape in a sparkling, white blanket. As I walked along the quiet street, I noted very few people had ventured out that early. Two-story residential buildings stood in neat rows along the clean streets. Skeletons of trees lined the road, while forgotten flowerbeds lay dormant along the walls.

As I neared Gretchen's apartment, I stalled in my tracks, trying to understand what I witnessed. This could not be happening! Nervous perspiration dampened my underarms, and my heart pounded as, helplessly, I watched the Gestapo lead Gretchen away. The uniformed man seemed to take some care, offering his arm to steady her as she walked down the three steps leading to the street. A Brown Shirt opened the car door, and she climbed inside, offering no resistance. The officers were oddly polite. *Brutes with manners,* I thought bitterly. I wished I could see her, just once, to let her know I cared and knew she had done nothing wrong.

Tinted windows kept me from seeing Gretchen's face for a final goodbye, but I watched for several minutes, waiting for the car to pull away. The sleek, black vehicle stood in dominant contrast against the snowy landscape, like a dark predator, a symbol of uncontested power.

Why had they come for her? She didn't deserve this unfair treatment. Gretchen possessed sweetness like honey lavished upon warm bread. She reminded me of everyone's grandmother. A woman of faith, Gretchen solved problems with a cup of cocoa and a dose of common sense. Common sense to her meant a refusal to sign a mandatory pledge of loyalty to Adolph Hitler. This defiant action, combined with an adamant refusal to give the Hitler salute, must have been what led up to the scene I witnessed.

My blood froze in my veins as I stared from across the street. She had tried to tell me. Her words blazoned themselves in my brain like a prophetic branding iron: "Oppression is like the bruising of an apple," she had said. "It starts as a spot which, if not cut away, will eventually eat into the very core of the fruit." Now, for her, it ended with a ride in a long black car with smoky windows.

There were a couple of people who shared the street with me that morning. A woman walked her dog, and the dachshund raised its leg to water the naked tree.

A man strode toward the spot the car had just left. Could he be Gestapo, as well? Our eyes met, and I looked away. Did he recognize me as Gretchen's friend? Would it seem suspicious to anyone if I ran from the scene? My thighs tensed, but instead of hurrying, I turned to walk onward. The rattling of a trashcan lid caused my heart to beat against my chest. The neighborhood bustled with activity where moments ago it had seemed so quiet.

I quickened my steps, certain I could hear the crunch of footsteps in the snow behind me as I came to a bend in the street. The church stood only a few blocks away, its white cross beckoning me to hurry on, a promise of safety against the snowy sky. I fixed my eyes upon this beacon. Certain I was out of sight from the scene of Gretchen's abduction, I turned and ran. It was all I could think to do. The wind stole my breath, and the cold dried my throat, but I could not stop.

The church bells rang, flooding my heart with hope. If I could reach the church, there would be sanctuary from the chaos filling my mind. Father Julian, who had been pastor there since I was a little girl, could help me make sense of all this. A stitch in my side became a stabbing pain, but absolute fear commanded my legs to pump harder, propelling me ever closer to my destination. I wanted to hide from the memory of what I had just seen and seek refuge in the one place where life would make sense.

At the top of the church steps I tripped, my foot slid, and I sucked in a breath to brace for impact, certain I would sprawl unceremoniously. When my face didn't hit the pavement, I realized I had been caught. A pair of strong arms held me at my waist and held me close.

"Oh, *danke schön*, thank you!" My relief came out in a rush. Placing a hand on the leather-clad arm, I steadied myself to stand upright and look my rescuer in the face. His eyes were blue as a summer sky, framed by golden hair neatly clipped above his collar. My throat closed up again, and words failed to escape from a parched mouth. A square jaw dominated the chiseled Nordic features. His straight, sharp nose gave him a look of intelligence, while the cleft in his chin made me think of the classic marble busts in the museum, masculine beauty preserved for generations.

Say something, moron, I coaxed myself, as shyness took over once again, and the cold wind stole my breath before the words ever formed. Swallowing hard, I forced words from my throat. "I've never seen you here before."

The corners of his mouth upturned slightly. I looked away from the blue depths and realized he still held me, and my heart leapt as though I were sledding downhill.

"I'm from Munich originally." His voice poured over me like melted chocolate. I felt that for a moment I'd found a safe harbor. I could see his breath when he spoke, and a flurry of butterflies erupted within me. I gently pushed away, taking a step back, suddenly too aware of his closeness. The clean smell of soap riding on the crisp wind threatened my equilibrium. The excitement of the downhill racer touched me once more.

"Let me help you, *Fräulein*." The man's gentle baritone voice wrapped me in velvet warmth. His square hands were ungloved despite the cold. Releasing me, he moved with slow deliberation. Easing his arms from around my waist, he moved a gentle hand to rest on the bend of my elbow. I straightened, brushing strands of unruly hair off my face. I thought of Gretchen and how the Gestapo officer had held her, steadying her by her elbow, assisting her to her fate. I pulled away, needing the sanctuary of my church.

"I really should go." I pointed toward the building, easing nearer the front door.

"Were you being chased?" he asked, looking back the way I'd come, his eyes following my path in the snow.

"No, not chased." I felt grateful the lot was empty of people. No one followed me, and no black car seemed intent on finding me. What if he were one of them? Fear overloaded the circuits of my mind. Could this man have seen me across the street from Gretchen's abduction? No, he couldn't have seen me there and then show up here so soon, could he? My imagination ran wild. I had to get away. I had to get answers, but the answers wouldn't be here on the church steps.

Backing up toward the church door, I felt for the handle. The need to escape returned with a vengeance. I turned quickly and, pulling the door open, smacked myself in the head and winced in pain.

He was at my side in a moment. The man moved quickly for someone so large. Head and shoulders over me, the stranger caught the door and held it open. I rubbed my forehead.

I had to tilt my head to look into his face again. Then, allowing my gaze to slip, I noted the leather jacket gave him the appearance of a large bear, exaggerating the size of his arms and chest. "Will you be all right?" His hand traveled along my forearm to take my hand. I jerked away as though burned.

"Of course. I'm all right. Really." Hand to my

chest, I hurried into the sanctuary. Breathing in the warmth of the church, I commanded my body to quit trembling, even as I willed the peace of the sanctuary to overwhelm me. Peace would not be had. I trembled from his nearness. I needed to reach the safety of the holy place where I could hide behind my safeguards against the world.

Here, away from the world outside, candles glowed, incense scented the air, and familiarity calmed me. The sun shining through the stained glass windows splashed patches of color across those parishioners prayerfully seated. I moved to join them.

That morning's events were not conducive to feeling at peace, so my rescuer never had a chance. I'm not skilled with talking to men. It isn't shyness so much as my mouth gets ahead of my brain, and I either freeze up or say something that makes them wonder if I am borderline retarded. It wouldn't matter. My handsome rescuer from Munich would forget about me easily enough. I was certain I would never see him again.

"Lord, keep me from turning into an ice sculpture around men." I wished I had my mother's talent for conversation. Men from sixteen to sixty seemed enchanted by her wit, though it could be tempered with sarcasm easily enough. I had made peace with the idea of being single, though it was the bane of my mother's existence as more young girls from the church became brides while she worked in the bakery decorating yet another beautiful wedding cake for someone else's daughter.

"Lord, if it isn't too much trouble, I would like to find someone. If I am not meant to get married, could you please break it to my mother gently?"

I rose for the hymn, palms resting on the pew in front of me, eyes closed, face tilted upward. My spirit rose with the sound of the music as though I could ride the melody to a peaceful refuge safe from worry.

The soft rustle of robes told me Father Julian made his way toward the altar. His regal bearing exuded confidence, bold strides carrying him forward, rather like a lion quietly ruling his domain until ready to pounce.

"You may be seated." The priest addressed the congregation. We moved as one while the priest studied the room. I glanced around me. Most occupants looked attentive. Uniformed SS and Gestapo were in the pews. Even some altar boys wore the Hitler youth uniform under their robes. Despite this, Father Julian always spoke as though determined his words would strike home, as would a blacksmith's hammer, shaping ideas into an acceptable form, never censoring his words. I closed my eyes, ready to channel each word and embrace its meaning.

His feet firmly planted, the determined man began to speak. "The angel appeared to Joseph in a dream and told him 'Wake up! Take the baby and flee to the land of Egypt, for the king wants to kill him.' They fled to safety in a foreign land and remained until the king died."

Father Julian was a man dedicated to the truth. He never expected it to be pretty or popular; he simply expected it to be. He never sugarcoated a fact; he knew the seeds of truth, once sewn, would either take root or die. I listened as he continued. "The Christmas story is more than a story about the birth of the Lord. It is a story about promise and victory in the face of adversity."

Father Julian spoke with authority, undeterred by the number of Brown Shirts among the flock. His palms on either side of the Bible, his thoughts centered on it, his commanding voice could not be ignored. "The Reich has not honored its promise to allow Catholics to practice the faith unmolested. Our schools have been closed and our newspapers are censored. Most upsetting is the new law regarding involuntary euthanasia. Involuntary mercy killing. Isn't there another word for that?"

His words challenged, and I noticed many parishioners shifted their gazes or moved to get comfortable. I wondered if the Brown Shirts felt guilty. Those who had arrested Gretchen weren't in church this morning, but I found myself looking across the church. No uniforms were moving toward the altar. I tried to relax. Father Julian continued. "As you know, last month a massive, violent riot took place against our fellow Germans. In response to this incident, the British parliament has agreed to open her borders and allow ten thousand German children to flee to the safety of a foreign land."

I felt fear begin to gnaw the corners of my mind as Father Julian spoke. "The Kindertransport will be offered to those with the greatest need, like children who have had one or both parents arrested, or who are living in one of the resettlement centers."

Leave the country? Why would children have to leave the country? *It is safer than living here,* a small voice in the back of my head answered. I had worked the night of the riots, the night of broken glass. I wanted to tell myself what I had heard were exaggerations. Gossip got juicier with the telling. The truth was, however, that people were scared. Whispers gave way to cautious looks over shoulders to be sure no one overheard. A once-unified German people became more disunited as liberties were chiseled away a piece at a time. How desperate has a situation become when a parent exports his child to give her a chance at the liberty being denied him or her at home?

I heard Father Julian sigh, as he paused to sweep his gaze over the people. I wondered what he searched for. Outrage? Concern? Did he see the hideous neutral mask that comes when a situation mustn't seem to concern the individual? For myself, the idea that such a thing could be necessary numbed my mind. What had happened to us? How could we turn against defenseless children? I held my arms close to my body and listened. "Parliament requires a bond of fifty pounds sterling as a resettlement fee per child. Registration is to be held in all the major Jewish temples. The transport will take these children by train to the Netherlands. From there, they will be ferried to Harwich or Southampton, England. I am asking you to wake up and pray for the success of the transport and for the compassion of our *Deutsches* German leaders."

He emphasized the nationality. I realized he was telling us that as Germans we were connected, and that as Catholics we should have social justice as a priority. Would there be a time when faith and duty would be at odds? My heart went out to Gretchen. I knew I would never see her again. Head in my hands, I rocked back and forth. Where would this end?

Resettlement. Children would be leaving in a mass exodus to England, without their parents. I felt for those children who did not speak English. How frightening for a child to be sent away from his or her family to live with strangers, unable to even speak to them, in some cases. Had things really gotten that bad?

Of course, they had, another part of my mind chided. The police had been replaced with Gestapo. Catholic schools were closed three years ago. Only carefully worded articles appeared in Catholic newspapers, and Catholic youth groups, even the Boy Scouts, were disbanded.

Now my friend Gretchen had been taken away, missing, as were others from the hospital. I would speak with Father Julian after the service today. He could give me advice. After Gretchen's arrest, I was sure I should quit my job. It could easily have been a hospital employee who reported her. I shifted in my seat and glanced at my watch, urging time to move a bit faster. The church seemed so crowded, and I feared someone could link me with Gretchen. I shook the thought from my head. I wouldn't submit to fear.

I closed my eyes and listened to the words of the priest—most of them, anyway. I heard the words, but my brain refused to translate what they meant. Unconsciously I began to tap my foot, causing my leg to tremble. *Relax*! I commanded myself.

"Turn to your neighbor and offer the sign of peace." The priest was the picture of tranquility as he spoke from the pulpit.

I turned and shook the hand of the person next to me, offering a sign of peace. The ritual was meant to promote peace among fellow Christians, showing we are brothers in Christ. I turned to the person sitting behind me, offering my hand as I did so, and felt as though the floor had fallen from beneath me when I discovered my rescuer sitting behind me.

"Peace," I chimed softly.

"To you, as well," came the deep baritone voice. His blue eyes looked into mine once more as his large hand clasped mine gently yet firmly. Electricity seared through my fingertips, jump-starting my heart. At the sound of his voice I was a marshmallow melting over a flame, yet I nodded politely, averting my gaze to avoid his eyes. His thumb brushed along the bare flesh of my hand. I pulled away slightly, and the stranger slowly released me.

He left as the last song played, a practice I thought rude. It is bad manners to leave before the priest, yet, I, too, yearned to get out of the now stifling building.

Chapter 2

The rectory was a small house where the parish priests made their home. In addition to the common room and reception area, each priest had a private office. Making my way up the path to the door, I tapped on the rectory door with a gloved hand. Opening the door a crack, I announced myself. There was no response.

The short hallway led to the sitting room, and to my right was an office. I was certain Father Julian was here, as he was not outside speaking to the parishioners. I pocketed my gloves and placed my hat and coat on the coat rack in the corner before peering into the office. The large desk was vacated, its surface neatly organized. I had often teased Father Julian that a true genius preferred a creative mess.

I heard the murmur of voices down the hall. Padding along the wooden floorboards, I made my way toward the sitting room, then paused to listen. One of the voices sounded unfamiliar. Hairs stood at attention as I heard the words more clearly. "If you can't watch your mouth, watch your back."

Insulted at the tone used toward the priest, I rested against the wall to listen.

"Rick, I have a responsibility to two things: the truth and the people." This was the voice of Father Julian.

It was rude to eavesdrop, but curiosity overcame bad manners as I continued to listen, hoping to identify the second speaker.

"Very noble. What good will it do when you are

arrested? I would hate to see the church lose its spiritual leader."

I could hear the calm self-assurance in Father Julian's voice, the cool logic he used when he counseled. If he was being threatened, he didn't sound concerned.

"I cannot hide behind the pulpit. I have a duty to lead."

"Well, you can't lead from prison! Need I remind you the Gestapo sits in your church? Hitler Youth serve as altar boys!" Harsh, stabbing words sliced through the air, startling me. Prison? I placed my fingers over my lips as I pressed myself against the wall.

"Duty to God comes before duty to state," came the cleric's unruffled reply.

"Can you maintain your duty to God without a target on your back?"

"What would you have me do, Rickard? Pretend I don't see what is going on? Thirty thousand people were arrested last month! Am I to believe they all are guilty of some heinous crime against the state? If I say nothing, is it not the same as condoning this action?"

"You are challenging the Gestapo."

"Have I said anything untrue?" he asked. I could tell the other man's words had missed their mark. Father Julian was not a man who strayed from what he believed. I wondered if the priest was in some kind of trouble. Should I back out slowly, unnoticed, or should I make myself known and let Father Julian know he had my support, regardless of what anyone else said?

"Truth is not the issue. Trust me, you do not want to be questioned by the wrong people."

"Trust you?" the priest responded with his usual calm, and then laughed.

I peered around the corner. The fireplace

dominated the back wall with its stone hearth stretched across it. Large bookcases adorned each side of the actual fireplace. No swastika blighted the room. No portrait of the Führer blemished the walls, and no Nazi symbolism marred the décor. Instead, the pale blue walls and rust-colored carpet accented the dark furnishings. A cocoa-colored loveseat rested against a wall, and a dark wood coffee table sat in front of it. Large, overstuffed, dark blue chairs formed a circle about the table. The source of the strange voice had his back to me. Father Julian, if he happened to turn his head, would see me. Was the unknown man issuing a threat, or a warning, or just stating a fact?

I was helpless to aid Gretchen, but I would not leave the cleric to face this harassment alone. Taking in a breath for courage, I prepared to make myself known.

"Losing you would be a great loss. Detainment centers are not pleasant." The man's whispered voice had grown harsh, and I bristled at the sound. No one would threaten Father Julian. I'd lost Gretchen, and I would not stand by and risk him, too.

Anger destroyed reason as I burst through the entryway. I would defend him no matter what. "How dare you speak to the priest in that tone."

I stood fuming in the doorway and looked at the two men. The priest tilted his head toward the sound of my voice, seemingly unaffected by my sudden presence. The other man stood quickly, fists clenched at his side, his eyes boring into me.

I gasped sharply and took a step back. The voice was of the stranger I'd run into earlier, the man who had sat behind me during the service. I felt small, like a mouse suddenly confronted with a housecat, its claws unsheathed and extended, ready to pounce and do severe damage. Nevertheless, I swallowed my fear and steeled myself for confrontation. Losing

Father Julian would rip my world apart. I refused to back down.

"What did you hear?" The stranger's nostrils flared. His words shot like poisoned arrows. I froze to the spot, holding my breath in defense against his hard gaze.

"Relax. She comes in peace," Father Julian's voice commanded. "Tell the man, Erika."

In my mind, an image of the neighbor's Rottweiler flashed. The dog would play happily one moment, yet jump in defense of his territory the next. I raised my hand in front of me as though warding off attack, certain the blond man would lunge toward me. Instead, he relaxed his shoulders and uncurled his fingers. Recapturing my lost breath, I took a careful step sideways toward Father Julian. The priest relaxed against the back of the chair, his fingers splayed in a pyramid under his chin. "Good morning, Erika."

The simple phrase startled me. While my mind struggled to shift gears, I fought to slow my heart rate. The priest was his usual picture of calm. Rick, as Father Julian had referred to the man, resembled a bull, ready to charge. I looked from one man to the other.

Unblinking, Rick's challenging gaze dared me to speak. This was the man who had kept me from falling. My rescuer. The handsome features were stone. Any sign of his former gentility had completely disappeared. Avoiding his gaze, I still felt the weight of his stare, and I grasped the lapels of my jacket and held it close, feeling exposed. I directed my statements to the priest as I fought not to stammer. "I heard voices."

Father Julian rose from his seat and motioned me to a chair. "Please sit and be comfortable."

Nodding, I eased myself onto the sofa while I tried to understand what was happening between these two men.

"Is there a problem, sir?" I asked Father Julian, not sure what I should do now, as it was obvious the cleric was not concerned about either person in the room. The priest gave a lopsided grin in response.

"I have known Erika from the time she was in grade school," Father Julian addressed the man. "She has been a member of this church since babyhood. How old are you now, dear?"

He chose to glaze over my worry with small talk and avoid my question. I looked to him, as though an answer could be found in his eyes. My lips trembled as I tried to remain casual, but I found myself looking away from the stranger, whose stare ripped into my core. I had obviously interrupted something. Something big. Something important.

"This is Herr Rickard Sankt. Rick, Fräulein Erika Lehmeier. She was a student of mine at St. John's." Father used that maddeningly unruffled voice that made me certain he would stand in the path of a speeding locomotive without flinching if he believed it to be his duty. Was I ever going to learn what transpired between the two? Rickard rose to his full height. With the leather jacket now gone, the dark sweater clung to a boxer's torso. A nationwide dedication to fitness was being promoted. By the well-muscled look of the man, he'd taken this directive to heart.

"It's my pleasure, sir." My voice trembled. "Why were you concerned about Father Julian being arrested?"

Rickard leaned toward me. I forced myself to stay still. I wanted to run. His voice the low rumble of an engine, his breath tickled my cheek. "I expect my conversations to be private. Understood?"

"Understood." I studied my knees a moment before looking to him once more. I hated feeling like a chastised child, but I couldn't let my friend be bullied. I raised my chin and focused on Father Julian. He leaned to take my hand.

"I am lucky to have people who care for me," Father Julian soothed. My jaw unhinged. My bold rescue was dismounted. "It would appear certain teachings go unappreciated by the powers that be."

Rickard crossed an ankle over his knee, filling the chair he occupied. "You would do well to remember that."

Father Julian kept his warm gaze on me, unaffected by Rickard's words, while I tried to find words I wouldn't trip over.

"How can I help you, Erika? You came by for a reason?"

I moved to speak but shifted uncomfortably on the cushion, uncertain how to start.

"Perhaps I could wait until Herr Sankt is finished. I did interrupt, after all." I might have been jumping at shadows now, but what I'd witnessed earlier was no shadow.

"No, I've said all I need to say," Rickard responded.

"Well, it was nice meeting you." I paused, assuming he would excuse himself and leave. Instead, he seemed to relax against the arm of the chair, listening politely.

"*Sehr angenehm*. Nice to meet you, too." Rickard made no move to leave.

"Well, sir, if there is nothing else, perhaps we will meet again." Again, he made no move. I began to wonder if a blunt object thrown to his head would be too subtle. I looked toward the door and back at Rickard. "I apologize if I seem rude, but would you mind terribly?"

I smiled and waited for him to get the hint, but he remained motionless.

"Do you have a confession, Erika?" Father Julian asked.

I bit my lip. "No, but I would like to talk to you privately."

Rickard looked toward the door. I was sure he would take the hint now, but instead he stretched an arm across the chair and said, "We're alone."

"I meant Father Julian and I." I was exasperated. "Will you please go?"

The two men remained quiet a moment before the priest spoke. "Speak freely, Erika. Rickard is here to help us."

I started to protest, still wondering why the two were so persistent in staying in the room together. I took in a huge breath, hoping I could relay the story without breaking into hysterical sobs. "I saw my friend get arrested this morning. We worked at the hospital together. I think I should quit my job at the hospital before they arrest me, too."

I tossed my hands in a motion of surrender.

"Were you having issues? Did you give notice?" Father Julian asked.

"No. I invited my friend to mass. When I went to her apartment, the Gestapo was there." I rubbed my temples to ward off an approaching headache.

"Were you questioned?" Father Julian asked.

With what appeared to be obvious concern, Rickard put the tips of his fingers to his head. Father Julian listened intently, as well.

"No. I saw from across the street." I looked at Rickard again. If he were Gestapo, Father Julian would not have him here, unless he had no choice. I was losing my mind, seeing demons around every corner, I decided, so I went on with my story. "Gretchen and I would read together on our breaks. She is a Jehovah's Witness, and she likes to talk about the Bible with me. I was fine with that. It was interesting to exchange ideas. I assume someone from work reported her."

"Did you report her?" Rickard asked.

"No! Why would I? She is my friend. We studied together, which would mean we are both guilty. It's not as though we were doing anything wrong."

"Guilt would be assuaged if you turned her in. It would make it look like her rebel ideas offended you. It would make you an ally of the Gestapo instead of a dissident." Rickard's smooth voice held a hard edge I found offensive.

"Rebel? Her? She's a sweet lady who would never hurt anyone!" I felt tears burn my eyes. "Father, I would never do that."

"Rickard, please." Father made a staying motion with his hand. "She is very upset." He turned back to me. "A group of Jehovah's Witnesses were arrested for printing church material. Practice of their religion is illegal. Did you make it obvious you were reading a Catholic Bible?" Julian asked.

"She used the King James Version. She never brought pamphlets."

"The Führer's assurance that Christianity is the backbone of German culture apparently applies only to certain Christians. I'm sorry. If you say you didn't turn in your friend, I believe you."

I wiped my eyes with the back of my hand. I reasoned he couldn't be blamed for the accusation. Gestapo encouraged notification of anything that might be construed as anti-Nazi and therefore damaging to public morale.

Relief washed over me at his words. "*Danke.* I took an oath of loyalty after nursing school, an oath to my country and the Führer. Of course I want what is good for Germany."

A part of me was leery. I wanted Rickard to know I was a loyal German. I loved my country, but I would never betray a friendship. I hoped the two loyalties would never conflict.

"What about Gretchen?" Rickard urged.

"She refused to sign the oath. It conflicts with

her beliefs. She told me about some instances where people were told to sign a document denouncing their religion or be arrested. It happened in her church."

Father Julian leaned toward me. His gentle, paternal manner gave me a small amount of courage. "So, did that make you doubt your decision to take the oath?"

"No. Military people make pledges to the flag and promise to serve their country. As long as God is first, then that is all right. Right?" I looked for confirmation. Father Julian smiled. Rickard's face was devoid of expression.

"She was arrested for refusing to sign," Rickard confirmed. It was more a statement of fact than a question.

"There were a few things she didn't approve of. We were working on the maternity floor, and she wouldn't turn in the names of retarded or handicapped babies. There is a bonus given for every name turned it. She called it dirty money and told our supervisor she wasn't interested."

"Erika was going to ask to work a different floor." Father Julian explained to Rickard. I began to wonder what his interest could possibly be in all of this.

"Yes, so I wouldn't be confronted with the same problem. Am I a coward?"

"No. They gave you an option to change floors?"

"They let other nurses transfer."

Rickard listened politely to us, nodding whenever the priest spoke.

"Have you done anything to deserve suspicion?" Rickard said in a matter-of-fact tone that grated.

Annoyed, I crossed my arms over my middle. "No, like what? I love my country."

"She just isn't wild about current events," Father explained.

"When did nursing become some sort of political job? I became a nurse so I could help people." I tried to keep from whining, but the situation was overwhelming.

"Erika, I want you to consider a position at Grafeneck Castle," Father Julian stated. I was curious. A new job would be an easy answer.

"Grafeneck? I thought that was a monastery." Rickard's eyes perked with interest.

"It is. They house children with disabilities. Erika is wonderful with children. She used to work in the church nursery." Father smiled, and I cleared my throat. He had my interest.

"Do they need a nurse? I believe in rehabilitation. Some of our veterans who lost limbs during the war have learned to compensate for the loss and live very happily, I know."

"You can serve the children well with what you have learned from the veterans."

Rickard nodded as Father Julian spoke. I was encouraged by the reactions of the two men. "I was thinking the focus on the handicapped might help to raise public awareness and make more opportunities for rehabilitation. The state is already setting up clinics, right?"

"Right." Rickard seemed distracted while Father Julian spoke. "Rickard has helped me monitor the moods of the people. His job allows him a certain freedom of action." The younger man frowned slightly as the priest continued to speak. "This could be fortuitous that you have met. When can you start?"

"After the holidays, I would like to see the castle."

"I will make an appointment for you to interview."

"I'd like that." I gave my foot a gentle sway. New energy surged through my veins, and hope filled my heart.

"Did you go to the Catholic school?" Rick seemed to change his mood with this simple statement.

"Yes. I received all of my education in the Catholic school, so I suppose that leaves me with no excuse for misbehaving." I intended only a respectful response, but I couldn't stop the memory of his touch. Smiling to myself, I felt grateful for the change in topic. Dancing on proverbial hot coals was decidedly uncomfortable.

Father Julian let out a laugh. "Ah, but do not think that ever stopped her. Five detentions, five!"

"Well, five detentions in her entire school career is not so bad," Rickard commented.

"Five in six months! She and her friends were taking impromptu biology classes in the girls' bathroom." Father Julian's mirthful glance became unbearably embarrassing.

"We were learning," I protested as heat rose to my cheeks.

"She looked at naked pictures," Father explained.

"It was art!" My cheeks burned.

"That is what she tried to tell Sister Monica."

"Michelangelo!" I countered.

"I do not believe David was meant to be viewed for that purpose," Father replied in mock sternness.

"It was purely an educational endeavor."

"Sister was scandalized."

"I had no access to medical texts!" I countered.

"Sister Monica had to have a lie down, shocked as she was."

I giggled. The look on the nun's face when she took the book from my hands was comical, at best. Seems a lady did not concern herself with such matters, medical curiosity notwithstanding.

"You have an interest in art, then?" Rickard sounded clearly amused.

Feeling the heat rise, I hung my head in my hands, and then shyly glanced up. "Well, medicine, actually. It all started in Bible study, when circumcision was mentioned. I was not sure how to recognize one. Well, it is not as though I make a study of that sort of thing." My face grew hotter as I forced myself to regain composure.

"Sounds to me like you were making an effort," Rickard stated. Sitting up straight, he looked at me calmly, mischievous eyes twinkling.

I cleared my throat, determined to harness my discomfiture, and tried to look serious. "I was merely seeking to learn the difference. Medical curiosity."

"Of course it was." Rickard's amusement was obvious.

"Michelangelo studied medicine, as well." I decided to change the conversation.

"He was a grave robber who studied the dead to better his artwork," Rickard corrected.

I angled my head toward Rickard and released an exasperated sigh.

Father Julian regarded us with interest. "It appears the artist was not aware, himself, of the truth. David was a proper Jew and would have been circumcised; the sculpture is not. Perhaps in the future you should enjoy a nice landscape." The priest smiled at me.

"There would be no studies in medicine without research." I strove for a normal voice. Discussing male anatomy was not what I would have intended, especially in present company.

Rickard rubbed his chin. "Well, a dedication to research is admirable."

"It is important. Medical advancement depends on it." I found myself smiling, finally able to relax after a harrowing morning.

"The League of German Girls is sponsoring a New Year's dance. I think you should go." Father

Julian changed the subject abruptly. "I think you and Erika should go, together. I myself won't be there."

I was taken aback and wondered when Father Julian had gotten into the matchmaking business. "We just met. I'm sure Herr Sankt has plans for the holiday."

"Work makes it difficult to socialize." It was Rickard's turn to vie for a graceful exit. It was not forthcoming.

"You have time off for the holidays." It was a statement, not a question, coming from the priest.

"Yes, but I might be traveling," Rickard countered.

"Business over Christmas? Surely not."

"Regrettably, my car is in the shop."

"You can borrow mine," Father Julian replied brightly.

"What of my other responsibilities?" Rickard kept an even tone.

"Your dedication to duty is admirable." Julian laughed.

Rickard narrowed his eyes at the cleric.

My smile faded, unsure of what exactly was being said, or rather unsaid, between the two men. "I'm nineteen. I don't need an escort."

I might be dateless, but I would not have this man forced on me, though it did sting a bit to be turned down.

"I'm afraid you might, dear." The priest turned his attention to me. I studied his face. It was the usual picture of serenity. Whatever he thought, he hid it well.

"What does that mean? What has happened?" I looked from one face to the other for an answer.

"I suppose moderation would be advisable in duty as in all things." Rickard's tone was resigned.

"Wait. You aren't telling me why I need to be

escorted to this. It's only a dance, and I am not going without a reasonable explanation as to why."

Rickard cleared his throat. "A parish outside Stuttgart had an incident. A priest spoke out against the mercy killings and several boys from the Hitler Youth made a move to threaten him. An altar boy, frightened by the harassment, rang the church bells to signal trouble. All the men and boys who responded to the bell stood up to the youth, and they fled."

"Overreaction, I'm sure." Father Julian waved his hand dismissively.

"The Hitler Youth were outnumbered. Next time they might not be. The warning should ring clear."

"Rickard, there was no violence."

"Because they were outnumbered," Rickard countered.

"You think Father Julian could be targeted?" I inquired. In my mind's eye, I could see Gretchen's apartment with the sleek black Mercedes before it, the obscene blot against the purity of the snow banks lining the quiet street. It had snaked its path, like a silent predator, down the road of no return.

"Anyone could be targeted, and Catholics are not in favor right now." Rickard's stern looks softened with this response.

"Father, maybe you should listen to Rickard. What if the Gestapo made a list outlining the desirable teachings from the derelict? You could be put on that list." I worried my lip.

"Such a list would relieve people of the burden to decide for themselves what is derelict. Every effort is made to promote proper thinking," Rickard mimicked the priest's cool logic.

"Erika, you did not serve in the Hitler Youth." Father Julian seemed to ignore our concern as he addressed us. "My concern is that she will not be recognized as a member. I am being overly protective of a favorite student. That's all." His voice was too smooth, the tone the one he used to settle a scared child after a nightmare. The wave of his hand and the look in his eye told me different.

"You never served?" Rickard raised a brow.

"No, it has been three years since participation in the Youth became mandatory. By then, I was seventeen and entering nurses' training. I fell through the cracks, I suppose." I shrugged. Actually, I had never given it any thought.

"I had to work in the Labor Corps for a year before I could go to University," Rickard mused.

"Go to the dance. The two of you should have a good time." Father Julian smiled.

"What is it you want us to do there?" I looked into the eyes of the man who'd guided my path my whole life. After my own father, he was the most important man in my life.

"I want you to have a good time, but, most importantly, please feel the mood of the people. It will help me serve if I know how they feel."

"All right," I agreed. Rioting. Arrests. Threats to the clergy. Rickard was right to warn Father Julian to censor his words. I forced a smile at Rickard and offered him a graceful exit. "I understand if you have other plans." I wanted him to have a way out if he didn't really want to go with me.

Rickard nodded. "I have plans. With you."

Chapter 3

I am a girl with a mission, I told myself.

The Catholic Youth Organization was outlawed, but Father Julian wanted to meet secretly with a group of like-minded individuals. 'Like-minded' meant those who would be willing to go beyond the law to promote Catholic ideals.

It was the same issue Gretchen had faced: stay lawful and stay out of trouble, or cross the boundary, practice our religion, and risk arrest. My friend stayed true to her faith, and she paid the price. Had she illegally printed religious tracts and practiced her faith with other people? Proselytized? I really didn't know.

Catholicism was allowed, though its practices were pruned like a tree grown too big. Its branches had been cut back to what the ruling power considered manageable size. We could run our presses, although words were censored and ideas and traditions pruned to make room for Reich dogma.

Banding Catholics together would give us the comfort of our faith and the support of our fellows. *What the Gestapo doesn't know won't hurt them.*

We could meet under the guise of a book club or a hobby, like stamp collecting. Then we could speak freely without the prying eyes and ears of the state. I wouldn't have to face the fear alone. I would have friends.

I couldn't be sure how to feel about Rickard. I'd barged into Father's office ready to defend his honor, only to raise Rickard's ire. The priest had been borderline amused at the scene.

I stared into my closet. It was too late to help Gretchen, but I would do all I could for Father Julian.

"Erika, are you listening to me?"

"Yes, Mama. Sorry." Truth be told, I hadn't heard a word my mother had said, but she beamed. Happy I was going out for a change, she'd decided to help me prepare for my big night. She meant well, but a silk purse would not spring from this sow's ear. I could easily guess the part of her conversation I'd missed. How girls my age should be meeting people, doing things, not locking themselves away, reading, on their time off. I would never find a husband if I kept to myself. My mother had made it her mission to liberate me from spinsterhood before it was too late.

"If you work," she continued, "You should also cook and sew for your husband." This preamble was followed by a list of my shortcomings as a woman, and another list of ways to improve myself. *At least tonight I have a date*, I thought.

"Tsk, tsk, tsk." My mother sighed as she fussed over me. Holding me at arms' length, she examined the marketability of such a creature. "You are too thin. Running around the hospital has caused you to lose weight, and now you have the shape of a nine-year-old boy."

Being petite and small-breasted, lifting patients gave me some muscle definition in my arms, but the curves were not forthcoming. I'd stripped down to a slip and underclothes, and my mother scrutinized every lack. "You will never bear children with those scrawny hips. Maybe you should work in the bakery. More strudel would fatten you up."

My mouth twitched. There was no use in arguing. An hour-glass figure would never be mine. I was not like the curvaceous women in the movies.

Average height, thin, nothing about me really stood out and said, "Wow."

My mother turned, holding two handmade fillers for the cups of my bra. They were an invention of hers. They looked like beanbags. Snapping them into the cups of the brassiere would enhance what nature forgot to give me.

I moaned my protest.

"You need all the help you can get." She handed over the dreaded padding to place inside the cups, covering my insignificant buds, before snapping the filler squares into place. My mother turned me from side to side and frowned. "Well, it's a little better than nothing."

I sighed and began to file through my clothes.

"Wear a full skirt, so you look like you have some shape."

"Yes, Mama." I rolled my eyes as I spoke. It was true. This would be my first date since school, if you could call that high school debacle a date. That evening had started with ice skating and ended with my date and friends meeting at the cafe and telling fart jokes. The boys I'd known in school had treated me like a kid brother, and I sounded like a drunk with a speech impediment when I tried to talk to men I'd never met.

I thought about Herr Sankt...Rickard. I had assumed he was threatening Father Julian, which caused me to rush to the defense. *He only wished to caution him*, I reassured myself. *Did anyone warn Gretchen?* I wondered why Father Julian had insisted Rickard and I go to the dance. All social groups save for the Hitler youth had been disbanded, yet he would risk arrest to establish a church group to meet in secret, so they could have their spiritual needs met. "The Reich might prune the branches, but the roots belong to God," he had said. Gretchen was part of the those roots, in a way. But Catholics would never turn on their pastor—would they?

I struggled with whether or not I should tell my parents the truth. No, telling them about Gretchen would only scare them. All I could do was pray Gretchen's age and gentle demeanor would cause her captors to treat her with kindness. I kept the bitter secret of her arrest along with the premise of the upcoming dance. There had to be other people like me, feeling the tug-of-war between church and state. According to Hitler, Christianity was essential for guarding the soul of the German people. If that were the case, why were innocent women being dragged away for practicing it?

Catholics were indeed now feeling the fist of the Reich tighten about them. Father Julian was right. We needed to learn where our loyalties lay, so we could reach out before our faith was choked to unconsciousness by Reich doctrine.

"Erika." My mother waved her hand in front of my face "You seem distracted."

"I'm a little nervous, Mama." She gave me a reassuring pat.

"Why? Does this man have two heads?"

"He's handsome."

"Good point. Let's shoot him."

"He's gone to college."

"Good-looking and smart. Why are you so quick to dismiss him?"

"I'm too dumb to know a good thing when I see it."

"No, you're not." I pouted and she gave me a one-armed hug.

"My child, running yourself down isn't helping. You're a woman now, and you need to find out who you are."

There was more. It wasn't *what* he'd said in Father Julian's office as much as *how* he'd said it. He'd changed moods the way one changes hats. If

31

one doesn't fit the occasion, wear another one. Rickard had been determined to hear what I had to say to Father Julian. Perhaps he'd wondered if I might have heard anything about complaints against the priest. Or worse, he might've worried whether or not I could be trusted.

As for my mother's instruction to find out who I was, I had always wanted to be a nurse, but then the hospital turned foreboding overnight. How could I continue in such an atmosphere?

My mother helped me slip into a full skirt and fastened it at the waist for me. Topping off the skirt, with a full-sleeved blouse, I added a black velvet vest. I would need a warm coat to go outside. She surveyed me once again and gave my pigtails a tug.

"Not sure about the braids. It makes you look like a schoolgirl."

"But the Führer said no one can resist a girl in braids."

Mother stared at me in disbelief. "Tell you personally, did he?"

"No, but I heard it somewhere. It keeps the hair off my face when I am working."

"You are not working, now. And from the look of that man's hair, beauty tips are the last thing he should be giving."

"I never liked the mustache, either."

"Tsk! A man should be clean-shaven. Facial hair looks dirty to me."

I smiled at my mother. It felt so good to just talk, even about little things. Sometimes, my mom's sharp tongue made for some funny conversation. She could be the poster girl for Aryan motherhood. Inga Lehmeier had a proud bearing, a Viking beauty, and a warrior spirit when she chose to use it. Always a devoted wife, a decent businesswoman who, if crossed, could send a grown man running from her verbal assault. Her sharp tongue could be tempered with good humor, but one tongue-lashing would suffice for even the most stouthearted.

I grinned as I pulled the braids loose so my mother could brush my hair. She brushed from the very bottom to release tangles, inching her grip along the section of my hair after each smooth stroke.

"I promise I won't grow a beard," was my solemn reply to her remark.

Inga shook her head slightly while keeping to the task at hand. "So where did you meet this boy?"

"In church." I smiled. "Father Julian thought it would be nice for us to go to the beer hall together."

"Oh, is he a matchmaker now? I suppose I should be grateful. At the rate you've been going on your own, it will take divine intervention for you to find a husband." Mother smiled. "So what is he like?"

I opened my mouth to speak but paused. *What is he like?* Upon first meeting, Rickard had seemed protective and caring. I could still feel his touch as I thought about how he'd kept me from falling, chivalrous and polite. Then in the rectory he'd become a different person. His eyes had gone from warm to a smoldering glare, leaving me feeling exposed and wondering which persona was closer to the true person. Of course, my mother herself could give varying impressions, depending on the circumstances, I knew.

I wondered if I should mention what I had overheard. What would she think? *No.* Even though Father Julian did not ask for secrecy, I thought it best to remain silent.

"He seems nice. He had business with Father Julian at the rectory, and that is where we met. We mainly talked about me." I realized I didn't know anything about Rickard, except Father Julian had called him Rick. If the priest thought him nice enough for me to date, then that would suffice.

"And he liked you anyway?" My mother seemed surprised and tapped my arm playfully. "I assume you know his name?"

"Rickard. Father Julian calls him Rick."

"No last name? I assume he has parents?"

"Stop bullying the girl, Inga." My father's voice preceded him into the room. Touches of silver interspersed in the reddish-gold strands gave his hair a sparkle to match his eyes. "Erika finally has a date. Apparently, Father Julian has a soft spot for lost causes." I gasped in protest. "You look very pretty, my dear."

I realized it must be a father's job to praise his daughter, but the compliment warmed my heart, nevertheless. Making a quick decision, I told him, "Papa, I quit my job."

"You liked that job." He leaned against the door jam, one hand on his hip as he listened patiently.

"Yes." I sighed. Mother swept my hair back in a bun and covered it with a black snood. I motioned the two to come nearer. "Gretchen, my friend from work, was arrested."

"Oh, *mein Gott!*" My mother placed a gentle hand on my shoulder.

"Why?"

My father looked concerned.

"She didn't do anything wrong. She was supposed to sign a loyalty oath to Hitler. It's against her religion, so she refused. It's the only reason I can think of."

"Has anyone said anything to you?" I had Papa's full attention. Mother finished my hair and then put an arm about me.

"Well, I took an oath of loyalty in training, but that doesn't interfere with my religion. Hitler isn't replacing God."

"I should say not." Inga patted my shoulder.

"Nursing honors God, *Liebchen*."

"Yes, Mama, but I'm scared of what they might require next." My shoulders sagged. "I went to talk to Father Julian about it, and that is where I met Rickard."

"What did the priest say?"

"That he would get me a job at Grafeneck Castle."

She stilled and cast a questioning glance at my father, who said, "It's the monastery a few miles out in the country. I know it. If Father Julian approves, and you are happy, then I think it's wonderful."

I exhaled. "A job at the monastery will be a refreshing change."

"Now, you know I don't like to criticize—"

She was cut off by a snort of laughter from her husband, but her icy glare caused him to choke back the guffaw. He began to cough.

"Sorry, my dear, must be a cold."

"As I was saying." My mother cleared her throat, her husband motioning politely for her to continue. "I find it odd most of your jobs have you working with the elderly, pediatrics and men who have taken a vow of celibacy."

Papa crossed the room to put his arm around me. "Maybe you should stay in the bakery and work with us." I knew he tried for a compromise, hoping to make both of his girls happy. My parents exchanged looks.

"Grafeneck, you say. What will you do there?" Mother asked.

"Help the retarded and handicapped children. I thought I might learn more about therapy and rehabilitation."

"You'll do well there." She smiled. She had let me make my own choice, proving her sincerity about letting me find my own way. I gave her hand a squeeze.

A knock sounded at the door, and we all came swiftly to an unsaid agreement. We would not let the outside world make us forget who we were. "Enough talk for now. Let's meet your suitor."

"Mama," I protested, but her hand was already on the door latch.

Rickard was there, and I felt a wave of nausea. I could tell him I was ill, but my mother would never lie for me. I inhaled deeply.

"*Guten Abend, mein Herr. Kommen Sie herein, bitte,*" I heard my mother say politely. I echoed my mother: "Good evening, Rickard. Won't you come in, please?"

Rick stepped into the sitting room with purpose and with the grace of a jungle cat. I felt my confidence being sucked into a downward spiral as the realization struck me that I had no idea how to get through this night. My insides did a back flip at the prospect of a whole evening stretching ahead, an evening in which I would need to make conversation. On top of that, although I didn't want to disappoint my mother, I couldn't consider this a date when Father Julian basically was sending us on an errand. I felt sure Rickard had agreed to escort me only as a favor to the priest.

"*Bitte,* have a seat," I offered sweetly, fighting the urge to run. My mother moved toward him with her hand proffered, and Rickard took it gently.

"*Guten Abend.* I'm Inga Lehmeier, and this is a pleasure."

"Frau Lehmeier. *Sehr angenehm.* It is very nice to meet you, as well. My name is Rickard Sankt." A proper gentleman, he remained standing until after mother and I took our seats. He looked comfortable, sitting on the couch, hands clasped in front of him, as he listened intently.

"Ah, so he does have parents." Mother crossed her legs, leaning toward Rickard.

"Two, actually." The corners of his mouth lifted. He leaned toward my mother as I watched with interest.

"And only one head."

"Ma'am?" He looked inquisitive, his head tilted toward her.

"You don't look like a hell-spawned creature of the damned."

"Mama!" *Oh, just shoot me now,* I moaned inwardly.

"Honestly, Erika, you should be kinder when speaking about your friends." Now I did think I might throw up. "Why does a good-looking boy like you need a priest to fix you up?"

Rickard seemed unfazed by the playful banter. In fact a small smile quirked his lips as he replied, "I'm new in town, so, after the exorcism, Father felt I needed to make friends. I can only hope the ritual took."

"Well, that makes two of us," Mother confirmed.

Rickard winked, and she raised an elegant brow and nodded in approval.

She likes him, I thought to myself.

Papa observed unnoticed for a few moments. Rickard seemed polite, confident and possessed of some semblance of intelligence. At least he proved bright enough not to get on the wrong side of my mother.

"A sense of humor, I like that," she said, relaxing in her seat.

Rickard crossed an ankle over his knee, leaning against the arm of the chair, resting his chin on his fingertips as he said, "Humor is a sign of good mental health." He kept a friendly tone.

"Yet, here you are," she retorted.

"The foolhardy rush where the brave fear to tread."

"So bravery breeds stupidity?"

"Or the other way around. The jury is still out on that question," Rickard added, his playful tone underlaid by a seriousness that surprised me.

I looked to my father, who just shrugged as he quietly entered the room and took a seat on the sofa next to Mother.

"Christoph, this is Erika's friend Rickard."

"*Sehr erfreut,* Herr Lehmeier." Rick stood to shake the older man's hand with a firm, confident handshake my father would appreciate.

"Mama just accused Rickard of being crazy for taking me to the dance."

"Ah, well, the moon isn't full, and she's had her shots, so you should be fine."

"Papa!" I held out my hands. My father laughed, unrepentant before turning his attention to Rickard.

"How long have you been in Marburg?"

"Only a few months. I went to University in Munich, and my work brought me here."

"One of the best schools in Europe," Papa approved. "How is it you know Father Julian?"

"He spoke in a comparative religion course I took. He even took the time to speak with some friends of mine after class—a very intelligent man. I enjoyed his course."

"He's been everywhere! He told us all about his trip to the Louvre after he came back." I loved to hear the priest talk about the places he had seen.

"Yes, Erika has a keen interest in art, I understand." Rickard gave me a wink. My mouth fell open. *Wasn't there a law against your parents and your date ganging up on you?* I rubbed my forehead. Papa watched us with interest, and I decided to change the subject.

"Where did you say you worked?"

"The Department of Property Appraisal and Site Development," came the smooth response.

"Does your job involve travel?"

My mother might have been disappointed that the bantering had stopped, but I would content myself to learn more about my date.

"It might in the future. For now, we are trying to estimate the future needs of the community after all the expansion."

Papa nodded politely. The expansion to which Rickard referred had to be the acquisition of Austria, the Rhineland and Sudetenland. Personally, I was certain flaunting the violation of the Versailles treaty would lead to war. I said nothing. My father rose from his chair. "It was nice meeting you. *Liebling*, let them get out of here so we can have the house to ourselves."

My mother giggled. She rose gracefully from her seat to take her husband's hand. Papa kept an arm about her as he spoke. "Midnight curfew, but have a good time."

Papa shook Rickard's hand one more time and kissed me on the cheek. I closed my eyes, hoping I wouldn't make a mess of the evening. As I headed for the door, Rickard placed a hand to the small of my back. His touch made me tremble. My throat went dry. It was going to be a long night.

Chapter 4

The streets looked strangely normal. Snow had
been shoveled off the sidewalks, and the bordering
snowy embankments glistened in the evening sun
like diamond dust. Curtains of small icicles adorned
the overhangs of the homes we passed. New Year's
Eve parties were in progress, people celebrating
prosperity, the end of financial depression, the
emergence of one of the strongest economies in the
world. A new year would bring a new chapter to my
little church where young adults, meeting in secret,
would grow in faith, despite the confines of state
restrictions.

My heart fluttered as fear and excitement vied
for dominance in a tug-of-war of emotion. I needed to
talk.

"How did you meet Father Julian?" My voice
broke on the question. We were alone, and I felt
vulnerable. Maybe if I'd gone to the dance with a
couple of girls, I would have been a bit more relaxed.
With Rickard so close, I became tongue-tied and my
heart skipped a beat, feeling his nearness.

Rickard shook his head and glanced at me. He
asked, "Do you always keep your hair tied back?"

"My hair? It's comfortable. Don't change the
subject." Annoyed, I fingered the hair behind my ear.
I thought the issue of being on the same side had
been established. He had put me off. Why?

He drummed his fingers along the steering
wheel before he answered. "We met at the
University. Professor Braunstein taught a class in
comparative religion and invited Julian as a guest

speaker."

"He's a smart man. Priests are very well educated."

"More dollars than sense in some areas."

"You were right to warn Julian about being arrested. Thank you." I placed a hand on Rickard's arm. He didn't flinch, but he stiffened at my touch as though unused to contact. He watched the road intently.

"As Father Julian pointed out, newspapers are censored. Catholic schools have been closed. We are being watched, and the state is in no mood to suffer fools graciously."

"Has he said anything wrong?"

Rickard snorted. "That depends on your point of view. Did he say anything wrong meaning untrue? No. Could his opinions cost him his freedom? Yes."

"A reading from the Old Testament, and then a reading from the New Testament. If he stuck strictly to saying mass without commenting on politics, would he stay beneath Nazi radar?"

"We both know this won't happen. Julian will put his flock's spiritual wellbeing before himself, personal risk aside."

"Father Julian is more than a priest. He's my friend. He's always been there for me."

"A mentor." Rickard kept his eyes on the road, but he nodded his understanding. "Professor Braunstein was my mentor. He always answered a question with a question and made us think." He cleared his throat. "The professor was a friend to me, too. We had talk sessions, in a group, about history and current events. I never talked about my personal life much, but we were close."

His lips quirked downward; for a moment he seemed far away. I stroked his forearm. "Is he still teaching?"

Rickard's whitened knuckles gripped the

steering wheel.

"No," came the one-word response. I watched him. He straightened in the seat, a look of determination etched in his features.

"He disappeared before the riots?" I realized he had lost a friend, as well. For the first time, it occurred to me Rickard might have a personal grudge against the Nazis.

"Right. A book burning. Teachers disappeared, and then came the replacements. The new teachers had been indoctrinated to promote Nazi ideals. The end of free thought."

I sensed something more, so I urged him forward with a pat of my hand. I could see the mental gears turning while he planned what to say. I gently queried, "How did your friends react?"

"We saw the changes. Civil rights were being chiseled away piece by piece. First there were restrictions against business, and then came the marriage and sterility laws. My friends and I met, and we talked about the changes in laws and what the changes represented."

"Do you ever see your friends from school?"

"Hans works at the mayor's office now. Sophie, Hans' sister, is still in school. She wants to set the world on fire. I imagine she is still active in the Hitler Youth. She loves kids. Mike went back to England. I still see Gregor."

"Do you worry something similar will happen here? Father Julian could be arrested as easily as your teacher."

"Hans' father was arrested when he criticized the Reich. We were all questioned, and I haven't seen him since."

Finally, the pieces came together. I saw him as I saw my friend Gretchen, a fellow countryman being deprived of freedom. "What did he say to offend the Führer?"

"Well, he never liked the violation of civil liberties. There are times when mail is censored. A woman was arrested in a movie theater for an offhand remark against Hitler. When questioned, I tried not to offer anything specific. Mr. Schmidt, Hans and Sophie's father, constantly criticized the government, but I couldn't admit that. I played dumb, hoping to make it look as though it was a one-time thing, but when the interrogators quoted him exactly, I knew someone close to him had reported him to the Gestapo."

"Was he actually sent to court over a simple statement?"

Rickard snorted, his lips thinned. "The police still keep order. They handle theft, public disturbances, and the usual. The Gestapo, the secret police force, deals with crimes of a political nature, treason, for example, or undermining public wellness—a pretty way to say 'criticizing the government.' Hitler Youth work with the state; they're the eyes and ears of the Gestapo. Children have turned in teachers and parents because they are told to, and so they do."

I weighed the words I heard. "Children are encouraged to report their parents?" I removed my hand. "What happens next?"

Rickard nodded. "When this happens, the Hitler Youth step in as a surrogate parent. Poor kids think they are doing something good until mom or dad is arrested. Their family is broken, leaving them ripe for indoctrination."

I chewed my thumbnail before I could stop myself. I felt myself go cold. "Any misspoken word could lead to an arrest." I whispered to myself more than him. "The ride in the long, black car." I shuddered at the thought.

"Now you are catching on. In some cases, instead of detainment a person may be eligible for re-education."

"Which is?"

"What it sounds like. You get to spend time relearning who you are—or, more accurately, who the Reich says you are."

"What happens if a person can't be re-educated?"

"You get a government-paid vacation to a detention center, a euphemism for the work camp."

"I suppose the smart thing to do would be to fake it, pretend to be rehabilitated, but Father Julian, for one, would never pretend." I could almost picture the priest behind bars, preaching the truth from prison, gaining followers. I shifted my body toward Rickard. "But the church has a contract. The Reich is supposed to leave them alone."

Father Julian had mentioned this in church, I remembered. A mirthless laugh broke through the hard lines of Rickard's face. "Ah. The Vatican-Reich Accord. An interesting line in the contract reads, approximately, 'The church will be allowed to handle its own affairs as long as it shows it is competent.' I am curious as to who determines competence, and how."

I could picture him and Father Julian working together, and I wondered how far into the Resistance he operated. I could understand better, now, his demand to know what I had overheard in the rectory. The two of them plotting secret meetings would not be welcome news to some. I pondered his face. Rickard was concentrating as one would on an algebra equation. I noted concern there and longed to comfort him, to let him know I indeed sided with him.

"Father Julian told me the writing of the Accord was like a chess match. When the Vatican insisted on a right, the Reich countered with a requirement of its own."

He glanced quickly toward me, the intensity of

his countenance softened. "It was all a waste of time. Any agreement written was violated before the ink was dry. Article Thirty-One is what gives the Church the greatest cause for concern: simply stated, Catholics will be given freedom to practice their faith unhindered. Because of the restrictions, the Vatican responded with a letter just short of a declaration of war."

"Father Julian isn't protected, is he? The law won't defend his right to preach?"

"No. Like it or not, there is no free speech, and if he steps out of line, he will be arrested."

"That is what he wanted us to see when he was talking about the schools closing and the transport."

Rickard frowned. "The transport." He whispered more to himself then to me. The words hung in the air like morning fog. "Look, Erika, you heard what I said to Father Julian. Political dissidents are sent to Dachau for protective custody. Dachau is a work camp, a prison, really. There is no pretty way to say it. People disappear, and we are watched constantly. Don't assume anything about anyone."

"Even you?" I meant for this to be a playful question. I wanted to show him I trusted him.

The sky grew dusky, and the fading light made it harder to read his face. In the shadows, the blue eyes clouded over, and his expression hardened at my words.

"Not even me." We had arrived at the beer hall. Rickard backed his car into a space near a rear exit, cut the engine, and turned to me. "I am new in town, and you are showing me around. We don't mention Julian or the church."

The sounds of laughter emanated from the building. The band would be starting soon. Rickard placed a hand on my knee, startling me. His eyes softened as his thumb stroked my skin. "You look like you want to back out. Do you?"

"I admit I'm a little scared." His gentle touch soothed, making me feel warm all over.

"If you want to back out, just say so."

I smiled at his concern. Looking into his eyes gave me courage. I refused to let Father Julian down. "I don't understand. I thought the whole purpose of our being here was to gather allies to protect the church in case of incident."

"Yes, but remember: we want to feel out the mood. You don't need to do or say anything. Most people want to stay blissfully ignorant. They don't want to be involved."

"Don't borrow trouble." I looked at Rickard's hand and scooted against the car seat.

"Exactly. We don't want to hold a meeting. We came to dance, have a beer, and talk with friends. No one is going to come right out and say they're against the Reich. They need to trust us."

"Just act normal." My new maxim, I decided.

"Right. If someone else brings up church or something, listen, but don't offer information which would make someone think you are anything but a good German girl who loves her country and acts accordingly."

"I am a good German girl who loves her country."

"Then this should be easy."

Chapter 5

League members greeted us at the door. They welcomed everyone who came in, probably hoping to make the guests feel comfortable. The smile on my face was genuine, as I entered: I recognized many faces.

The band played on a raised platform opposite the bar, which dominated a corner of the hall. Bar stools lined the wall in a row along the edge of the dance floor. A storage area for beer and supplies opened up behind the bar stools. People could come and go through the rear exit inside this storage room. Had Rickard realized that when he parked? More than likely, I decided.

League girls arranged tables in long sections, and the varnish on the dark wood floors looked well worn, a testimony to years of use. The mandatory picture of Adolf Hitler was displayed prominently over the bar. I wondered whether the sight of his image made people drink more, or less.

The blood banner stood proudly in a distant corner. Would I ever see the proper German flag again? It had been three years since its replacement by the twisted cross on a red field.

The League of German Girls had a banner along the back wall, reading: *Be strong. Be pure. Be German.* In the League, Catholic and Protestant girls mixed with girls of no religious upbringing at all. Background wasn't important in this setting. The message was loud and clear. We were the future mothers and caregivers of the next generation. All of us were equally important.

Rickard only nodded in greeting to the people around us, while I smiled a lot. We were here to have fun, so I played the part. The hall looked great, decorated with homemade decorations, the bar sporting a newly polished shine. The old place came alive with sounds of revelry and excitement for a new year.

A table off to the side of the dance floor a few feet from the bar caught my eye. "Over here. This is a great table, and we can see everything!" Rickard allowed me to lead him to it by the hand while he continued to study the layout of the area. My mood escalated with the upbeat tempo of the music, and I tapped my foot to the beat. Music had not gone unscathed in the Nazi quest to quell the morally tainted. Jazz was termed degenerate, and listening to music from England and America was now illegal, but polka music filled the air of the hall. As much as I liked Wagner, there was nothing more fun than a lively polka.

Rickard scanned the room as though looking for something specific, taking note of each area of the hall and glancing back toward the exits. He studied the band and watched the bar a few moments, his eyes intently searching for something, I didn't know what.

"Do you want a beer?" I quipped. If he wanted to act natural, the hawkeyed scrutiny needed to be relaxed.

"Not now." His eyes quickly shifted. "Do you see anyone you know?"

I combed through the crowd. The place was only half full, and I caught the eye of a neighbor.

"Johanna!" I waved, bouncing on the balls of my feet.

Rickard moaned. "So much for a low profile."

The pretty red-haired girl sailed over and hugged me. "Rickard, this is my friend, Johanna

Becker. We went to school together."

Johanna's hazel eyes twinkled as she shook his hand with a bright, "*Guten Abend!*"

Rickard looked like he was late for the door.

"Are you still dating Henry?" I asked in an attempt to ease the meeting.

Johanna rolled her eyes. "Ancient history. He joined the army. I'm still in the League of German Girls, and I'm working with the younger girls."

"Do you like it?" I offered Johanna a seat.

"Sure, the activities are fun, and it lines you up for a good job down the road."

"I've heard that." I smiled. "How is your brother?"

"Dirk is a policeman now. He's here somewhere."

"Excuse me, ladies." Rickard nodded toward us. "I think drinks are in order." And he made his way to the bar.

"Who's Mr. Delectable?" Johanna grinned as she watched Rickard's retreating form.

"Rickard Sankt from Munich. Father Julian introduced us."

"I have got to spend more time in church."

"The Lord takes pride in his work." I giggled. Johanna's tongue darted out to stroke the corner of her mouth. "Great pride."

We giggled in unison. I hid behind my hand as Dirk strode toward us. Lean and muscular, the red hair betrayed him as Johanna's brother. He asked, "What are you two cackling about?"

"New cock in the henhouse," came Johanna's breezy reply. I felt my cheeks burn. She was too outspoken at times. Dirk's face broke out into a boyish grin.

"Why do I ask?" he chuckled, lifting his hands in surrender. I squashed my inclination to ask if they had heard anything about the incident at the other parish, the one Rickard had spoken about.

"Our *kindlein* has a date." Johanna pointed toward Rickard. "They grow up so fast." She teased. I crossed my arms to stare her down. She fluttered her eyelashes innocently.

"He is only a friend of Father Julian. I'm just showing him around," I explained.

"There are a couple of things I'd like to show him." Johanna's eyes danced, her tongue tapping the corner of her mouth.

"Johanna, behave," Dirk chided. Her posture straightened as Rickard walked over and set three mugs on the table.

"I suppose we need one more?" he addressed me, and then looked to my friends.

"Rickard Sankt, this is Dirk Becker, Johanna's brother. We all went to school together."

Rickard paused a minute before shaking hands with Dirk. Dirk responded with an open grin. "I am two years older. I went to school with Erika's sister, Helga."

"Ah, you have a sister?" Rickard asked.

"Yes." I replied, as Dirk took a seat beside me.

Without missing a beat, Johanna asked about Helga. "Is she here tonight?"

I shook my head. "Helga is at a clinic."

"What's wrong with her?" Rickard interrupted. I had forgotten he didn't know about Helga.

"She contracted polio as a child. Her doctor recommended treatment for the aftereffects of the illness."

"I see. The League of German Girls..." Rickard changed the subject abruptly, his blue orbs deepening in color as he looked at me. "They promote the Reich ideal of church, children and cooking. What is your stand?"

Surprised at the question, I thought a minute. "Taking care of home and family is pretty traditional, really. It is important to stay healthy and be a good mother. I'm not much of a cook."

He smiled, leaning on his hand while he studied my face. It felt for moment as though I were being teased.

"Why do you ask?" I was curious.

He leaned into me, and his scent was fresh and masculine. "You have a job. That isn't necessarily traditional."

Dropping my gaze before I fully met his eyes, I laughed. "I'm a born rebel."

He took my hand in his and brought it to rest against his chest. I felt like a marshmallow melting over a flame. I didn't know what to expect. Realistically, this wasn't a date, but a favor for a friend. In the back of my mind, I wanted Rickard to be charmed. I wanted him to see something in me, a smile or a word that would wedge its way into his heart and let me live there. *I'm an idiot.* At least it was New Year's Eve, and, if nothing else, I could expect a kiss. My heart fluttered at the thought.

"Let's dance."

He led me to the floor. Nothing else existed as we faced off. He held my right hand against his chest, and I fought the nervous giggle that tried to rise in my throat. His face loomed so near to mine I was certain he could hear my heart pounding as he took a step closer.

"I know the box step." Rickard explained. "My mother insisted I learn one dance, despite my protests." His husky voice sent shivers across my skin.

Ah, he doesn't dance. I decided to lead him gently. His thumb brushed along my knuckles as he curled his fingers around mine. When I drew closer, he placed his free hand on my waist tentatively, and I saw the uncertainty in his sapphire eyes as he hesitated, and we stood a moment, the aura of warmth from his nearness making me lightheaded.

"You'll be fine." My words quivered, and I drew in a deep breath filled with his essence, the clean scent holding me near him even before his fingers entwined with mine, a gentle touch despite his large hands. My free hand was on his shoulder, fingers splayed.

His first step landed on my foot. He tried to compensate by moving back, pulling me toward him, and I stumbled. As he held me close to him, a rush of electricity ran along my spine. I laughed and held up one finger, motioning for him to stop.

"*Entschuldigen Sie, bitte*, sorry," he muttered. His breath caressed my face.

I shook my head. "Relax."

As he placed his hands on my shoulders, he drew in a big breath, as though steeling himself to try again. I encouraged him with a smile and a palm laid gently against his jaw, and his hand slid the length of my arm until he captured my hand in his. The velvet touch slid across my fingers in a soft caress before sliding into place.

I felt the timid left hand slide along my arm, stopping to caress my elbow. Our eyes met, and my heart thudded. He moved from my elbow to my midsection. I swallowed hard and closed my eyes. The warmth of his touch traveled along my side, melding itself along the curve of my midsection to rest on my hip. My feet shuffled restlessly, while I tried to calm the eruption of butterflies within my stomach and fought to focus on the music. I nodded, and my mouth went impossibly dry. I wet my lips. He overstepped, causing me to lose my balance and stumble again as he drew me closer. Trapped in the circle of his arms, my heart leapt with as much excitement as if I were sledding downhill. I found myself longing to be kissed as his cheek brushed against mine. The warmth of his presence awakened a longing for more. He whispered, "You keep falling for me."

I licked my lips again. The sound of his voice made my heart race. Taking a step back, I decided a dance lesson was needed before we could continue. I rested my hand on his chest before I spoke. "It's simple. Move toward me, and I step." His hand glided along the small of my back. The heat spread across my flesh. I closed my eyes to refocus. "Think about the points of the compass. North. Come to me." I stepped backward as he moved close. "Good. South, take a step back." I stepped toward him, bumping into his still form. He felt solid and smelled warm. I breathed him in again. He paused a moment before taking a delayed step back. "East. A move to the side." His hand glided across my midback to the curve of my waist. My breath hitched. "West." We moved as one. "Then we start over. Just like a box, hence the name."

Holding me closer, he bowed his head to rest against my forehead. I felt as though I floated. If he let go, I would sail among the clouds. Rickard focused intently on the steps, swaying to a rhythm no one else heard. North. South. East. West. We kept the same controlled pace. If we weren't in tune with the music, we were in tune with each other. I ignored the beat of the music and kept to the rhythm of my heart. His nearness awakened a need in me, a need spreading throughout my being, a need for completion. I brushed my cheek against his as I pulled back a bit. "You seem distracted."

"No. Counting steps," he responded.

"The music has stopped. The band is taking a break." We had danced without the band for a few moments. It felt natural to be in his arms, and I was loath to stop.

"Right." He stood to his full height, drawing away from me. My hand slid off his shoulder, but not before I noted the mass of muscle beneath my fingertips. As we turned to leave the dance floor, he took my hand and again entwined his fingers in mine. I smiled up at him just as his face suddenly contorted into a snarl. A second man had approached and slapped him on the back. I stepped back in surprise. Rickard, dropping my hand, took a moment to greet him. "Gregor."

"Didn't think you were going to show." The good-natured deep voice belonged to a tall, lean, platinum blonde man in well-tailored clothing. Angular, sharp features dominated his face.

"Last-minute change in plans," Rickard stated.

Gregor kept a hand at Rickard's back, while holding a beer in the other. The duo walked ahead of me back to our table. By the time I reached my seat, the usually polite Rickard had already sat down and looked quite at ease, an arm flung across the back of his chair. He saw my inquisitive look, and his response came in a single word as he pointed toward the tall man. "Gregor."

I smiled and extended my hand.

"What a crap introduction, Rick. Herr Gregor Eisen, at your service."

"Erika Lehmeier. *Sehr erfreut*. Pleasure to meet you."

"Yes, it is." The man took my hand in both of his, caressing my palm with his thumbs, a wolfish grin on the aristocratic face. I gave a little laugh and pulled away.

He gave my hand a light squeeze before releasing it, smirking while his look roamed across me. "It's sweet of you to bring Rickard along. How did you manage to drag him out of the house?"

"I drugged his coffee."

"Oh, I like this one." He directed his comment to Rickard, but the steely blue orbs never left my face. Rickard sipped his beer, flicking his gaze back to Gregor. I quickly took a seat next to Rickard, placing him between Gregor and myself.

"It's unusual for Gregor to visit among the peasants. We should feel privileged," Rickard explained. He seemed to take the other man's arrogance in his stride.

"Privileged we are." Gregor raised his glass. A smile played across his lips. "To 1939."

We raised our glasses, tapping them together.

"To 1939. A new year." Rickard lifted his glass toward me.

"How do the two of you know each other?" I watched the duo. Rickard looked to Gregor as though waiting for him to respond.

"We went to University together," Gregor replied. He gulped from his beer stein. "Had classes, and then training."

"Like graduate school?" I asked. Gregor shrugged and nodded. Rickard said nothing. The words hung in the air, weighing heavily in the silence. I wiggled in my seat, watching the two.

The quiet was mercifully broken when Gregor responded. "The finer points of German history, science, and ancient culture."

Gregor's face betrayed no emotion. He wore confidence with ease, like his expensive suit. Alert eyes took in his surroundings and quickly judged most things to be beneath his notice.

"Ancient culture sounds fun. I love the Greek myths and the artwork of different people. I always thought it interesting. The same ideas are repeated." Though relieved to resume conversation, I was thankful to be next to Rickard. Gregor was overwhelming. Rickard silently glanced from me to Gregor, who smirked back at him.

"The emphasis was on Germanic cultures— Germanic culture and Teutonic history," Gregor went on to explain.

"Land of poets and philosophers. That's us." I

smiled as I sipped from my stein. The amber fluid warmed my throat.

"Erika has studied the arts. She has a particular interest in form and function, if I remember correctly." Rickard winked at me, and heat rose to my cheeks.

"Well, as a nurse, it is important to know where everything is!" I wailed in mock protest. I felt relieved. The icy demeanor was melting. Rickard was playful again, although it seemed obvious he wasn't entirely comfortable with Gregor there. I wished the man would go and find a partner, so Rickard and I could resume our evening together.

"You're a nurse?" Gregor's tone flattened like air from a tire. It was true some people viewed nursing as an occupation held by lower class women. Apparently I had established myself within his caste system. I looked to Rickard for support. He shrugged, apparently accustomed to Gregor's condescending manners, but I wanted to defend myself. Nursing was a noble profession, and I was proud to be a nurse. Rickard brushed aside Gregor's rudeness and took my hand before I could speak.

"It's time for another lesson," Rickard said with a smile.

Gregor stood. "Oh, no, don't put her through that again," he protested. "Erika should dance with someone who knows how." He stood behind my chair. I met Rickard's eyes, and he quirked his head to the side as if to say, "Go ahead."

The chair groaned its protest as I slid it away from the table. Gregor took my hand from Rickard. I resigned myself to one dance. His hand in mine, I noted the silver ring he wore. The skull dominated the center of the band, and bones lay behind it. On either side of the skull, triangular runes contained what looked like a reverse 'N'. I recognized the German symbol for victory.

On the dance floor, he placed my hand in his, holding me close as the music swayed our steps. He was an elegant dancer, but I found it difficult to meet his eyes. They seemed to study me as though I were a specimen in a lab. Moving in time with the music, I looked at anything but his face, even the buttons on his shirt. Nevertheless, I heard rather than saw the explosion.

There was a gasp from the crowd, and my mind fought to register what had happened. Gregor's arms wrapped about me, shielding me with his body, one hand protectively covering my head while the other held firm along my back. The starched shirt scratched my cheek as I fought to free myself from the headlock trapping me. "Gregor, what is happening?" The smell of smoke permeated the air, and I could hear panicked voices and feet running toward the exits. "Let me go. If anyone is hurt, I must help."

Gregor held fast, turning his body in the direction of the explosion. I could feel the hardened planes of chest as he held me prisoner against him.

"*Stille.*" His one word command made me stiffen.

Quiet? I cannot believe he just ordered me to be quiet.

"Gregor, you are crushing my nose." I struggled to be free of the iron grasp.

"I said, be still." He looked about. "Smoke from the bar. My guess is, the explosion came from outside."

"Would you let me up so I can see, please?"

Finally, I was released from his imprisoning embrace. I stood tall, flexing my back to stretch a bit as I stood. Most of the crowd had disappeared.

"I must find Rickard and investigate. *Bleiben Sie hier.*" He walked toward the bar, leaving me to simmer in frustration. *Stay put? Who does he think he is?*

Ignoring his command, I followed several paces behind him. Both exits were opened fully now, and the cold air lent refreshing relief to the smoky room. Behind the bar was a storage space, and within this room was a delivery entrance, well away from the main hall, where Rickard and Dirk seemed to be conferring.

"Hey, Gregor." Rickard barely glanced up. He and Dirk had been crouched on the floor, searching for anything that might give a clue as to what had caused the explosion, and I thought I saw Dirk slip something into his pocket, but I remained silent.

"Looks like smoke bombs were placed here in the storeroom, while firecrackers of some type went off in the truck." Dirk said as he rose to meet Gregor's gaze.

"What demented bastard attacks a beer truck on New Year's Eve?" Rickard looked outside from the door. Gregor placed a comforting hand on his shoulder, his head bowed in respect. "Be strong, Rickard, be strong."

"I don't think that's very funny. Where is the driver? Was he hurt?"

Dirk started at my voice. Rickard grinned when Gregor turned quickly in my direction. "I thought I told you to stay put."

Our eyes met. Refusing to back down, I crossed my arms. "You did."

Making a point of disregarding him, I went to stand by Rickard. The beer truck had been backed up to the door so barrels could be removed and rolled into this room from the truck. Now, some barrels still on the truck were cracked, and beer drained from leaks in the casks, flowing freely in a foamy waterfall from the truck to the pavement.

"Does beer explode?" It was a stupid question, but I couldn't understand what had happened.

"Not without help," Rickard answered. "Looks

like a set of firecrackers may have been set off in the truck, along with some smoke bombs in the storeroom."

"A prank." Dirk tried to dismiss my concern with a gentle pat on my back. "It was just a prank, Erika. Too much partying."

"It's a prank unless we find gunpowder residue, and then this prank steps up from criminal mischief to attempted murder," Gregor stated.

"Murder? No, that couldn't be. It was just silly partygoers who got out of hand, *nicht wahr*? Wasn't it, Dirk?" I wanted him to agree and put my mind at ease.

Gregor pushed past us to look inside the truck. "It was lucky the explosion happened inside the truck. The sides contained the blast." Gregor examined the sides and floor of the large vehicle.

I had never seen anything like it. The building was unaffected, but the truck's interior was blackened. The truck had taken the brunt of the blast, protecting the building and those inside.

Dirk put a brotherly arm about my shoulders. "Rickard, why don't you take Erika for a walk?"

Rickard nodded, replacing Dirk's arm with his own. He guided me out the door and past the assaulted vehicle. We walked around the building toward his car. I noted it would have been only a few feet from the large rear exit of the hall. His windows had been soaped, across the windshield. The writing said, "*Freiheit*. Freedom." He paused, brows furrowed, then sighed in resignation. When I moved to speak, he brought a single finger to his lips. I was silenced.

Vandalism didn't stop with the cars. Across the side of the building were painted crossed-out swastikas, with slogans like "German Freedom, *Deutsche Freiheit*, or German Bondage" and "Three Reichs make a wrong."

"Sometimes they use tar," Rickard stated casually.

"They?"

"Resistors. Protestors. They must have assumed we would all be inside, to give them time to do this. I surmise the Resistance is keeping their displays as non-violent as they can. Someone who can make a smoke bomb could have made a much more harmful explosive. They keep out of the way of any high-traffic areas, which lessens the chance of getting caught, but it makes me think they do not want to hurt anyone." Rickard was right about too much noise drawing police attention.

"This explosion was none too subtle. Didn't they assume it might call attention to themselves?"

"Long fuse. Depending on how long the fuse is, they'd have plenty of time to run or to mingle with the rest of the party."

"You think they may still be here?" I looked around, suddenly very cold, and my muscles tensed to run.

Rickard gave me a squeeze. "Let's go back inside. You are getting cold."

I allowed myself to be led. The party was beginning to resume. Most people believed it was merely a prank and decided to stay; only a few decided to go home. I sat on a bar stool next to Rickard, and we watched as Dirk and Gregor strode back in. Dirk was saying, "Clever. The use of a firecracker on New Year's Eve wouldn't bring suspicion like a big explosion would. Someone knows his chemistry. The firecracker and the smoke bombs were all homemade."

Gregor addressed the men in the group, and my presence seemed to go unnoticed. "It looks like the firecrackers were set off just as the smoke bombs went off."

"Probably they just wanted to get folks out of the

building to see the messages they wrote outside."
Rickard joined the conversation.

"It's hard to believe there are no witnesses,"
Gregor fumed.

"It is New Year's Eve. Most of us were inside
enjoying the party. It is a bit cold to wander out
here," Dirk responded.

"So you don't think it's a prank?" I leaned
toward Dirk for an answer. Gregor acted as though
he saw me for the first time, and he frowned. "Erika,
this is no place for you."

"I have as much right to be here as you, or more
so. Marburg is my hometown, not yours." I may have
sounded petulant, like a spoiled brat, even, but
Gregor was not my father. I refused to be treated
like a little girl who was in the way while the
grownups talked. Now committed to my stand, I
stared him down and continued to speak. "Who
would have done this?"

"Pirates." Gregor's one-word answer left me with
more questions, and I figured I would get the same
answer to the same question from both Dirk and
Rickard.

"Pirates?" I crossed my arms and tried to keep
from rolling my eyes.

"The Edelweiss Pirates. Bastards run in splinter
groups, like packs of rats," Gregor replied. He wasn't
kidding.

The Edelweiss Pirates? Was that the name of a
Resistance group? "I've never heard of them. What
do they want?"

"They are protesting the Reich," Rickard
explained. "Generally non-violent protests."

"This isn't non-violent," Dirk added darkly. "The
smoke bombs are made easily enough, with sugar
and saltpeter. The explosive part looks like
gunpowder. I'm just glad it wasn't any closer to the
gas tank."

"That would not have been pretty," Rickard added.

"Gunpowder. Isn't it illegal?" My question was received with amused looks from the three men. I cleared my throat and pressed onward. "Gun ownership is outlawed, so how would a person get gunpowder?"

"Outlawing makes a thing illegal only to those who choose to recognize it as such." Dirk smiled. I had to love him like the friend he was. He never made me feel stupid.

"This will not go unpunished. The Pirates have attacked Hitler Youth in the past, but usually uniformed paramilitary. I have never known them to take aggression out on a League function before." Gregor's tone was dark, his stormy eyes angry.

"At least the Hitler Youth can fight back," Dirk replied. "I don't suppose anyone saw who wrote these messages."

"The ones we talked to hadn't," Rickard answered. I didn't volunteer the fact that we'd never asked.

"Won't the police handle this?" I queried, now worried about who might still be about.

"I *am* the police, Erika." Dirk smiled at me. "I think you should go home now, *Liebchen*. Rickard, I could use your help."

Rickard responded with a sharp nod. I was dismissed, like a child sent to bed after supper. I started to protest.

"Gregor, take Erika home. I've already told Dirk I would help out until the police investigators arrive." Rickard placed a gentle hand on my shoulder, and Gregor took me by the arm.

A trio of hard stares directed themselves toward me when I sputtered in protest, looking to each face on the chance someone might take my side. There were none to take my plea. Exhaling sharply, I held out my hands in surrender.

"Fine," I muttered. Gregor put his arm around my shoulders, his arm gliding down my back.

"Come." Gregor pressed against the small of my back. I balked.

"Wait. You are not my father, and you cannot just send me home."

Rickard took my hand. "Please, Erika. I am responsible for your safety. I will see you at church."

He motioned me to go. It was 11:30. I had gotten no New Year's kiss. I squeezed Rickard's hand.

"Happy New Year," I muttered. Hiding my disappointment, I reached up to kiss his cheek.

"I'll take care of her," Gregor promised. Rickard gave a half smile. Dirk looked toward the blackened wall of the storage room.

"I bet you ten Reichmarks this didn't happen," I heard him say as I was led away.

I shivered and knew the whole thing would be covered up, like Nazi dirt under a rug.

Chapter 6

After months at Grafeneck Castle, I was adept at preparing meals for six children. One morning I set out cereal, and cut up oranges for breakfast. The simple meal started out innocently enough, until the children got creative. Wilhelm gave Lara a wide grin revealing the orange wedge pressed against his teeth. Lara responded in kind with her own orange wedge smile. Without warning, cereal went flying across the table, a spoon used as the catapult device. The twins loaded their spoons and sent the contents hurtling across the table.

Not to be outdone, Wilhelm began spitting seeds across the table into Luis' bowl.

"Point!" he announced, arms raised in victory as the airborne seed hit its target.

"*Kinder, genug!* Enough!" I chided. Out of nowhere, an orange landed in my cereal bowl, splashing milk onto my dress. I sighed. The children were suddenly quiet. "Fine. You're not hungry, so let's go outside. You may be excused."

The restless children flung themselves from their chairs and ran for their coats while I dropped my napkin on the table. I would clean up later. They were so full of life and spontaneity, the force of nature embedded in their beings.

"Lord, give me strength," I muttered, only to find them all stopped short, little faces pressed against the window by the wardrobe at the door as they watched a silver Mercedes SSK skid to a halt on the slushy driveway. The two men who climbed out made their way up the walk: one a platinum blonde in a leather overcoat neatly tailored to fit his frame; the other carrying a large box, his gold hair like an announcement of spring's triumph over the gray of winter.

"What are they doing here?" I wondered, annoyed at the invasion. Not a word in weeks, and Rickard just breezed up the walk, unannounced.

"Do you know them, Miss Erika?" Wilhelm looked over at me. I nodded. It was all he needed. Six children gathered around me at the open door to look at the strangers. Wilhelm braved the cold and stepped toward the men.

"Get back inside, and get coats on," Rickard ordered. Wilhelm started at the authoritative voice but didn't move. Gregor ignored the little inquisitors, while Rickard and Wilhelm faced off.

"What's that box?" Wilhelm was undaunted.

"Toys for children with good listening ears." Rickard smiled in response.

The children looked to me and back to their leader as though unsure of what to do. I stood firm against the doorjamb.

"Get your coats, children. Then we can go outside." Little faces looked up at me. I motioned, and they went to get their coats.

Rickard nodded. "I'm impressed."

I grinned as the gaggle of children retreated to the wardrobe. Wilhelm, however, plodded his way toward Gregor, the braces on his legs slowing his pace. Gregor ignored him, and Rickard handed his friend the box and picked the child up to carry him inside. "Spring fever has laid siege to the castle," I explained. "The kitchen is a shambles from breakfast, and you are just in time to help."

"I can't believe you let him go out like that." Rickard placed the child on the floor.

"There was no stopping him. I knew he would come right back in when he realized how cold it was.

It's important to pick your battles, and keeping him in was one I would lose."

"Mutineers, eh?" Rickard responded with a wink to Wilhelm. The children, curious about the visitors, watched from a little distance, coats forgotten, as Gregor set down the box, giving the twins a warning look to stay away. They took a step back.

"Aye, captain." Wilhelm gave a salute.

Gregor joined us, kissing my cheek. There was a mixture of "ick" and giggles from the children. I was suddenly embarrassed. Rickard glanced away.

"Good morning, beautiful," followed the kiss.

"Hello. This is a surprise. Children, these are my friends, Rickard and Gregor. They are guests, so we need to use our best manners." Then, to the men, I said, "We were going to spend the rest of the morning outside. When we come in we will put another log on the fire and have lunch, if you would like to join us?"

The children gave assorted greetings. Josef threw his arms around Gregor, who visibly stiffened at his touch. Disentangling himself from Josef, he took the child's hands and let them fall. Rickard ruffled Wilhelm's hair and then went to the fireplace in the sitting room.

"One log, coming up." Rickard tossed the log on the grate with the others. "This will burn slowly and warm the room while we're out." Wilhelm watched his every move with interest. Undaunted by Gregor's lack of response to the hug, Josef asked him, "Are you going to play with us?"

Gregor stepped away from Josef in annoyance. He answered, "Rickard and I are here to see Erika."

Rickard poked the logs before setting the fireplace screen across the hearth. Pointing to the box, he explained the reason for the visit, "Delivery. Toys. Courtesy of Father Julian."

"How sweet! Thank you. We have exhausted

every game available this winter. Spring couldn't come fast enough." I hated to admit I'd missed him. "Will you stay long enough to join us for *Mittagessen?*" Hope sprang within me.

"Lunch sounds great." Rickard took Wilhelm by the hand to rejoin the adults.

"We're staying for lunch?" Gregor deadpanned.

"Time with a beautiful girl is never wasted," Rickard countered. I looked from one man to the other.

"Thank you, kind sir." I smiled to hide my suspicion. "What conspiracies are you two cooking up?"

"Conspiracy? Us?" Rickard was the picture of wide-eyed innocence. I folded my arms.

"Yes, you. I have not spent the winter with a houseful of children to misread mischief when I see it. What are you up to?" It had been several months since I'd seen him. Feeling unsure, I searched for motive.

"Erika, I'm shocked you would question the intentions of your most ardent admirers." Gregor put a hand to his heart. His feigned lovesickness made me roll my eyes.

"Okay, Rick. A straight answer, if you please."

He answered with a smile that sent my heart over that imaginary hill once more. "Father Julian wanted me to check on you. Knowing I have a car, he asked me to deliver the toys and see to it you were in one piece and staying out of trouble. *Bestimmt.* That's it."

"How thoughtful." I addressed Gregor next. "And you?"

"I came along for the ride. Well, you know what a chore it is to keep you out of trouble." Gregor smiled. Rickard winked. I shook my head in disbelief.

"Welcome to Grafeneck Castle. It is nice to have

visitors. We are a bit isolated, and there are only so many things to talk about with a ten-year-old."

Gregor watched the children, his lip curled in derision. "What is your usual routine?"

"Generally, they wake between seven and eight. We eat breakfast and take medications. They play outside most of the morning, when the weather allows. The monks usually watch them while I make lunch. Story time and naps follow lunch. During naps, I get any charting done."

"They follow instructions well?" Gregor asked.

"They are children. There are some instructions they follow more quickly than others, but they are good children, for the most part."

"When they aren't bored," Rickard teased.

"That can become perilous, yes." I beamed with pride. "You'll get to know them a bit better at lunch. When they get accustomed to you, they will be vying for your attention."

"Tell me more about Grafeneck," Gregor interjected. His manner seemed more suited for a job interview than a visit with friends.

"We would love to see the place." Rickard ignored his friend.

"I think we can arrange a tour." I grinned. "Outside first, of course." Gregor did not wait for a response. He strode toward the door.

"I'll help get these coats on," Rickard offered. Wilhelm took his hand to lead him to the wardrobe.

"It will be nice to have the odds evened a bit. These guys gang up on me, so don't let the innocent faces fool you," I said.

"Forewarned is forearmed." Rickard took a coat from the closet. "Who belongs to this?"

Lara stepped forward, and Rickard helped her into her coat, buttoning the crippled arm inside. She smiled up at him while he buttoned. "There you go, sweetheart." With the last coat button, he knelt down to Lara's eye level. "Now you're ready to take on anything!"

The twins made another play for the mystery box until Gregor approached them. Snapping his fingers, he pointed to the door, and they stepped away from the box and ran together to the closet, grabbed their jackets, and lined up with the others at the door. I bundled up Josef and Wilhelm, with a casual glance noting how nicely Rickard helped the girls. Gregor approached. "You seem disorganized."

I folded my arms. "Really? You stay cooped up all winter with six children and see how well you hold up." I gave the signal of permission for my charges to go outside, and they eagerly obeyed.

"No, thank you," Gregor sneered.

"Come on, Miss Erika. You play, too." Josef took my hand. I gave his head a loving pat. The twins were already peering into the windows of the silver Mercedes.

"Stay away from my car!" Gregor roared. I redirected the children's attention to play in the courtyard.

"Josef, go find Wilhelm, so the big people can talk a bit." Josef graced me with a wide grin before running off.

"This is what you do all day?" Gregor surveyed the area as he spoke.

"We've built a routine, but today is the first day of real spring weather after two weeks of cold rain and wind and snow, and the children are a bit wild."

"Cabin fever?" Rickard commented.

"I'll say. They were bouncing off the walls at breakfast."

I looked my visitors over. "It's been a while. I was wondering what happened after I saw you last." I tried to sound indifferent.

Gregor responded, "Work-related."

The short response would have to suffice.

"You work together?" It hadn't occurred to me to ask where Gregor worked.

"Yes. We have been checking out building sites," Gregor said. Maybe that explained the absence, but a phone call would have been nice. He went on to explain a few details that I realized later were so generalized he'd told me nothing.

The children had decided on a game of tag. Wilhelm would have been the easy target. The leg braces slowed his speed, making running difficult. He was rarely it. The children let Wilhelm escape while they went after someone else.

I pressed my lips together and, putting on a casual air, asked, "So what brings you two out here?" I wanted to make the most of this visit.

"We thought we'd check on our favorite girl."

Gregor added, "And congratulate you on your new job."

The compliment fell on apathetic ears. I wasn't in the mood for false flattery. I was hurt by Rickard's lack of attention but determined not to show it. "The children will like the new toys. Thank you again, and thank the church women."

I wondered how often Rickard saw Father Julian, as it was unlikely the women's group actively involved him. Did he offer to bring the toys as an excuse to see me? Part of me hoped so, though part of me was angry about the way he'd sent me off with Gregor from the dance.

"Always doing a good deed." Gregor nodded his head toward Rickard. "At least his mother loves him."

Rickard chuckled. "Nice place here."

"Grafeneck was built in the 1500s and inhabited by royalty for a time, before it was bought and renovated by Samaritan House. It became a monastery first, and then also a home for disabled children."

"Are they all retarded?" Gregor's blunt statement made me pause, but my professionalism put me in a teaching mode. As a nurse I often found myself in a position to correct misinformation.

"No. None of them are. The twins are developmentally slow. Given their..." I cleared my throat, "creativity, I would not say they are unintelligent at all. I think people think differently. They are smart in different ways."

"Some are mechanically inclined while others are artistic," Rickard added.

"Exactly. One isn't better than the other, just different."

Rickard touched a finger to his nose to let me know he thought I was on target. Gregor studied the dirt path leading to the castle. "You could do with a paved driveway and a parking area."

"We get few visitors, though it might be nice for the parents to have a place to park."

"A circular path leading from the drive to the front door would make patient transfers easier." Gregor seemed to envision the suggestions as he spoke.

"We only have six children, and all of them can walk to the car. I hate to bother the grounds, and I prefer the grassy courtyard over a paved driveway."

"In the event that an ambulance has to take them to the hospital, it would be better," Gregor maintained.

"I see. The monks would have to decide on something like that. I have never given it a thought, truthfully."

"More parents are institutionalizing their children. It may become busy here." Gregor continued to study the grounds.

"We would have to see how much room we would have, to determine how many children we could accommodate. Again, the monks would decide," I explained.

"Tell us about the children, Erika." Rickard smiled as he watched the children at play.

"Each child is a gift. It is amazing how they adapt to their handicaps. Lara Huber was born with a shriveled arm. She came up with the very creative, albeit messy, idea of finger-painting with her feet. Heidi Völker is Lara's roommate, a sweet girl with a liking for American movies and cartoons. Mickey Mouse is among her favorites." I spoke with pride as I pointed out each child. "Heidi is epileptic. She goes into an occasional trancelike state. It is as though her mind takes temporary leave of her body. She is the dreamer in the group, an empathic girl who likes to make friends happy."

"I met the girls as I helped with their coats, and they are adorable." Rickard leaned toward me, touching his shoulder lightly against mine.

I continued, "Luis and Helmut Bauer are the twin terrors. They are the inventors of the catapult spoon, among other instruments of chaos. They like anything that makes a loud noise when it falls. They feed on a steady supply of action, always willing to contribute their own, if necessary."

Gregor scanned the grounds, barely hearing what I was saying, while Rickard studied the children, matching names and faces. I went on, "Josef Farber is a ten-year-old born with Mongolism and an inability to hate. The boy loves everything and everybody. He's always the first to help and cheer his friends on, often encouraging the twins in their latest episode of crash and bang. Finally, there is Wilhelm Schuster, the gentle leader of the group. The braces on his legs prevent his body from keeping up with his mind. Great imagination." I smiled at the group. Rickard's arm brushed against mine.

"You are dedicated. They are lucky to have you." Rickard's compliment touched me deeply.

"I'm the lucky one. I wish people could see how they thrive. I've learned so much about love from these kids." Our eyes met, and I cleared my throat and looked away. The brisk wind whipped around us, and the sun glistened brightly off the snow. "We'll let them play for an hour or so and then bring them in for lunch."

I smiled up at Rickard.

"What's that?" Gregor pointed.

"Stables. We have two horses, Sugar and Spice. When it gets warmer, I want the children to ride them. Animals and children seem to have an affinity."

"They do. I had a dog, growing up, and I swear if I was sad or upset about something, he knew it." Rickard seemed so natural right now. Catching him unaware like this showed me a different side of him. I leaned into him.

"We have chickens, too. Wilhelm loves his chickens. He feeds them every day, and the children have named them all. Farther down the path are bees. We have a fresh supply of honey in the spring." I beamed. "Grafeneck has become a second home to me. I love to talk about the castle."

"It's a nice place." Rickard's arm barely touched mine. The warmth of his body warmed the cool air around me.

"I love it. The children have grown to love it, too."

"Do you ride?" Rickard asked.

"Excuse me?"

"The horses. Do you ride?"

"A little. They need exercise, too. There are the side yard and paths in the forest where we can ride." I shuffled from foot to foot as I responded.

"Rickard, I'm going to look over here. Gregor pointed to the stables. "You check the back."

His voice startled me. I had forgotten he was

there.

"Come, children, let's explore," I called out to the group. Rickard picked up Wilhelm and walked toward the rear of the castle while Gregor went off by himself to look at the stables. The forest caressed the castle on one side, and its trees brushed along the ancient wall. We strolled into a copse of trees until Rickard found a desired spot. The tall tree had a generous trunk and a low hanging branch. Rickard jumped. Holding onto the lowest branch, he hoisted himself up. The boys cheered, urging him to climb higher.

"What's up there?" Luis stretched his hands over his head, but to no avail. The lowest branch was too high to reach. Rickard waved. "I can see the castle. Don't stand naked in front of an open window, Erika." The children giggled as I sputtered in protest. "Yes, I see a window and lots of trees."

"That's the forest!" Helmut squealed.

"*I* think you're right." Rickard pulled his lips into a grin. "Hey, Earth mother."

"Me?" I looked up.

"Yes. I say we build a tree house."

"I don't think it's a good idea."

"We can make it safe."

"Strength might be an issue." I hoped he would understand.

"You get stronger by testing limits." Rickard made his way down from the arms of the tree.

My jaw clenched. "Do I really need to explain to you this isn't a good idea?"

He stood on a high branch, surveying the area. I shook my head.

"Okay. Maybe a tire swing." He smiled.

"We will have to get permission." I frowned. It was unfair to get the children's hopes up for something that wouldn't happen. Or worse. His good intention could cause an injury that could have been prevented.

"So what will Gregor find on the other side?" he asked.

"The stable, as I said. Trees run along that side of the castle. The bees are kept on that side. Of course, the chickens and horses are in the stable."

"There is a store here, as well?" Rickard seemed genuinely interested.

"Sure is. The monks sell eggs and honey. It doesn't bring in a fortune, but it helps keep things running," I responded. I met his eyes and quickly glanced away, unsure of what to say. I pointed at the trees. "It's all forest back there, and a pretty clearing if you go deep enough." I pointed toward a hidden path.

"We're going to look at the woods. Who wants to show them to me?" Rickard addressed the children.

"Miss Erika, can we build a tree house?" Josef's brown eyes gleamed as he spoke.

"A tree house? I'm not sure," I answered gently.

From his perch in the tree, Rickard scanned the area, the thickness of the brush, the density of the trees, and the canopy of branches overhead.

"This tree is begging for a fort," he announced as he patted the trunk. Taking a pocketknife from his pocket, he carved an initial into the bark.

"Watch you don't fall." I worried my lip.

"I'm fine." He looked toward the castle and beyond the trees ahead of him as he scaled even higher.

"Rickard, come down." Worry tinged my voice. "I don't want the little ones to try to climb."

A small limb broke off and he turned to look down. "On my way," he announced with a jump. Laughing as he landed, he caught his balance when he placed both hands around my waist. Our eyes met again for the first time since the dance. I refused to act flustered, but my heart refused to calm its thunderous beating. The hands encircling my waist followed a trail to the small of my back, holding me close. Our lips brushed lightly before melding into a deepening kiss. My hand caressed his cheek before playing with the short silky strands of golden hair and my knees went weak as I melted against him. Nothing else existed, save the magic of his touch. A peal of giggles followed by Wilhelm's declaration of "icky" pulled me back to reality. I pulled away and straightened the bodice of my shirt.

"Rickard, I am pleased you were able to jump unharmed from the tree," I stammered.

"I am quite well, thank you. It was most kind of you to break my fall." He seemed to push back a laugh as he spoke.

Butterflies erupted within me, making my heart flutter. "We really should go in for lunch."

"Your wish is my command." Rickard smiled. I held his eyes with mine for what seemed several minutes, until Gregor walked up, a chicken bundled under his arm.

"He's got Tania." Wilhelm smiled at the feathered bundle. Wilhelm and Josef went to stroke the soft bird.

"Does he like you?" Josef smiled.

"A chicken will sleep when you put his head under his wing. It's not just an old wives' tale." Gregor gently moved the head from its protective spot under his wing and gave it one quick jerk. With a clean snap, the head drooped over his hand. I gasped and stepped into Rickard. Heidi whimpered and buried her head in Rickard's side. Wilhelm, mouth agape, watched the head dangle lifelessly in Gregor's hand.

"You make dead!" Tears collected in the corners of Josef's eyes. Gregor shoved the dead bird at me.

"Make dinner while we tour the rest of the castle," Gregor ordered casually, as he turned back toward Grafeneck. Rickard took the newly dead bird from him.

Anger burning, my words exploded in a heated rush. "She was our laying hen! What are we supposed to do for eggs, now?" Wilhelm muffled a cry. Josef ran to his side and put his arms around him. Over his shoulder to Gregor, Josef admonished, "That was a bad thing to do."

Heidi hid her face. Gregor shrugged and reached into his pocket to hand me some money. "That will cover a few chickens."

I snatched the money from his hand. "It isn't just the chicken." I ran my fingers through Lara's hair. "Do I really have to explain?" I asked through clenched teeth.

"We may as well cook her so her death will not be in vain," Rickard soothed. He patted Heidi between the shoulders as she sniffled into his pants leg.

"Erika, we will do the cooking and try to make this up to you," Rickard offered. I still shot daggers at Gregor with my eyes, not trusting myself to speak further with the children present.

"Go. I will try to calm them, but we will be having a discussion." I barely recognized the lethal tone as my own. Rickard cleared his throat and motioned Gregor to follow him.

Chapter 7

I took the children to the water closet to wash up. Wilhelm's eyes were still leaking generous tears onto his cheeks. I wiped his eyes with a towel and urged him to splash some cool water on his face. "I'm sorry, darling. I don't think Gregor understood how you loved Tania."

I tried to soothe him with words I myself didn't believe. The chickens were castle property, and any idiot should know, at the very least, you ask permission before you use another's property, let alone kill a pet. *Moron.*

"We can get more chickens with the money he gave us. I am sure he is very sorry." I hoped my voice did not betray how angry I was. Wilhelm's lower lip trembled, and my heart broke. I most certainly would be having a word with Gregor. Helmut and Luis seemed to stand away from the other children, and an unsaid agreement passed between them.

My blood boiled with anger. This was the children's home. Gregor could keep his attitude outside the castle walls. Grafeneck was a fortress against outside prejudice. I would show the boys around the castle after lunch. Boys? Technically, they were men, but until Gregor could gain more maturity, I would refer to them as boys. We would have a talk about how to treat the children. I tidied the bathroom as the children went downstairs.

Easing down the steps, I glanced toward the fireplace, Rickard had the twins in a huddle, and smelling mischief in the making I eased over to hear what they said.

"Uncle Gregor is grouchy because he doesn't have enough fun, so we must make him laugh." Twin smiles responded. I opened my mouth to protest, but my voice caught in my throat; instead I listened in on the conspiracy.

"Now, the best way to deal with grouchy people is to give them something to grouch about," Rickard continued, an arm around each of the boys' shoulders. His mirthful tone made me pause. Maybe a small lesson in manners was just the thing to teach Gregor humility. Father Julian would call it a teaching moment. I neared the trio, clearing my throat softly, waiting to be noticed.

"Can we show Gregor upstairs?" Helmut's innocent voice asked.

I held Wilhelm close to me. "Yes, you may see to our guests; that is very gracious of you," I replied. One twin looked to the other, and they left the room. I was focused on Rickard and too distracted to consciously note the sound of footsteps taking two different directions, while his smile made him look like the picture of innocence.

"I should get started on lunch," Rickard said, as he happily rubbed his hands together.

"Do that." I didn't want to smile in return. I was angry over the chicken, but there was more to it than that. The Reich saw the handicapped as less than they were. I had seen ugly posters in shop windows, proclaiming them a burden. The emphasis on health was positive, but perfection was the only standard to be tolerated. I watched with suspicion as Rickard made his way to the kitchen. I thought about the picture show Gregor had persuaded me to see with him the week after he had taken me home on New Year's Eve.

We had gone to see the film *I Accuse*. It was a rave among critics. The hero ended the life of his bed-bound wife and, as she drifted blissfully into death, asked, "If you were a cripple, would you want to be forced to endure a half-life such as this?"

When I'd moved to get up, Gregor had placed a restrictive hand on my wrist. He waited for the crowd to disperse, as if royalty might wish to have the way clear of the peasantry, so he could make his way unobstructed.

"Let the rest go. No need to fight the crowd." I resumed my seat, realizing Gregor saw himself as above the crowd. His head always held high, he paused when addressed, as though assessing the person's worthiness of his time before deciding whether he would respond at all. His clothes never had a wrinkle or seam out of place, and he invariably looked as though he'd stepped off a magazine cover. For me, if it was clean, it was wearable.

"Did you enjoy the movie?" he'd asked.

"Yes and no. It's so sad."

"Would you want to be forced to live as a cripple?" It almost sounded like a challenge.

"If I were in great pain, I might not. But otherwise it's just sad." Life was a precious gift from God. Labeling a person as inferior was an affront to His creation.

"It's sad to be confronted with that decision." Gregor's tone softened as he took my hand.

I looked away from him as I responded, "We discussed euthanasia in seminars at work. I can understand in the case of the terminally ill or the criminally insane, but most handicaps are manageable. Our veterans, for example, live happy, productive lives, despite war injuries."

"Society has to protect itself," Gregor amended.

Protect from what? I needed to change the subject. "I suppose so. Next time, let's watch a romantic comedy."

Gregor had responded with his usual smirk, an

indulgent gesture meaning he would consider what was said.

I realized now, thinking of his rigidity with the children, a genuine smile from Gregor was a rarity. I loved these children, and no handicap made them less valuable to me.

Following Rickard, I heard voices in the kitchen and paused behind the swinging door to listen. It sounded like Rickard was indeed cooking. Gregor would watch lazily as his friend bustled about.

"Are you going to eat Tania?" Luis asked. I put my hand to my chest.

The poor angel, I thought.

Gregor responded, "She has died for a noble purpose."

"Gregor is sorry, aren't you?" Rickard had a warning tone in his voice. I was glad at least he understood.

I could hear the icebox door open with a slight squeak, and then Luis' voice. "Miss Erika likes this."

"Careful." Rickard spoke nicely with the children, without resorting to baby talk. I liked that.

"Are you going to eat with us?" Luis inquired.

"Yes, we are. Maybe we can become friends," Rickard answered.

"I can help. I'm big," Luis stated with pride. I hoped the corpse was not in plain view. I wasn't sure if the sight of it would be upsetting.

"You sure are! Erika is very proud of her children. I bet you are very helpful," Rickard encouraged. I felt guilty, listening, but I remained where I was.

"It will take some time to cook. Should we tour the castle?" Gregor's bored tone asked.

Luis stated with enthusiasm, "This is the kitchen."

Rickard laughed, "Yes, it is."

"I got to go potty," Luis announced. It was my

cue to scurry into the sitting room undetected.

"You go ahead, and we will meet you upstairs," Gregor stated with impatience. Pushing past Luis, he climbed the stairs. "Cretins," I heard him mutter.

Luis simply watched him go. They did not notice me on the settee. Luis and I climbed the stairs together. Mine was the first room, closest to the stairwell.

"This is Miss Erika's room," Helmut announced as we passed along the hall. Gregor opened the door. Handmade pictures lined the walls, and the desk had piles of papers strewn about. A file cabinet was next to the desk, and a small cot was pushed to the far side of the room. Beside it, a small dressing table stood, looking lonely. The room was sparse and closed-in, with only one window, overlooking the forest.

"It is quite comfortable," I answered, sparing Gregor a warning look and informing him there would be a later conversation. "It is pretty simple, but it is home." I smiled. Gregor nodded curtly. Rickard took a quick peek himself.

"This is mine and my brother's room." Helmut continued the tour. The twin beds dominated the area. A pair of dressers lined the wall. The bedrooms were much the same, spartan rooms, containing only the necessities. I noted it appeared the dresser drawers had been rifled through.

"What about the third floor?" Gregor had little use for small talk, and none for socializing with the children.

"The monks live there. We respect their privacy and keep to the first two floors. I know there is a ballroom they use for church services, and then they have personal quarters there."

"Catholic-owned," Gregor stated flatly.

"Yes, a monastery."

"You're a babysitter."

I hid my annoyance. "I am a nurse. The children require medication, and there are some treatments, as well. We keep the parents informed of the children's progress, and their activities are charted." Unsure what to make of his comments, I clapped my hands. "Shall we resume our tour? There are a couple more rooms to see before we go back downstairs."

Josef led the way as Helmut watched. The rest of the tour went one way, and Gregor walked toward the stairwell leading to the monks' bedrooms on the third floor. I was hoping to make the children forget about Tania's demise and trying to think how I would handle the eating of the beloved pet. At the girls' room, Rickard stayed outside the threshold while Lara showed him her dolls and her music box. Artwork was displayed on the closet door. When Helmut rushed to Rickard's side, the crooked smile and disheveled hair warmed my heart.

"Hey, you, are you staying out of trouble?" Rickard asked, ruffling the boy's hair further.

As if on cue, a voice down the hall screeched, "*Scheisse!*"

It was Gregor. I gasped. Lara giggled, and Heidi looked aghast at the source of the sound. Helmut took Rickard's hand, looking up at him in wide-eyed innocence.

Rickard made his way ahead of the group to find Gregor waving his hand in disgust. "Problem, Gregor?"

"One of these idiots put shoe polish on the banister."

Rickard swallowed a laugh. "They were with us the whole time. Could it be slick from polishing?" Rickard leaned against the wall, grinning ear to ear. Gregor stuck his blackened hand in Rickard's face. "Oops."

Rickard was unrepentant.

"When I find out which of these nasty, little…" Gregor didn't finish his sentence as I had arrived with the children in tow.

"Are you all right?" I had heard the conversation, but I would not let on.

Gregor's expression softened. "Just a slippery spot on the floor. Where's the bathroom?"

"I'll show you!" Helmut beamed. He took Gregor by the sleeve. Rickard winked. I smelled a plot.

"Thank you, Helmut." I motioned the children to follow me down the stairs.

Luis put napkins at the place settings. The table was set with mismatched tableware. The tea pitcher sat in the middle of the table along with butter, salt and pepper, and a bowl of sugar.

"What a wonderful helper! Nice job, Luis." I beamed. He smiled at the praise.

Rickard commented on the twins. "They are identical, save a few freckles running across the bridge of Helmut's nose."

Luis beamed at his new friend. His twin moved closer to Rickard when he heard Gregor thunder down the steps, muttering. Rickard turned to me. "Let me help you in the kitchen. Gregor, just in time to entertain the children while we serve."

"Joyful day." Gregor's monotone reflected annoyance he tried to hide. "Go look at the toys."

He pointed to the box. The children scrambled to bring the parcel to an open spot on the floor, where they up-ended it and poured out its contents. I noted Gregor tugging frequently at his pant leg. It was an old prank. A thin coating of honey or corn syrup on the toilet was not noticeable until the victim sat, sticking his skin to the seat. I chuckled as two things became evident: the classics never die, and the twins had just declared war.

"I'll be right back." My honeyed voice dripped as I moved to go to the kitchen, leaving Gregor looking disgruntled. "I'm going to help in the kitchen. You children be nice to Uncle Gregor."

Rickard didn't bother to hide his smirk, even as Josef smiled up at him. Gregor looked like he wanted to punch something. *But it had better not be a child,* I thought.

In the kitchen, I poured milk into nine mugs and placed them on a serving tray. I glanced up at Rickard as he entered the room, and then I went about my business. I refused to fawn over him like a schoolgirl with a crush. He smiled. My heart flipped.

"Hey," he stated warmly, his voice relaxing me like a dip in a hot spring, until I remembered to be cool toward him.

"Hello." I resumed pouring the milk as he moved closer to me. I bumped into him as I tried to pick up the tray.

"I can carry this tray for you," he offered.

"Thank you. That would be nice." My cool tone had a tinny, fake sound. He placed his hands on the tray, momentarily trapping me in his arms. I brushed him aside and moved toward the stove to check the potatoes, then poured the steaming water through the strainer. "I suppose it would be simpler to serve these boiled, with a bit of butter, rather than make a potato salad."

I forced small talk, willing myself not to care at all that I had had no word from him all winter.

"Let me take the chicken out of the oven for you," he offered. I had never noticed the kitchen was so small. With every move, our bodies seemed to make contact in some way. I made a point of not looking at him, my unspoken anger at his neglect looming larger by the minute. Rickard placed the bird on a serving tray. "It's been my experience that how angry a woman is can be measured in direct proportion to how angry the woman tries not to act." His comment was met by silence and an apathetic shrug of my shoulders. "Erika, I owe you an apology," he gently stated.

"Yes, you do!" The pan in my hand rattled on the stove as I slammed it down, causing its contents to jump within it. "Gregor. I didn't even know him, and you just dumped me on him." The dam had burst, and angry words surged forth from my lips.

He placed the tray on the table. Taking me by my shoulders, he had barely begun to speak when I interrupted him, "He was talking about those people. Those pirate, gang people! How do you know he isn't one of them?"

"Edelweiss Pirates? He isn't. Trust me."

"You dumped me! How am I supposed to trust you? You let him take me home, and it hurt. I got no New Year's kiss, and that hurt." I pulled a knife free from the butcher's block. Rickard took a step back. Wielding the knife with precision, I began to victimize the chicken. I brutally stabbed the chicken, ripping the knife into its breast, hacking off hunks of meat to put on a plate. Rickard swallowed as he watched.

"Again, I apologize." Rickard placed a restraining hand on my wrist, ending the assault.

"Well, thank you for escorting me. I suppose the incident cannot be blamed on you."

He leaned in to whisper. "Funny how it never made the paper, and nothing on the radio, either."

He was right. I had called the paper myself. I didn't have to wonder. A demonstration would run counter to public morale. The story had been hushed.

"Let's just get this served." I moved to leave, when his hands wrapped around my waist, stopping me.

"Erika, it wasn't you."

"I know it wasn't me." I brushed past Rickard, serving tray in hand. He may have had his reasons for having Gregor take me home, but there was still the matter of no phone calls for two months.

Gregor still studied the fireplace as the children explored the new treasures. The toys were in small piles, according to whether they were girl toys or boy toys, Gregor having sorted the booty. The children would take the newly claimed prizes to their rooms.

"Here we are." Rickard cheerfully set the trayful of mugs on the table. "Are you joining us, Gregor?" Rickard summoned the other man from what seemed to be a daydream.

"I wouldn't miss it." Gregor's smile did not reach his eyes as he took the chair at the head of the table.

"That's Miss Erika's seat," Lara pointed out. He ignored the little girl. Sitting ramrod straight, he reached for a drumstick. Noting the mangled remains, his brow arched.

"It put up a fight?" Gregor asked, holding up the mangled leg, pierced by his fork. Rickard shrugged in response.

"I want that one." Wilhelm pointed to the impaled chicken leg.

"He likes the drumsticks," I explained, expecting Gregor to graciously give the child the leg. Instead, he bit into the meat, ripping it from the bone while he stared down at Wilhelm.

"No food until we pray." Josef placed a hand on Gregor's wrist. It obviously took great control on Gregor's part not to slap Josef's hand.

Ignoring the child's protest, Gregor scooted his chair forward. "Don't put your hand on me. I'll get something on my shirt."

I failed to force a smile. My glare must have said it all, as his lips drew into a thin line. Rickard stood to offer me the head chair opposite Gregor. I politely refused. *"Nein, danke, es geht,* it's fine. He's company. I will take this prime seat next to Lara."

The men may sit at the head of the table, but

they do not rule this castle, and I will see to it this is understood.

I sat at Rickard's left side. Our hands brushed against one another.

"Sorry," I whispered.

Rickard gently smiled.

"Everyone seated? Heidi, can you lead the prayer?" I asked, noting with satisfaction that Wilhelm had managed to get the second drumstick. Heidi was a delicate brunette with pale blue eyes that looked from one stranger to the other. "It's okay."

"Thank you, God, for food," Wilhelm shrieked.

"And snakes," Josef chimed.

"And snow sleds," the twins spoke as one.

"And toys." Lara glanced shyly at Rickard as she whispered. He took hold of her hand and kissed it.

"You are welcome, *Liebchen*. Heidi was going to speak, so let's have quiet, please." Rickard's soft voice made Heidi look up at him, giving her courage to start the blessing.

"Bless us, oh, Lord, and these thy gifts, which we are about to receive," Heidi said timidly.

The other children joined in with the words they knew: "From thy bounty, through Christ our Lord. Amen."

"Amen," I finished.

"Amen!" Wilhelm exulted.

Gregor took another bite of the chicken leg still in his hand, ignoring Wilhelm. He was losing ground with me. No matter, charm would always serve him. Leaning toward Heidi, he tried for a child-friendly voice. "Thank you for showing me the castle."

Heidi's eyes locked onto Gregor's. She moved her lips to speak, but she seemed frozen. Gregor leaned closer, looking into the child's eyes. They were open but far away at the same time, as though she wasn't really seeing him.

"What's wrong with her?" Gregor asked.

"She's having a seizure." I jumped up, along with Rickard. He was by her side in a minute. "I'll get her medicine. Keep her from falling," I instructed.

Gregor didn't move, but he studied the child dispassionately. "She's not spastic," he noted.

Rickard put an arm around Heidi and eased her onto the floor, cradling her in his lap.

"Not all epileptics are. Maybe she doesn't have grand mal seizures," Rickard explained. He was rocking her gently, I noticed, when I came back with her medicine.

"Heidi goes on a trip," Josef explained.

"She does?" Rickard looked to him.

"Yes, but she comes back," Josef added.

"Sometimes with stories," Lara added.

"Interesting," Rickard stated. "I am impressed at how calm the children are. It is a testament to your care. They seem to understand Heidi's condition."

"Well, I believe in explaining things. Understanding one another helps us care for each other." Heidi's eyes fluttered open, and I took her hand. "Heidi, are you all right?"

She nestled against Rickard as he stroked her hair. She nodded.

"Heidi, where did you go?" Wilhelm asked. "Were we there?"

Gregor looked curious. "What do you mean, where did she go?"

"She can dream with her eyes open," Lara explained.

"Sometimes she sees us in the dream, and it happens," Josef added.

"Interesting," was Gregor's only comment.

After our meal, Rickard volunteered to tell a story and the children gathered in a circle on the floor around him, giving him full attention. I was grateful. Deciding it was now or never, I tapped Gregor on the shoulder. "Gregor, a word, please. We can talk while I clean up."

Gregor had reached to hold me but stopped in his tracks when he noted my face. "Can you forgive me? I am helpless around children, not having had much experience with them."

Gregor used his charming voice. I wasn't moved. "Not when it hurts my children. Why on earth would you do such a thing? Those chickens are like pets. The children love them."

"I am truly sorry. I honestly thought they were being bred for food. I would never seek to cause those poor angels trauma." It was an oily, unbelievable lie. Was he not listening when I'd said the children had names for all the animals? "I did pay for the chicken. My heart is in the right place."

If he wanted to avoid a confrontation with me, it was too late, and I spoke forcefully. "You will *not* upset the children. This is their home, and they deserve to be treated with courtesy."

Gregor's lip twitched. He was not one to be told what to do, I realized. It was time for him to appreciate there were some things he would adhere to or leave. Gregor put his hand to his chest. "I am so sorry. They are very lucky to have such a loving headmistress."

"The money won't calm their fear, but I did try to explain you meant no harm."

"Simply explain we eat chicken all the time. It is the way of nature for the weak to yield to the strong." He moved to stroke my chin. I shied from him, narrowing my eyes with my next breath.

"Yes, but they aren't friends with the chickens at the butcher shop. You will apologize to them. Furthermore, you will need my permission before you go upstairs again or touch anything on this property again, or you will not be welcomed back. Am I clear?"

"Yes, madam." Gregor gave a half smile that was beginning to grate on my nerves.

He wasn't sorry. He didn't even acknowledge he had done anything wrong when he continued. "I'll make it up to you. I'll take you to a party."

"You don't get it! You disregarded my authority entirely, not to mention upsetting the children in my care." I dumped the pots into the dishwater.

"I've been a monster. Let me learn from you. In time, I promise, you will have no worries about the children."

I offered no comment. Turning on my heel, I went back into the sitting room, where Rickard was regaling the children with an adventurous tale. "Nap time, darlings." The children muttered in protest at my announcement.

"Get some rest." Rickard offered a hand to Wilhelm, helping him stand. "We'll be back to visit again."

I wondered if it were true. Would he come back? Rickard was good with the children, kind and funny. The time had gone by so quickly. I wondered if we might form a friendship, via our mutual love for children. At least this way we could be friends, and the seeds of friendship often bloom into love. The thought spread warmth through me.

I pretended to chase the children up the stairs while Rickard carried Wilhelm. Gregor waved them off from his seat on the couch. Josef hugged Gregor before scurrying up the stairs. Gregor stiffened, his arms at his sides. "*Guten Abend, auf Wiedersehn!*" Josef called back from the top of the stairs. I stood just outside the door to watch Rickard tuck the boys in. He helped Wilhelm take the braces from his legs and tucked him into bed carefully.

"Do you think we will have a tree house?"

Wilhelm asked.

"I will be very nice to Erika and hope she says yes," Rickard responded. Wilhelm smiled while Josef jumped into his bed, his arms outstretched for a hug. Rickard gave him a squeeze. "Thank you for showing me around today." He brought the blanket up under Josef's chin and tucked it in between the mattresses. "Comfortable?" he asked. Josef nodded yes.

"Two down." I blew the boys a kiss before following Rickard to the next room. The twins opted for a pillow fight, jumping across the divide from one bed to another, throwing a pillow in mid-flight. I approached the door just as Rickard crossed the threshold.

"To bed, ye scurvy rogues!" Rickard teased as pillows came at him from two sides. Armed with two pillows, he swatted each twin, and they promptly hid under the sheets.

"*Stille*! Calm! You are supposed to settle them." I sat on Luis' bed while Rickard wrestled with Helmut. "This isn't calming!"

"Yes, captain!" Rickard gave a salute. "Boss lady says to bed!"

I rubbed Luis' back while he settled. "You boys were a big help today."

I always found reason to give praise. I felt it encouraged good behavior. Rickard and Luis exchanged knowing glances. "More than you know."

Rickard's wink was accompanied by a half smile.

With the children settled, I made my way down the stairs and toward the kitchen, but my steps were interrupted by the ringing of the phone.

As I listened to my mother's voice, I paled and fell into a chair, then dropped the phone into its cradle and looked at the men in the room. "Will you give me a ride home? My sister has died."

Chapter 8

I barely remember the drive home. Trees and buildings all blurred into some unreal vision, alien to my memory. My one thought was to be home with my parents, to comfort them and to find comfort myself. Gregor was at the wheel with Rickard in the front seat. I could only stare out the back window with my head pressed against the glass, hoping this was all a mistake. We stopped at the curb alongside my house, and I stared at the place I called home, now devastated by grief

"Are you staying, Rick?" Gregor asked.

"Yes. You go ahead. I can get a ride home."

As I got out I thanked Gregor for going out of his way. Watching his car ease away from the house, I barely noticed Rickard, who stayed by my side all the way to the door, where I braced myself for what would come next.

"I have to be strong for them," I whispered. I was determined to push away my own sorrow and comfort my parents in theirs. Commanding my courage, I stepped into the kitchen.

Confirmation of my sister's death was like a dagger driven into my heart. Embedded, it twisted sharply as I saw my mother's overwhelming grief. Her sobs tore through the silence of the house. Her normal animation gone, she sat crumpled at the kitchen table, where I wrapped my arms about her shoulders.

"I am here, Mama," I whispered. My voice seemed an obscenity in the stillness shrouding the room. How could I find the words to comfort her, when the news gnawed at my own soul? I looked into her tear-stained face, wishing I had the words to heal her pain.

"She was doing so well. We got reports from her doctor, and she was responding well to treatment. Therapies were successful, they said." My mother's dreamy tone sounded surreal to me. Tears ran in a track along my own cheeks as I listened. "And then we got this." She ran her fingers over a letter on the table. I hadn't noticed it earlier. She thrust it away from her, as though horrified to have it so near, handing it to me and indicating I should read it.

It was an official document from the hospital, signed by the doctor and his staff nurse. My eyes jumped randomly across the page.

"We regret to inform you... despite all efforts... she succumbed... died... cremated to prevent epidemic... condolences..."

I had no words. A creak of the floorboards told me my father had entered the room. Papa crossed the room in a few easy strides and began to rub Mama's shoulders. She broke into a sob, and he whispered in her ear. "Come, angel. Lie down a while."

Mama stared blankly as Papa took her hand. He led her to the bedroom.

On some level, I sensed Rickard near as quiet footsteps approached. I felt a gentle hand on my shoulder and rose to my full height to look into the sky-blue eyes. Looking at Rickard brought me back to reality. He helped me into the chair my mother had occupied moments earlier.

"You drove me home." I realized I hadn't thanked him. *"Danke."*

"Yes, Gregor dropped us off. Would you like me to leave?"

"Leave?" The word sounded foreign to me, like a sour note hit by accident. "No, I need a friend."

"Erika, I'm sorry." His caring words, strong and gentle, reflected the compassion in those eyes. I leaned into him, to draw strength from him.

"I'm sorry, too." I looked away and stared out the window for a moment, just in time to see Father Julian pull up to the curb.

Automatically I went to the door to greet him, and found him looking harried, as if his strength had faded. Bluish circles hung below his eyes. Worry-scored lines in his face told me something was up. I saw him peek into the bedroom, where Papa was caring for Mama, before he sat next to me and whispered, "Erika, I just got word this morning." The priest gave my hand a squeeze. I nodded and handed him the letter. His eyes scanned the page too quickly, almost as if he'd seen it before. "Erika, I need to speak with you about the funeral."

He stopped speaking when Papa entered the kitchen.

"Let me make coffee. I think we can all use something to warm us," I offered.

As Rickard respectfully approached my father and shook his hand, it seemed once again Rickard would be witness to personal discussions in my family.

"My wife is resting. This has come as a great shock," Papa explained in a mumble. "More upsetting is that there will be no funeral mass." My father's tone was forced.

"What?" I turned quickly. The water I was pouring into the percolator splashed onto the floor. Flustered, I hurriedly set down the coffeepot and wiped up the spillage.

"Cremated remains are not allowed in the church," Father Julian stated.

"Why?" Rickard asked.

The priest shifted his weight before responding. "Eucharist cannot be celebrated in the presence of said remains; therefore, no funeral mass. Church rule." Father Julian shifted in his seat as he spoke.

"That isn't right!" I threw the soaked towel into the sink. "It isn't Helga's fault this happened."

"However, I could justify adapting the rite if we can show anti-Christian motive," Julian stated.

Rickard blinked. "Show what?"

"As I pointed out, Helga was cremated without family consent or knowledge. Show that, and I can handle the rest," Julian assured.

I was outraged. "I have no doubt of Helga's place in the afterlife. There was no one with a heart as beautiful as hers, but to be denied a proper burial due to something beyond our control is not going to happen if I have anything to say about it."

"Erika, Christoph, I will do all I can. If no funeral mass is permitted in the church, then we will have a service here, and I can certainly offer a mass on her behalf, at any time." Julian's voice softened. "I will do everything in my power to see she has a proper burial. I promise."

It was then I rose from the chair. The urge to move drove me onward. "Rickard. I have an idea. Could you take me to the clinic?"

****

Rickard and I drove to the clinic in Father Julian's car. The ordered streets were clean, and the new road systems made travel quick and easy. Troubled, I fell into an old habit of mine. I spoke my thoughts aloud as I tried to fit the pieces together. "I am trying to understand. Pneumonia? Helga never had asthma, never any condition that would have made her vulnerable to respiratory problems."

"Hospitals are cold, and sometimes so many sick people make a person more apt to catch something," Rickard offered.

"She survived polio," I countered. "She was strong. Maybe I just don't want to accept the truth.

Denial, that's what doctors call it when a patient won't accept a diagnosis."

"I think that covers a myriad of conditions. Not only the medical ones." He smiled at me consolingly.

"As a nurse, I know pneumonia is treated with Vitamin C. There are also radiation treatments available, Roentgen therapy, although that treatment is harsh."

"I'm sorry. I don't follow." He cocked his head to the side, waiting for me to explain.

"The reports contradict. If she had pneumonia, she would have poor appetite and extreme fatigue. If she were undergoing Roentgen therapy, she would have decreased energy and appetite. All the reports Mama got said she was active and eating well."

"The doctors never mentioned Roentgen therapy? Do you think they made a mistake?"

"I want to believe they did." I couldn't tell Rickard my gut railed against all logic. Helga had been strong and vivacious. She would not have succumbed to something like pneumonia. It had to be a mistake, a gross error. She had survived polio, and only a catastrophic illness would lead to her undoing. I had to discover the truth.

"Are you going to mention this to your parents?"

"No. It is only speculation. Doctors are trained professionals. It is presumed they did all they could. Even so, I want to see her charts. I'm a nurse, and I know what to look for."

"What are you thinking?"

"She was cremated. There can be no funeral mass for her."

Rickard furrowed his brow in confusion. "These rules make no sense."

I gasped. "I thought you were Catholic?"

Rickard rocked his hand in a so-so motion. "I was raised Catholic. But I don't practice."

"Well, when she appeared terminal, a priest

should have been notified immediately, so Helga could have her last rites. No one was notified. End of story. Discrepancy established."

The car rolled into a parking spot in front of the clinic. Rickard cut the engine. The center was beautiful, brightly decorated—maybe too bright, and too cheerful. Two long hallways had rooms on both sides, and the nurse's station sat in the middle between the two wings. A young nurse sat at the desk, watching cautiously as we approached.

"*Guten Tag,*" she greeted.

"Good day. I was just curious. Which is your quarantine area?" I asked.

The receptionist smiled politely. "We have no quarantine area."

"If patients are isolated during a serious illness, where would they stay?" I pressed her.

"We have no isolation rooms at this time, though if one were needed, we can transform one," the nurse stated. She watched me closely.

"Has there been a need lately?"

"I'm sorry. Who did you say you are?"

"Erika Lehmeier. I am a nurse."

"Are you looking for a job?"

"Yes," I lied, hoping she would be more forthcoming with a fellow caregiver. Rickard remained silent, leaning against the desk and watching. He inched his way further out of her range of vision to where the charts were kept.

"You sound as if you are specialized in terminal patients. Even so, we have no positions available at this time, but you can leave contact information and check in periodically."

"Wonderful. What about religious preference?" I asked. "If a Catholic patient dies, or is dying, is it policy to respect their wishes regarding religious counseling and visitation?"

Rickard casually glanced at charts sitting on the

long countertop.

I kept a friendly tone, hoping she would speak freely without getting suspicious.

"If the family has requested a preference, a priest is summoned," she replied, never noticing Rickard's movements.

"What is the hospital policy about cremation?" I asked lightly.

"I'm sorry?" She furrowed her brow.

"Cremation of those who have died," I pressed.

"We don't do anything like that here." Her furrowed brow nearly united her eyebrows when she frowned. "Who did you say you were?" Her voice cracked, and her eyes darted back and forth across the papers on her desk before meeting my gaze again.

"Reich Health Ministry. Heil Hitler," Rickard responded. Jumping at the sound of his voice, she did a double take, as though confirming his presence. He wore gray pants and a blue dress shirt, nothing to reveal he worked at the Ministry. I hissed in a breath, hoping she would not think to ask for identification.

"Heil Hitler," she repeated.

"I need the records on a patient. Miss Helga Lehmeier."

The nurse pulled the requested chart.

"You may use my office, sir. There you will have privacy." She pointed to a small office alongside the nurse's station.

"Thank you." He smiled as he led me into her office. I flipped to the patient information. The page listed Helga's full name, address, diagnosis, and—as I suspected—religion. Father Julian was listed as her clergyman, along with his address and phone number.

"They only had to look to know she is Catholic." I pointed to Julian's name.

"Does this show anti-Christian motive?" he asked.

"Well, obviously they had to know she was Catholic, and they deliberately ignored her religious preference and never notified her priest."

"In the case of medical necessity, wouldn't that supersede religious preference?" Rickard was playing Devil's advocate, I realized. Preventing an epidemic would be reasonable cause to ignore religious ritual.

"That's hard to say. I suppose if they were preventing an epidemic, then legally and morally they did the right thing." I hated to concede that point.

However, if there was no medical necessity, then I had established anti-Christian motive in the clinic's failure to act according to established procedure, I reasoned. I flipped through the nurses' notes and read.

"I don't see where Helga ever complained of anything. These notes are pretty routine, and they barely mention anything outside the usual activities."

"The symptoms we are looking for, again?" Rickard asked as he scanned the page with me.

"Extreme fatigue, shortness of breath, chest pain or heavy feeling in the chest, a cough, especially one producing green or yellow sputum. These nursing notes are vague. There are no observations listed."

"You mentioned therapies." Rickard turned to the marked section of the chart. The lab section was empty. I skipped to the section labeled *Therapy*. It was empty.

"There are no doctors' notes. Her doctor admitted her but never put her in a therapy program. She was the victim of polio. There is nothing to indicate she was ever given any type of treatment or exercise. The whole reason she was admitted was to get therapy." I flipped angrily through more pages, until I saw a card signed by three different physicians. There were three red crosses next to their names.

"None of these are her doctors." I stared at the card before surrendering it to Rickard. The last page of her chart was a copy of the condolence letter sent to my parents. Attached was a notice of transfer. I showed this to Rickard, trying to hide my rage. When Rickard read it, his expression became dark. He abruptly stood up, closed the file and led me out the door.

"Where are we going?" I protested.

"We need to go. Helga never died here."

"What do you mean, she never died here?"

"No facilities for cremation. She was moved. No quarantine area. When—or if—she got sick, she was moved to a facility to be isolated from the rest of the population."

"Why?" I was stunned. "And why wouldn't the nurse simply tell me that?"

"She was ordered not to."

Chapter 9

The funeral done, a memorial mass was arranged by Father Julian. To fill the emptiness I poured my life and energy into the Grafeneck children. The winter had passed. Outside the castle, the snow melted, bringing blossoms of mountain flora to life. New leaves decorated the formerly barren trees. The warmth of the sun banished the cold gray of winter, allowing the sky to turn a beautiful shade of clear blue. I loved Easter; its promise of rebirth gave me hope for spiritual healing, something I badly needed this year, especially.

Tania, the chicken, had had a burial of sorts at the dinner table. Her bones were forgotten with the rubbish, but Helga was not so easily forgotten. I wiped my eyes with the realization this Easter would be the first without my sister.

Home for the holiday, I entered the church, hearing soft organ music as I bowed my head to pray. An image of David and Goliath flashed through my head. *Lord, will you show me what to do? Do I have to find a way by myself to prove the murder of innocent children by the government? A government I assumed worked for my best interest? What power do I have? How can I make a difference?*

Grief was beaten down again by a surge of anger. I found myself looking toward the altar, daring Father Julian to say something to soothe my soul.

"Who is deserving of love in God's eyes? Do we ever deserve it? Or do we fall short?" Father Julian spoke with his usual calm, but his eyes were warm with sincerity and blazed with passion.

Remembering what had happened at the dance, those months ago, I wondered if I could love the Resistance movement. An innocent prank could have turned deadly with a more intensive use of gunpowder and saltpeter, if Dirk was accurate. Were they trying to do the right thing for the wrong reason? Or the wrong thing for the right reason? Would they be demonstrating if the Nazis did not give them cause? Did I love either of these groups of people? If I was to answer honestly—no, I did not.

Father Julian's words brought me back to his sermon. "The Ministry of Justice Commission proposes those suffering from an incurable or terminal illness could request a mercy killing from their doctor if it is the patient's expressed wish. There is news of a father asking—no, begging—the Führer to take pity on his child. She was born severely handicapped, retarded. Hitler touts his great love for children. He listened to the man's plea. In an act of what he calls compassion, he murdered this child, per her father's request."

I grew dizzy at the last words. A father pleading to end the life of his own child? Could he honestly feel it was an act of love to terminate her life?

"Voluntary euthanasia has just become mandatory. The burden of care for our needy children has been taken from us." His strong words brought goose pimples to my arms, and I knew he was right. This case would act as a catalyst to promote the euthanasia of more handicapped children. No one moved, and not a sound was heard save the sound of his voice.

Involuntary euthanasia. The choice was ripped from the individual as voluntary gave way to legalized murder. I closed my eyes against a truth I couldn't accept. My sister had died in a clinic that didn't exist from an illness she never had.

My usual refuge from chaos, Father Julian's words now threw my thoughts into a tailspin. "Clause two of the euthanasia proposition states: a person who, because of incurable mental illness, requires permanent placement in an institution and is not able to care for himself may have his life terminated by painless medical procedure."

He read the law verbatim. It seemed reasonable to some, when the quality of life was in question. I could understand euthanasia in the case of chronic pain, coma or criminal insanity. But Helga had none of those. I would be hurting for the rest of my life because Helga's death left a void in my soul. It was something I would have to live with, missing her bright and cheerful spirit. Suddenly, in the second row, a man in military uniform started coughing, drawing Father Julian's attention. The priest stared directly at the coughing man and continued, "Who decides?" Father Julian's voice rumbled. "How do the incurable become curable without treatment? I ask you. More importantly, when will the state supersede the individual or the family?"

It already has. The words came from the back of my mind. It was a certainty. Helga's cause of death was euthanasia.

There was the sound of shuffling as I realized people moved from their seats. Father Julian continued to speak even as the brown uniforms moved closer to the altar.

I fought to swallow the lump in my throat. Brown Shirts approached Father Julian from both sides, grabbing his arms and knocking over the offering table. The chalice spilled crimson fluid, staining the white tablecloth. I froze at the scene. Frightened cries were heard from the acolytes, and the parishioners started in the pews. Some rose to make their way to the altar, and cries of protest rent the air. My own shout of "No!" was lost in the confusion. Father Julian was handcuffed and led to the exit. I wanted to run to him, to tell the Gestapo this was a mistake, but there were too many people between us to fight my way there.

He was led through the door and out of the church.

In a whirlwind of insanity and fear, Father Julian was gone...just like Gretchen, and just like my sister.

When would it all end? And how?

Chapter 10

Be strong in the Lord and in his mighty power.
Ephesians 6:10.

I put the Bible down. I scolded myself for my
weakness, but without Father Julian I felt
disconnected and lost. I found myself praying more
and going to church less. Were these two things as
contradictory as they seemed? My little church had
found a replacement for Father Julian, but to my
mind there was no replacement for the beloved
cleric. The new priest held strictly to the mass,
taking great care to leave the world outside, while he
preached messages of hope from the gospel. I
couldn't blame him. The people needed a spiritual
advisor, but Father Julian had been taken away in
handcuffs for his dedication to the truth and for my
right—and the right of others—to know that truth.
He'd made a stand that day, and he'd paid for it.

Reaching for him as he was hustled away, I'd
screamed a protest that fell on deaf ears and was
useless to stop the Gestapo, but I prayed Father
Julian was comforted to know so many had objected
to his arrest. I wiped the tears from my eyes. I would
be strong, for Father Julian's sake.

I chose to bury myself in work, and my
otherwise spare time was spent in research of each
child's medical history, as well as his or her family
history, and I cried myself to sleep most nights.
After the Easter holiday, I couldn't sleep in the room
I'd shared with my sister at home, so I decided to
stay in the castle most of the time. Grafeneck
became my safe haven, my refuge from the ugliness

of the outside world, where the streets were lined with posters reminding us that Jews were the enemy and the handicapped were like parasites, sucking the life force from the healthy and crippling us under the weight of their care.

I loved my children and was so thankful to have them to lavish attention upon. I gladly exchanged the mischief, the challenge and the chaos that came with being outnumbered by active children for the unconditional love they gave me in abundance.

I thanked God I could escape to this fortress, where He kept my angels safe from those deeming them unfit, safe from the State's efforts to brainwash the populace to look down upon the disabled. The love these little ones gave me was fully reciprocated.

It had been eleven days since Father Julian's arrest. I had gone to the police station and was told he was placed in protective custody. I was not given a location or a name of the jail, despite my insistence on an answer. It had been my intention to stand up for him in court, prove him innocent, and secure his release. In my fantasy, it was as easy as that. In reality, I couldn't get a straight answer on where he was being held, let alone when—or if—he'd receive a trial.

At Grafeneck, we celebrated my birthday, easily forgotten because it was Hitler's birthday, as well. The rest of Germany went into a frenzy over Hitler's birthday, while my children made me the star of the show with a party just for me. We played Spin the Bottle. When the bottle pointed to the child, he or she had to tell a story and pick someone to guess the title. There were charades and a clothespin-in-the-bottle game and, a variation I noted with amusement, the monks had created a pin-the-mustache-on-the-Führer game.

Holding a black chicken feather, which was taped on the back, a child was blindfolded, turned around three times and told to pin the mustache on Hitler's picture. I stifled a laugh. Brother Rolf was no fan of the Nazis. I could only imagine what his first choice might have been.

I felt a certain satisfaction, as well. Hitler's birthday overshadowed my own, out in the rest of the world, and I couldn't help feeling vindicated, here among my children. I was a hero, and the mighty Führer was a party game. When Heidi was blindfolded and spun around three times, the black feather was placed neatly across Hitler's left eye. Heidi laughed and clapped her hands when she saw what she had done. She bounced up and down until, suddenly, she stopped and hid behind my skirts. I caressed her head, looking toward the hallway to see what had caused her shyness.

A figure approached, and then Rickard seemed to fill the room, his stern bearing exuding confidence.

"Happy birthday, Erika." He half smiled. "May I come in?"

"Yes, certainly. We were just having a party." I was surprised he'd remembered.

As he moved into the room, Heidi looked beyond Rickard. Then, satisfied he was alone, she ran to give him a hug. Gregor was not popular with the children after the incident with the chicken, although he and Rickard had been to the castle again since then.

Rickard knelt on bended knee to receive a hug, and as the other children followed Heidi's lead, he was overcome with a shower of affection. The children were relentless, and he gave willingly until the little bodies seemed to have him well pinned down.

"I surrender," he gasped, looking to me with almost a plea for rescue in his eyes.

I roared with laughter, a sound so foreign it

startled me. I could not remember the last time I'd laughed. But I took pity on him. "*Ganz genug*! Enough! Let the poor man breathe!"

Reluctantly, they released Rickard and allowed him to rise from the floor.

"Do you have treats for us?" Wilhelm asked.

"No, it's not your birthday. I have something for Erika." He plucked a velvet box from his pocket.

"Me?" I smiled as I took the box. "Is something going to jump at me when I open this?"

"No, I promise," Rickard answered, a sparkle in his smiling eyes.

Opening the lid, I was surprised to find a silver necklace, an Edelweiss flower pendant attached to a chain. I drew in a surprised breath, hand over my chest. "This is just beautiful! Thank you so much."

I took a step toward him, then an awkward step back, but Rickard closed the distance to place a sweet kiss on my cheek. The children giggled, followed by an "Ick" from one of the boys.

"Let me put it on you," Rickard suggested. I nodded my agreement and turned with my back to him, holding the chain so he could work the clasp. The backs of his fingers lightly brushed my neck, making me shiver.

"You always keep your hair up, don't you?" Rickard asked. The soft voice made my knees go weak, and the feel of his breath against my neck made me lean toward him, lightly brushing my ear along his cheek.

"It's easier to work with the hair out of my face." I caught my breath when he stroked the hair and tucked it behind my ear, letting his finger glide along the curve of my neck from ear to shoulder. I wet my lips. Once again a flurry of butterflies took flight in my stomach.

"Happy birthday," he whispered. His breath tickled my ear, and a rush of electricity ran along my spine.

"Thank you." His nearness blanketed me in warmth as I breathed him in. I played with the pendant between my fingers, memorizing its feel. The Edelweiss flower had a long history as a symbol of pure love. I had heard stories of lovers who'd died while braving the Alps to find this token of affection. I found myself smiling as we sat together watching the children play. Toying with the pendant, the smooth silver made warm by my touch, I wondered whether Rickard realized what the Edelweiss symbolized.

"The pendant is lovely. Thank you again."

"During the war, the Edelweiss medal was given to those who displayed valor in battle," Rickard explained.

"Fascinating." I sighed. That wasn't what I looked for, so I changed the subject. "I wanted to ask you about what happened those months ago, at the dance. I never told my parents anything, and I'm glad. With Helga gone now, they don't need another problem to worry over."

"The incident was silenced. The last thing the Nazis want is to encourage demonstrations by having them make the news. If the rebels are caught, I am sure they will be executed."

I gasped in surprise. "Executed? That seems so harsh."

"Harsh or not, any demonstration against the Reich won't be tolerated. The League of German Girls sponsored the dance. Therefore, a demonstration against them is considered a protest against the Reich."

"I see. Did you know Father Julian was arrested?"

In response to my question, he took my hand and caressed my fingers with his thumb.

I continued, "No one would tell me where he was

taken."

"Dachau. That is where the political dissidents are being held."

"He's not a political dissident! He was only preaching!"

"He criticized the euthanasia program. That is enough."

"I was there when the Gestapo took him. I tried to reach him and stay close, so he wouldn't feel alone." I hung my head. Rickard gave my hand a squeeze.

"I hoped to fight for his release, but I got nowhere when I spoke to the police."

"You asked questions whose answers were not in your best interest to know. At least, that is the point of view of the police," Rickard responded.

"I felt so helpless."

"Remember, the Nazis have control of the courts, the papers and the law. When we gave up on democracy, we gave up our personal freedoms, too."

"You tried to tell him, but he would never just go along. I didn't want to believe it, either. I always thought authority was established to safeguard the people."

"I believe it is going to get worse." Rickard placed an arm about my shoulders, and I leaned against him. The warmth of his body against mine seemed so natural. Secure in his arms, I couldn't imagine how anything could get worse.

Chapter 11

The Nazis seeped into every pore of German life, quietly invasive, like cancer, surrounding whatever was to be conquered by planting themselves on all sides before overtaking the target.

The children were in their beds for a nap one summer afternoon when I padded down the stone steps to Brother Rolf's small study, hoping to have a quiet talk with him. Instead, I heard voices through the open door and stopped short, a gasp of surprise escaping my lips.

The man wore the black uniform of the SS, decorated with a death's head pin and a dagger clipped onto his belt alongside a gun holster. What was he doing here? The appearance of an SS man brought instant dread, squeezing my throat to raw dryness. Brother Rolf sat across the desk from the SS man. The normally jovial face was somber, his white lips pursed as he spoke to the unwanted visitor. I knew the trooper wasn't here because he'd lost his way.

The men stood when I entered the room, and I bowed my head politely. "*Guten Tag*. I apologize for intruding."

"No intrusion, Erika. Please, come in." Brother Rolf forced a smile, betraying his relief I'd shown up.

"Good afternoon, Brother. I didn't know you had company." I stood with my hands folded in front of me, desperately trying for a look of cool professionalism. The SS man rose from his seat and nodded politely.

"This is your nurse?" The trooper scowled at my

uniform in derision. His tone was not unpleasant, though his voice brooked no compromise.

"She is." Brother Rolf's gaze darted from the visitor to me. "Erika, have a seat. This gentleman was asking about the castle."

I didn't wait for a chair to be pulled out for me but took a seat opposite our guest. I knew it wasn't a social call. Brother Rolf's friendly voice held a note of apprehension.

"Erika Lehmeier, sir. Pleased to meet you." I extended my hand in greeting.

"*Fräulein*. Captain Valentine Braun at your service." He nodded his head in greeting. The soft handshake he gave was an odd contrast to the steely ice blue of his eyes. Looking into them was like staring into a bottomless pit of cold darkness. He seemed nearly inhuman, and I suddenly felt the desire to hide.

Captain Braun, may I get you a drink?" I asked, instead.

"Nothing. *Danke*." He was polite but not friendly. Our words were scripted courtesy with no intent of genuine welcome.

Good. That means you can go away now, right?

As though able to read my mind, Brother Rolf squirmed in his chair. "Captain Braun has expressed interest in the castle." The air was thick with apprehension, though the monk tried to sound pleasant. I heard the tightness in his voice.

"Why?" was all I asked. The Nazi looked at me. My heart began to pound in defiance as well as a certain measure of fear.

"The SS has use for it." He looked through me, his voice a non-revealing monotone with no pretense of friendliness, only a naked statement not to be disputed. When his declaration was met with silence, as neither Brother Rolf nor I knew what to say, he continued, "Why don't you tell me about the castle?"

It seemed a harmless request. When I followed his gaze to the staircase, fear for the children wrenched my insides. I felt determined his shadow would never fall on them.

"Ours is a very quiet routine here, sir. Very little of interest, I'm afraid," I responded.

"On the contrary. It's quite lovely. The grounds are spacious, as is the castle itself. How many rooms are there?" He seemed amused at my discomfiture.

"Very small rooms. The castle is just big enough for a handful of children and a couple of staff." My hands wouldn't stop trembling. Hoping to hide my anxiety, I held them under the table.

"Nearly froze last winter," Brother Rolf followed my lead. "These stone buildings provide little heat. Dank, musty, dreadful after a rain."

"Horrible plumbing!" I added. " In fair weather, I encourage the boys to pee in the woods."

"Charming. How many children do you have here?" Braun's voice deadpanned as his gaze darted from me back to Brother Rolf.

"Six," Brother Rolf answered.

Like a she-wolf protecting my cubs, I steered the subject away from the children.

"In the interest of the Reich, I would like to point out that the castle would be of little significance to anyone. As I said, substandard plumbing is only one in a list of many, many flaws." My words sped across my tongue. My mind screamed at him to leave. *Go, and let my children be. Let Grafeneck be.* Would they not leave at least this one little corner of refuge, this one small piece of Germany, untouched?

His head turned slowly, and his eyes narrowed as if daring me to look away. "I do not recall asking for a list, *Fräulein*." His lip curled slightly, and the cold eyes betrayed no emotion.

"Of course not, sir." My voice fell.

Brother Rolf reached over to give my hand a pat. "I don't know how we managed before Erika came. She has been a blessing." The round, friendly face smiled.

"Thank you." I felt grateful for his support, and I only wished I could be more help and rid us of this unwanted guest.

"I'm certain she is quite competent. That is not the reason for this visit," Braun's cold monotone responded.

"Did you need directions to Marburg?" I asked with a smile. The steely gaze bore into mine.

The question was ignored. "As I said, the Reich has use of Grafeneck."

"Is Grafeneck up for sale?" I tried to keep the tremble out of my voice. Brother Rolf stiffened in his seat, casting a pleading look toward me.

"Nothing was said about buying it, *Fräulein* Lehmeier. The grounds are quiet, a perfect place to heal and rest. Surely, you would not hinder the best interests of our soldiers?"

I assumed his calm expression was meant to be a smile, but it pierced my soul. He studied me.

"Of course not. I confess renovations would be costly, and the overall damp of this old place might hinder the healing process." Why did we need an army hospital when we were not at war? I feared the rumors were true.

Braun rose gracefully from his chair. "It has been a pleasure meeting you. Heil Hitler."

I did not return the salute. I only watched as he regally strode through the door toward his car.

"They can't take the castle!"

"I'm afraid they can." Brother Rolf's tone was resigned, and he slumped in his chair.

I tried to protest. "Grafeneck is Catholic-owned. The Accord..."

He stopped my protests with a motion of his hand. We listened for the sound of an engine roaring to life. Brother Rolf placed a finger across his lips. "Hopefully, it is an interest that will pass."

He reassured me with a pat to the shoulder. Neither of us believed his words. I could only hope Grafeneck would not appeal to our rulers so much after a second glance.

Chapter 12

Brother Rolf called an emergency staff meeting at ten o'clock that night. The four monks and I met in the dining room downstairs. Brother Rolf took the seat at the head of the table. The children were in bed, while the SS slithered back to their homes. We were assured privacy at this late hour with little chance of interruption.

My flesh crawled as I felt the prickle of hairs standing on end. There had never been an emergency staff meeting called before, as far as I knew. It couldn't be good news.

Brother Rolf stood before us; with shaking hands he held a document that appeared to have been crumpled and then smoothed out. The creases were still evident as he read it to us. His once smiling eyes were flat and unfocused, and his voice droned dully, finishing with the dreaded statement: "Samaritan House has transferred ownership of Grafeneck Castle to the Third Reich."

His bloodshot eyes drooped sadly, and his shoulders appeared to slump with the weight of the words. There was a murmur of angry protest among the other monks.

"When will we have to leave?" Brother Heinrich asked.

"Yes, when does this happen?" Brother Stephan added.

They were visibly shaken at the prospect of losing their home. How could I blame them? Grafeneck had become my home, too, and I hadn't been there nearly as long as they had.

"The SS will take possession in September." The news fell like an executioner's axe.

What I feared most was about to happen. What about the children? Would they be shipped off to an institution, forgotten and alone until the end came as it had for my sister? No. There would be a way to keep that from happening. If it took my last breath, I would protect these children.

The silence remained unbroken, each of us thinking of how this would affect life as we had so far known it, until, "Why?" The word came out in a snarl. "What about our responsibility to the children?" Brother Stephan's voice was only slightly calmer now that the initial shock had worn off.

"Why Grafeneck?" Brother Heinrich voiced my thoughts exactly.

"It is my understanding Grafeneck will be converted into an army hospital," Brother Rolf quietly explained. "I don't like it any more than you do." The monk looked weary, as though life had hit him with one punch too many. His shoulders drooped in defeat as he spoke.

"Wait. Grafeneck is Catholic-owned. It is church property. Isn't there something in the Accord to prevent the takeover?" I grasped at straws, but the straws were my only lifeline against the truth I didn't want to face.

"I appreciate what you are saying, Erika. The Accord frees us in one way and binds us in another."

"How much do we lose before we say no?" I was railing against the wind, I realized, but I needed to vent. "Why doesn't this cursed Accord ever work in our favor?" I couldn't stop the anger, the pain at losing Gretchen, and then Helga and Father Julian, and now Grafeneck and the children. The bursting of the dam of emotion I'd held in check and forced back now exploded freely. "Article 31 says Catholics are free to practice our faith unmolested. Father Julian was arrested at the church. Isn't that breach of contract?" I scrambled for something substantial to use in our defense. "The Reich is a lawful institution. Lord knows they've passed enough ordinances to fill a large tome. Why can't the Vatican make them adhere to the contract?"

"Article 17 says we take an oath of loyalty to the Reich, which means submitting to their laws and decisions," Brother Rolf replied, seeming resigned though his eyes burned with fury as he again crumpled the document in his hand. I knew he agreed with me.

"Does loyalty to our country preclude a loyalty to our faith?" There had to be something overlooked, some loophole we could use to keep possession of Grafeneck. It was only then I noted the bruises on his hands, bruises absent before the SS had come to visit. They had forced his hand, literally.

"That is the reason for Article 32, Catholics will not be compelled to tasks running contrary to moral obligation." Brother Heinrich spoke for Brother Rolf now. Tempers bubbled over like boiling water as the brothers broke into discussion.

Brother Rolf rubbed the dark bruise on his chin, but his words came as if very carefully chosen. "Erika, we could talk about this all day. I don't like it any more than you do, but we have no alternatives. They take possession in September."

He turned away. The staff was dismissed as he rose from his chair. The conversation was over. Bitter tears stung my eyes. "This is how we compromise? The Nazis do whatever they want, and we Catholics sweetly comply?"

"Only if we want our church to survive, Erika. You must understand. *In burning sorrow.* That is the name of the letter the Vatican wrote denouncing the Reich. It was nearly a declaration of war. The Vatican publicly denounced Germany for its actions," Brother Stephan explained.

"And that left Germany's Catholics in the eye of a storm with nothing tangible to hold onto." I spat the words as if they were poison in my mouth.

"The Vatican is doing all it can to protect us," Stephan went on to say.

"What about the children?" I said.

"They will be relocated before the first of September," Brother Rolf replied.

I couldn't believe what I was hearing. All the authorities I had put faith in were failing me. Nothing made sense. Anger fueled my determination to find a way out. Any path to resistance would be made in small steps, but if there was a way to get past the Nazis and protect the children, I would do it. "That's it, then? The Reich barks an order, and we heel?"

"Or pretend to." For the first time, I saw defiance shine in Rolf's eyes. New hope caught fire in me from it, strengthening my resolve. For the first time since Gretchen's arrest, I was sure I was not helpless.

Chapter 13

Nazis stalked about the castle like sinister shadows lurking around each corner. Groups of SS men surveyed the lands, the stable, and the entrance to the castle. I kept the children near me, cloistered away from the shadows in a room filled with sunshine.

The gray-coated uniforms were an unwanted presence, but I had little choice other than to put up with the unwanted guests. It was obvious they were staying. The monks were planning to join another, larger, group of brothers near Berlin, while I was to remain at Grafeneck to tend the children and familiarize the new residents to the castle. I can't say the newcomers were rude to the children. I had to swallow my fear and run after the twins when they wanted to inspect the men clearing land.

"What are you doing?" Luis looked around.

"We are going to build something. Land is cleared first, and then we can put in the pipes and pour concrete. That is called laying a foundation." He smiled as he ruffled Luis' hair.

"I'll help!" Helmut scooped up dirt with his hands, which made the workers laugh. I watched the scene a few moments. Later, it would always make me wonder if the workers knew what it was they built.

"Boys, come on! Let them get their work done," I called to them. A few of the workers paused as I approached, and some smiled a greeting while others kept working. "I'm sorry." I smiled to the foreman. "Let's go find another place to play, children."

I extended my hands and each boy took one as we walked away from the building site. The grounds were filled with the bustle of activity, giving the children plenty to watch. I wondered what additions they would make to the current building for the hospital that would be opened. I learned the renovations would be done before Christmas and the facility operational by January. It was an ambitious schedule. I peered at work orders and began to befriend the workers, hoping to glean bits of information.

Then came the day when I was asked for information. From Berlin, a team of three doctors came to evaluate each child under my care. Their stated mission was to examine each child and judge the rehabilitation potential for each one based on diagnosis, response to therapy, and future medical needs. Each doctor, odd-looking in his own individual way, exuded a dark presence. I simply referred to the trio as 'the tripod.'

I sat at the table across from the tripod. Charts for the children were placed in a neat pile. These were inspected, one at a time. The charts were scrutinized, as was I. I felt like a germ under a microscope. The trio watched my every move and measured my every word. I forgot their names, referring to them simply as Bug Eyes, Snake, and Weasel.

In addition to prestigious letters and a title long enough to shroud himself, each doctor bore the attitude that I, a lowly nurse, should be content to simply bask in his presence.

The panel questioned me about each child. Bug Eyes did most of the talking. His protruding eyes looked as though they might pop in and out of his head at will. When he asked questions, Snake and Weasel focused on me and jotted down what I said. Taking a file from the top of the pile, he spoke the name of the first child.

"Heidi Völker?" Bug Eyes had the voice of one who wore his underpants too small. He squeaked the question in a small, almost girlish tone.

"No, sir. Erika Lehmeier," I sweetly answered.

"I refer to the child, Fräulein Lehmeier. Please, pay attention." Bug Eyes focused the protruding orbs on me.

"Certainly. My mistake." My honeyed voice hid my annoyance.

"Heidi Völker. Diagnosis?" Snake hissed the command.

"Epilepsy." I fought not to show fear. I felt dirty in the presence of the tripod, and I longed for a hot shower to cleanse myself as soon as these three departed.

"Overall health?" Snake seemed satisfied to ask the questions for now. His eyes bore into mine as though trying to pry the information from my mind before it could cross my lips.

"Very good. With medication, her condition is..." I was interrupted.

"You will answer only the questions asked," Snake hissed.

"Stable." I finished the sentence anyway. Snake and Weasel stared without blinking. I ignored them.

"Visible abnormalities?" Weasel asked.

I furrowed my brow. "She's a healthy little girl," I replied.

"You are not qualified to diagnose." Bug Eyes' eyeballs protruded ever further, giving me the urge to push them back into their sockets.

"Probable success of treatment?" Bug Eyes continued.

"As I said, with medication the epilepsy is controlled," I answered honestly. Luminol was used to treat the epilepsy, and Heidi's episodes were really very mild. If a person wasn't aware of the diagnosis, it might be assumed the child lost herself in daydreams.

"Will the condition remedy itself?" Bug Eyes continued. Of the three, he seemed the most interested in actual care of the children.

"I can't answer that. In time, science may find a cure. For now..."

Snake interrupted me. "It is genetic and incurable." Snake's words were slow and deliberate. He was a man with intense brown eyes and dark hair. Looking at him made my flesh crawl.

Weasel concurred. The tripod each marked a card in red pencil as Heidi's chart was placed by itself. I ran my foot along the back of my calf. Maybe Weasel was a newcomer. He deferred constantly to Snake and Bug Eyes.

"Josef Farber has mongolism?" Weasel's raspy voice oozed from his chicken chest, and I wondered how this man had ever passed a military physical.

"Yes, sir." I forced myself to sit bolt upright with my hands folded on the table. I would not flinch or show emotion, I vowed.

"Has he an aptitude for learning?" Weasel asked.

I smiled as I thought of the sweet boy who rushed to help in every situation. A child with no ability to hate, he was a great teacher of love.

"Yes, sir. He is easily taught." I couldn't stop a smile.

"So is my dog." Snake handed Weasel the red pencil. No other questions were forthcoming as the three made their marks. I felt hairs rise on the back of my neck. His file was placed in a neat stack with Heidi's.

Snake spoke next. I swallowed bile. His eyes glowed with malicious interest. "Luis and Helmut are twins?"

The boys were mildly retarded, but I could not

bring myself to say it. The diagnosis was in the chart. The chart was in their hands. I couldn't lie.

"Yes, sir." I wanted to run to my children, to protect them from this toxic man and his cold stare.

"They will be transferred to Berlin," Snake stated. His matter of fact tone would brook no argument.

"Why?" I demanded to know. The twins had no family in Berlin. Three heads popped up in surprise. I looked to each face for an answer.

Snake narrowed his eyes, and his gaze bore into me. He kept writing as he spoke, deeming my concern unworthy of notice. "They will be relocated. You need not be concerned." His voice was too precise, too smooth. "Their parents have, of course, been notified."

I was certain he lied, and I would find out soon enough. They ignored my question as the interview continued.

"Lara Huber." Bug Eyes resumed the questioning, but I stayed focused on Snake, wondering what he wrote.

"Lara is a healthy nine-year-old girl," I answered. Because of a birth defect, she would never have a normal arm. The three passed the chart and made their marks in red pencil.

"The last child." Weasel's mundane-sounding voice screamed in my ears.

Wilhelm. The Last Child. The. Last. Child. My heartbeat slammed against my chest. My breathing became heavy.

"Full rehabilitation possible. The leg braces will support his legs until they are strong enough to support themselves. He walks. He talks. He thinks like everyone else. He's a genius, in fact. Brilliant. Tests off the chart!" My voice became impassioned. He was smart. A genius? Maybe not.

Three sets of eyes stared into my soul. I wanted

to run, but I forced myself to hold my head high, taking time to look into their faces, each in turn.

"Thank you, Fräulein Lehmeier. That will be all." Three sets of eyes bore into mine without blinking.

"When are the children to be relocated?"

"Arrangements have been made." It was Snake. I hated him with a ferocity that scared me. Never before had I truly hated. People had annoyed me, embarrassed me, even hurt me, but nothing compared to the hatred I felt churn my insides at the sound of his voice. I rose with deliberation and held his gaze.

"Where are they to be taken?" I met his cold stare.

"You are dismissed." Snake raised his voice slightly. Nodding curtly, I noted the slogan *For blood and honor* written underneath the skull pin worn on his uniform. As I left the interview, the instinct to run overtook me, and I ran to the children.

Later, alone in my office, I began to leaf through the charts, curious to see the doctors' notes. I opened Heidi's chart to see what comments had been made by the three physicians. My heart stopped. The familiar letterhead caught my eye.

Dear Mr. and Mrs. Völker,

We regret to inform you there was an outbreak of pneumonia spreading through the wards of the hospital. Despite our best efforts, the disease could not be contained. Your child became infected and died in her sleep. We have sent an urn containing her cremated remains. Again, you have our deepest sympathy.

Regards,
Christian Wirth
Director, Children's Services

It was the same letter my family had received a few months ago, along with my sister's ashes contained in an urn. I looked at the letter again. I tore into all the charts. An identical letter was in each one. In each folder was a card with three red crosses signed by the three doctors who had examined the charts. The cards had information regarding the patients' diagnoses, mental state and rehabilitation potential. The categories were marked individually. My children all had three red plus signs on their evaluation cards. Fear had a chokehold on my tightening chest as I read. They were labeled "useless eaters" because of "Genetic disorders."

What is their fate from here?

I could take the children to Vienna and put them on a train to the Netherlands—from there, they would board a boat to England. Could I provide the fifty francs per child the British asked? This resettlement fee was to guarantee placement in a foster home. My sister had been promised a final placement, as well. I shook the thought from my mind.

Epilepsy. The word caught my eye as I glanced through the file. Heidi would occasionally stare at nothing in particular, but she had no seizures such as people normally associated with epilepsy. Heidi passed as normal, under most circumstances.

At least long enough to get her on the boat, I prayed. If, like Helga, these children would be taken somewhere to die, I had to keep them from dying. How could I reveal the truth to people? How could I rescue them? I took Heidi's folder. My decision was made.

I looked up from the file. I had not noticed the entrance of the man who stood there. The black uniform was in sharp contrast to the blond hair and made the sky blue of his eyes stand out. He removed his cap and came to the desk with confidence, as though he owned the very space he occupied.

"Erika?" It was one word, but the look in Rick's eyes made my knees go weak as I tried to stand, holding the edge of the desk for support. My stomach clenched into a fist of panic as my eyes took in the sight of him.

"You're SS?" My throat felt dried, my tongue shriveled and unable to form words. He had crossed the room in a few easy strides, and his hands reached toward me.

"Erika, I'm sure you're..." Rickard never finished the sentence. The sound of my hand meeting the side of his face echoed across the room. His head swung violently to the side with the impact, and his cheek quickly reddened with my handprint.

"Ouch." The man showed no emotion when he spoke. His voice was clear and cool, like ice. "I assume the doctors have been in."

"The children's charts have been examined." I stood tall. "I have found cards in the files. The doctors took note of the medical condition, potential for recovery and mental status for each one." My hands trembled as I picked up a file. Shaking the manila folder toward him, I smacked him squarely on the nose. "Your doom squad placed death notices in each folder. Six notices for six breathing, living children."

I wanted to claw his eyes and run my fingernails in bloodied stripes down his face. He responded coolly, his eyes weighing and measuring my every word. "Blue minus signs signify a condition that is treatable, generally non-hereditary. A red cross means there is no cure or the condition can be passed on to progeny. The three doctors must agree unanimously before a child is sent to a treatment center."

Did he say "treatment center"? My mind wrapped itself around the concept: a place to die from an illness you don't have in a facility that doesn't exist. I drew in a deep breath, hoping to calm the tremor in my voice. "In each folder is a card like the one we found in Helga's chart at the clinic. Three red crosses were on her evaluation, too. It didn't occur to me to find it odd, then. Not only that but the nurse at the clinic accepted who you were without question. It wasn't the uniform, and she never asked for identification. She had seen you before. She recognized you. She knew who you were." It was a statement rather than a question.

Rickard nodded.

"You son of a bitch!" I choked out the words as I lunged toward him to scratch at his eyes.

Rickard took hold of my wrists to keep me from striking as I continued to fight.

"Father Julian is gone because of you. He trusted you, and you betrayed him!" I hissed, and then tried to bite the restraining hand. Rickard forced my hands behind my back. The abrupt closeness made me snarl, where only days before it would have sent my heart to flight.

"I am not a traitor." Rickard's tone was controlled, yet his eyes blazed at the accusation.

"Liar." The tears broke free from my eyes and burned a path down my cheeks while I struggled against him, my heart frozen. The blue eyes, so warm days ago, pierced into my soul; the dark-clad figure pressed me against the desk, moving closer still.

"I am the same man you met earlier. Remember that." Rickard kissed me gently, brushing my lips tenderly against his.

Tilting my head away, I wet my lips with the tip of my tongue. With renewed breath, my head began to clear. I brought a knee up to make contact with his groin.

In a swift motion, he grabbed me under the

offending knee and lifted me onto the desktop. "That was rude." He held my shoulders firmly. The raspy voice hid pain, though I hadn't hit the mark as squarely as I'd planned.

A cleared throat caused us to look toward the door. I was too flustered to be frightened at the moment. Rickard winked. "Trust me," he whispered. I made no attempt to return his smile.

"You're SS," I hissed.

"What is going on in here?" Gregor's casual comment followed his trademark smirk, which somehow suited his black uniform.

"You're both SS?" My voice was faint, and white knuckles gripped the edge of the desk as sudden lightheadedness made me stagger.

"Erika just received word of the acquisition." Rickard's tone was pleasant, despite the handprint emblazoned across his cheek. I tried to keep a cool exterior. I wanted to rail against him, cry and demand an explanation. How could he be SS? How could I have been so wrong about him?

"The news was not well received?" Gregor lifted the corner of his mouth. I was certain he'd noted the handprint.

"I wanted to show her some self-defense moves. With more criminals being institutionalized, I thought it prudent she learn to protect herself."

I had assaulted an SS officer. Either man could press the charge against me, I was sure. I could almost see the black Mercedes beckoning with an open car door. I rubbed my temples, thus hiding my watery eyes with my hands. "If you will excuse me, I have a headache."

I hoped Rickard would take the hint. Instead, he walked over to a counter and placed a bottle of aspirin on the desk.

"Fortunately, you work in a health care facility. Do not let a headache interrupt your day." He smiled pleasantly.

"Yes, that would be a shame," I deadpanned. I fought not to roll my eyes as I took the bottle from his hand. It was going to be a long day. Gregor leaned against the doorframe, while Rickard sat next to me on my desk. "I thought you had a specific purpose for being here." I fought to smile, but my lips barely twitched as I spoke. "Will you be relocating the children?" My head pounded, and my stomach threatened to redeposit my breakfast onto my lap.

"Not me," Gregor answered. "There is a transport system for taking patients to treatment centers."

"Treatment centers," I murmured. The pounding in my head thundered across my temples. The children would be taken elsewhere to be killed, and the parents would believe they died of pneumonia. It was too much like a nightmare to be believed. I was certain Helga must have been taken to a treatment center. Had she realized what was happening, or was the lie convincing enough to keep her blinded to the truth until the very last minute? I hoped so.

"Erika and I are going to the gala," Rickard stated. I stared daggers at him.

"I am not going anywhere with you," I whispered.

Gregor crossed his arms. "Good. You will be able to learn more about what we are doing. Don't worry about losing your job. After the renovations, there will still be a need for nurses here."

My face froze. Was he kidding? He thought I had been crying over my job?

"What a relief," I choked out the words. "That would be preferable to working with criminals. What will become of Grafeneck?" I asked him. Was he just going to ignore what he'd seen when he'd walked in?

"Military hospital." Gregor's smooth response

burned like salt in a wound. He wasn't concerned, because nothing I said or did would stand against Reich authority. I could feel my heart race as I looked into Gregor's steel-gray eyes. I fully understood how the mouse must feel when cornered by the hawk. The lies were smooth, and the truth was hidden. I couldn't stand looking at Rickard. It hurt too much. It was too much to process. If he'd betrayed Father Julian, and if he'd known all along what had happened to my sister, to Helga, he was as guilty as those who did the actual deed. I kept my eyes on the file cabinet.

"Military hospital." I repeated Gregor's words with a bob of my head. "If you two will excuse me, I have work to do."

Gregor smiled. "Best of luck on defense lessons." He cast a knowing look to Rickard and left. Rickard remained.

"You never really understood the concept of the subtle hint," I stated coldly. I steeled myself to look into his eyes. The black cap was decorated with a silver skull pin. The black uniform enhanced his natural coloring, giving his features a sharper, more intense look. In nature, black and brown were colors of warning, colors of impending dangers. Interesting, that they were the colors chosen for those loyal to the Nazi regime.

Rickard stood still as stone, the cold eyes never blinking. My heart pained. I had forgotten about the small handgun lying in the corner of the desk drawer. I had borrowed it from my father as protection for when the monks left and I was alone with the children in the castle. Despite the ban on guns, he had never gotten around to turning in his service revolver.

"We hadn't finished our conversation," Rickard answered. I slipped off the desk and eased open the middle drawer.

"Let's finish, then." I pulled the gun from the drawer and aimed at Rickard. He sat casually on the desk, arms folded as though nothing unusual was happening. He studied the weapon.

"Deutsche Waffen und Munitions Fabrik 1916. Government issue from the war. Nice piece."

I shook the gun in front of him. My hands trembled. "You realize it may be old, but it can still kill you?"

Could I let the hate well up, surge through my veins as I wrapped my finger around the trigger, and release the tension with a pull? Rickard didn't seem to think so.

"You realize you are not scaring anyone but yourself?" His calm tone only served to infuriate me.

I held the gun at arm's length, looking down the gun barrel. I imagined a target on his forehead. "What I realize is you are a black-hearted miscreant who misled a good man into trusting him. Is that why the Resistance attacked at the dance? They knew you would be there?"

Rickard leaned on one arm, one leg casually draped across the desk. The other leg dangled alongside. He leaned toward me and whispered, "You are standing in a building under SS control. If you shoot me, you still have more SS than you have bullets."

I felt dizzy. I did not think I could shoot another person if I had to. Worse, I sensed Rickard was aware of that fact. "I have no desire to fight my way out of here. I will not have to—you will help me."

Trembling fingers betrayed the control for which I fought. Rickard grinned. He lacked Gregor's arrogance. His smirk was almost playful, as though he'd heard an amusing story.

"I am interested. What is it you expect of me?" He raised a curious brow. I saw no reason to try and lie at this point. Pulling a gun on an SS officer was a serious offense. I would either succeed or die. I took a breath and glanced at the files.

"We are taking the children out of here," I stated. Rickard pursed his lips.

"We are?" he queried. My thoughts raced in a fury through my head. I needed a plan, and I needed it now.

"The Führer is allowing children to leave the country. It is called the Kindertransport. England has agreed to take ten thousand children, and I plan to have these children on board," I explained, motioning toward the files on my desk. Rickard shifted to get more comfortable. He leaned closer to me, his leg still dangling off the edge.

"For this, you threaten me? Have the parents gone through legal channels?" Rickard asked. I understood why he responded that way.

"They are dead to the Fatherland, as you already know." I took a breath. Rickard inched across the desk toward me. "Do not move," I commanded. Talking about the children steeled my resolve to help them. His help would be like penance for his betrayal of Father Julian.

"Of course, I will help you." Rickard smiled, and then, like a flash of lightning, he swept the dangling leg across his body and knocked the gun from my hand. I squealed as the weapon hit the floor. Rickard rolled off the desk and pulled me close to him, grabbing under my chin with his free hand while the other wrapped securely around my middle.

"There is a fine line between courage and stupidity. The next time you cross it could be the last." Rickard's voice was a deadly whisper that left me shuddering.

I trembled under his touch as my words came out in a gasp. "Please. What is one less child to the Fatherland?"

Chapter 14

In the castle, the activity of government workers took on new proportions, since the Nazis would take possession the next month. I felt a warning letter should be written to each of the parents. I hoped that if the parents knew the acquisition would take place on the first of September they would move quickly to bring the children home before they could be automatically relocated. I would mail out the death certificates as instructed, but they'd be bogus.

I took pen in hand, trembling slightly, and I began to write. My stomach ached at the thought of the letters in the children's files. I took a breath to steady myself. Did anyone know I had seen the letters? I couldn't think like that now. I had been told the children would be relocated. Fine. I still had a job for six weeks, so I could reason the children were my responsibility until then.

My words flowed across the page:

Dear Mr. and Mrs. Völker,

I regret to inform you Grafeneck Castle is undergoing a change in management as of 1 September, 1939. Please, prepare to take your child home as quickly as you can after receiving this statement. Any delay may bring an automatic relocation of your child. Suggested date and time to arrive at the castle is August 25, noon.

Sincerely,
Erika Lehmeier
Staff Nurse
Grafeneck Castle

I wanted them all to come at the same time. It

would be difficult to lie to six sets of parents at once. I quickly skimmed the letter. The castle would be taken over in September. If they were gone well before the Nazis moved in, why would there be a complaint?

Movement in my peripheral vision caused me to look up. Gregor lifted a note from the pile and read it. My face burned with anger at his lack of respect for my privacy. How long had he been standing there? Gregor towered over me as he read my letter. When he'd finished, he looked me dead in the eye. "This is not necessary. Arrangements have been made."

I forced a smile again and tried desperately to keep my fingers from trembling. "Yes, but the parents should be informed, so they have the option to place their children elsewhere. Saves us the trouble."

I tried to hold my ground with an offensive glare, though I did not get the response I hoped for. In one swift move, Gregor scooped up the letters and tossed them into the fireplace. My effort to make a grab for the pages was futile. I watched the blackened pages curl as they burned, and anger rose within me, poised to strike. I bit back a scathing response.

"I understand your concern, but as I have stated, arrangements have already been made for placement." He moved in one fluid motion, like an eagle plucking a fish from the water, to take the pen from my hand.

At first, I wondered how much I should admit to knowing. I decided it was in my best interest to feign ignorance. "There is such a thing as being too efficient. I fear I am not much use with your team handling everything so well."

I tried to sound airy, but part of me feared arrest. I could almost feel the cold steel of the handcuffs when I looked into his eyes.

"From this point forward, you are to be working with the children as always. Any administrative duties will be handled by the SS." His voice was sharp as a razor, and the beaklike aristocratic features reminded me of a bird of prey. Again I glanced at the burning papers. Without realizing it, Gregor had effectively destroyed any evidence against me, but if it came to his word against mine, I was certain Gregor's would hold more sway.

"Just let me know if there is anything more I can do." I tried to make eye contact while willing myself not to be afraid. Gregor stood unmoving as his gaze bored into mine.

"There is one issue that concerns me." His predatory voice put me on alert as he took one step closer, invading my body space, looking down on me as he squared his shoulders. *Only one?* I thought to myself. I tilted my head as though curious about what he would say. "There is a policy of confidentiality to be strictly adhered to."

I shrugged my shoulders. "Of course. That is standard duty in nursing. Patient confidentiality." I wondered if he could smell my fear as he circled around me.

Gregor looked me over. He leaned closer to see if he could intimidate me. The hot breath tickled my ear. Each word was clearly stated with slow precision. His attempt at intimidation worked. He must have seen me flinch. "Understand me. A breach of these protocols will result in immediate legal action."

I took a tiny step back. He had swooped down for the kill. It was a threat. I turned and smiled sweetly, my voice like honey. "Then, please, explain the protocols."

His face was devoid of expression. I knew I could play the game, once I knew the rules. Gregor paused, probably believing I would run off like a scared rabbit. I was determined to face him head on. "The job parameters remain the same. You will see to the usual needs of the children, until they are transported from Grafeneck Castle. There is to be no discussion of patient conditions or relocation plans to anyone who is not on staff here."

"What happens at the castle stays at the castle. Yes, sir." I tried to smile, despite the painful clenching of my teeth. *The raptor won this round.*

"That includes discussion with the children themselves. There is no need to confuse or frighten them with details of the move."

I looked at him again. If I accepted all other protocols, this one bothered me the most. I nodded agreement and asked, "Where will they be relocated?"

Gregor shrugged. "Treatment centers. Hospitals designed to meet the needs of the patient."

I grinned softly. "Well, you can't ask for more than that. I will miss it here. The SS picked a beautiful spot for..." I paused. "What will it be used for?"

"Hospital for wounded soldiers," Gregor replied. I nodded. The SS was consistent with their story, I noted.

"Despite Germany's insistence for peace, we preoccupy ourselves with the threat of war. It's scary." I rubbed my arms as though warding off a chill. I wasn't sure what I wanted him to say, but I was tired of the innuendos and the sugarcoated lies. The truth might be ugly, but at least I would understand what really happened.

"Germany is well able to defend itself. Will you inquire about a job here? There will be recruiters looking for nurses to run the facility."

"It's an idea," I quipped. "I think I will spend some time with my parents, however. It has been difficult for my mother without Helga."

"Who?"

"Helga. My sister." Now I was annoyed. Gregor had little concern for anything that did not involve him.

"Sorry. That was sad. Helga was sick?"

"She had polio." I did not bother with the whole truth. She had survived the polio, yet died of pneumonia when she had no history of respiratory problems.

Gregor took me by the shoulders. His attempt to console me only made me seethe. "It may be for the best. At least she isn't a cripple."

My mouth twitched. His stupid, callous words drew blood. He'd found my soft spot and attacked without conscience. I forced the words out. "Yes, I suppose you are right."

His comment had hit a nerve, but I refused to lash out. I was a nurse. I was able to submerge my feelings if I had to. The letters had burned quickly and with them any hope of notifying the parents. Gregor would have me arrested if I tried again, and I wasn't completely certain he wouldn't still. Maybe he would simply hold the information over my head until it suited him to use it.

"What future do you see for the Third Reich?" Gregor folded his arms across his chest as though satisfied he had conquered the problem. His smirk indicated that, if he couldn't make me squirm, he would play with me.

"Austria has returned to the Fatherland. We have the Rhineland as well as Czechoslovakia. I would say we are growing and prosperous. The future looks bright." I smiled the sweet, comforting smile I used to lull my patients.

"So, are you willing to work in the hospital if called?" Gregor continued to study me with cold, gray eyes.

"I am a nurse. Of course I would. I care about people, Gregor, and I don't ask how many factories they own when I choose a friend."

He lifted a brow. I had managed to find *his* soft spot and bruise his ego. He was born into money, so someone in my position on the social scale would never warrant a second look. He looked down his nose at me.

"Just choose your friends carefully." The smirk came with a warning when he spoke, and I grew tired of it.

I placed a genteel hand on his shoulder, and my voice oozed sweetness. "Gregor, thank you for taking the time to be so concerned for me. Knowing you care just does something to me," I cooed as I batted my eyelashes. I knew he was peeved on a personal level, but I wasn't too worried.

"Remember what I said." His gaze was steady, his tone unwavering. Whatever he was after, I hoped I was able to give it to him. He obviously did not trust me, nor I him.

"Yes, sir, certainly." I gazed at him and sighed as I watched him leave the room, my painted-on grin contorted into a snarl.

Chapter 15

My parents had a social engagement of their own for the evening of the Nazi gala to which Rick was taking me. I was grateful to be alone while dressing in my room at home. My preference would have been to cuddle up with a good book. Instead, I prepared to go to a dinner dance only the high society of Nazi government would be attending. Rickard wanted me to pretend to be part of this pseudo-society. Hopefully, I would blend in and be able to listen and learn without drawing attention to myself.

I parted my hair to the side, swept it away from my face, and pinned it with a comb. My pink dress swirled to midcalf, and with its lace bodice, cut halfway down the back, I felt myself the picture of elegance.

I had borrowed my mother's pearl necklace for the evening. I stroked the smooth globes, appreciating the glossy feel as I ran my fingers across them. A pearl is created as a result of constant irritation. Would Rickard turn out to be a pearl? He could certainly be an irritant at times.

A soft knock on the door announced his arrival, and I went to let him in.

He had no sooner come in the door than he ran his fingers along the door jambs. Then he felt under the tables and the underside of the couch, moving systematically across the room.

"What are you doing?" I watched as he continued to carefully run his fingers along the underside of the counter in the kitchen, as if

141

searching for something.

"Checking for listening devices." I was stunned. Rickard raised a finger as though restraining me from commenting. "Outside, I heard bells as I rode up." His casual voice belied his intense search as he continued, on his knees, checking under furnishings, lamps and inside cabinets.

"Yes. They ring before church services. The Catholics have service on Saturday night." I copied the casual tone he used. The thought of outsiders listening made me feel exposed, violated.

"Spread the word. The confessionals are frequented by Gestapo." Brushing off his knees Rickard stood upright. He was now satisfied nothing was amiss.

"Gestapo listens in on people in the confessional?" That was outrageous, a direct violation of the Accord.

"They listen everywhere. A woman was arrested in a movie theater for making an unflattering remark about Hitler."

"Secret police," I whispered. The words were never uttered above a whisper. It was as though saying them aloud would bring the dreaded thing to view.

Rickard nodded. "That is why I did not bring Heidi here."

"Heidi? Where is Heidi?" A jolt of fear caused my breath to hitch as I reached for his arm. Rickard covered my hand with his.

"A safe house. The monks are alone at the castle. As far as they know, she was relocated early," Rickard explained as he made his way toward the front door. "If you are ready, maybe we should leave."

I breathed a sign of relief. "One down and five to go." I shut the door behind me. Turning, I walked into his solid form.

"Lock the door." It was a command.

"My parents will be home soon. There is no need." I smiled as I said it.

"Trust me. Lock it." His eyes held mine until I reached inside my purse for the key.

We never lock our doors," I whispered, suddenly fearful. I wanted to trust Rickard. If he were going to have me arrested, surely he would have done so before now. The black SS uniform was a constant reminder the world was changing. Had he said Heidi was in a safe house? Had the monks taken her there? If not them, then who? Since Rickard was concerned about my house, I could assume I was being watched. Father Julian had trusted him. I looked at Rickard in his black dress uniform, a color meant to force respect, along with the gun holstered at his side. He looked every inch the authority of the Reich at this moment. My hands trembled as I placed the house key in my purse.

When we arrived at the gala, I was amazed at the number of guests present and the political power represented. The manor was resplendent—huge pillars lined the front entrance, with long banners draped from the balcony, banners bearing the Reich emblem. I couldn't remember the last time I had seen the real national flag of Germany. SS uniforms were everywhere, swarming the steps as people moved in and out of the building. I turned my gaze from the sight of them and drew a calming breath.

"This party is being held to honor the SS. Many top-ranking officials will be here," Rickard explained as the car eased along the driveway. "This is where you will have your questions answered."

"A sheep in wolf's clothing," I muttered, silently praying I wouldn't say the wrong thing while in the wolf's den. Rickard drove around the large fountain, which grandly stood in the middle of a circular drive, and then he pulled to a stop under the portico over the front entrance. A soldier opened my door, greeted me, and extended his hand, which I politely took. Then Rickard placed his arm casually about my waist and guided me up the marble steps. I leaned into his touch. Whether he held me for warmth against the cool breeze or as a pretense of being a couple, I wasn't sure, but I welcomed his light embrace and the reassurance it provided. We crossed the marble foyer overlooking a grand ballroom where several people waltzed as the musicians played. Rickard placed his hands on my shoulders and turned me gently to face him.

"You look lovely. There are a lot of prominent people here, but do not be nervous. Everyone will love you." His words were sweet, his smile so convincing I nearly believed him. His hand moved to caress my cheek, sliding smoothly under my chin and tilting my face upward. He brushed his lips against mine, kissing me gently. He took my breath away as I kissed him back, wishing nothing else existed save the two of us in this moment.

"I won't be nervous with you here." I half closed my eyes demurely and wondered for whom we performed. Rickard wanted the guests to believe we were a couple. I had hoped the kiss was not simply staged. Part of me wanted to hate him, but for now Rickard felt like a safe haven in a world gone crazy.

"Rickard! It is good to see you. No sign of the guest of honor yet." The voice was that of an impressive figure clad in the SS dress uniform. Rickard heartily shook his hand and gave him a friendly pat on the back.

Turning toward me, Rickard made the introductions. "Herr Rittenour and I go back a long way. We met when I attended the University of Munich," Rickard explained. "This is my friend. Fräulein Erika Lehmeier."

"It is a pleasure, sir, *sehr erfreut*." I gently shook

his hand.

"A friend of Rick's is a friend of mine." His smile seemed genuine, though I hesitated to trust a smiling Nazi.

"Were you a professor, Herr Rittenour?"

"No, no." The friendly smile never left his face as he continued. "I am a recruiter for the SS. There was an uprising at the university a while back. Some young people became immersed in radical thinking. The problem was quickly resolved, and from this I was able to find my star pupil."

"So you were able to recruit Rickard into the SS from the university?" I felt my smile erode. My spirit sank.

"It is an honor to be chosen. We strive to represent the best of Germany," the man continued, giving Rickard a friendly pat on the back.

"I am sure I fall short." Rickard smiled. I stood silent. Rittenour put an arm around us and laughed.

"Rick, you are too modest. I assure you, *Fräulein*, you're on the arm of one of Germany's finest," Rittenour crowed, with a pride that seemed almost fatherly, while Rickard stood tall.

"Yes, of that, I am sure," I stated meekly. Rickard's eyes locked onto mine as though daring me to say a word. While the orchestra featured a beautiful violin solo, I decided to try to be charming and see if I could learn anything. "Herr Rittenour, I apologize if I seem forward, but may I have this dance?"

The older man glanced at me in surprise and looked to Rickard. "If your beau gives consent, I should love it."

When Rickard tilted his head and smiled, I took Rittenour's hands in mine.

"I am sure he will appreciate the respite. I am a bit awkward in this elegant setting." I hoped I sounded charming. If I had to be here, I would get honest answers to my questions, straight from the source, if possible.

"Nonsense. Just be gentle is all I ask." Rickard's self-appointed father figure chuckled. We moved to the dance floor. I wondered what the man had been like before the Nazis had conquered him. He was the type who made a person feel like family, the perfect mentor for a boy with no direction, who needed encouragement, or a friend. The Führer was no fool. He knew his people and used their strengths to full advantage. Because of this, my words had to be carefully chosen.

On the dance floor, my thoughts raced. I put Heidi out of my mind. It sounded mad, but my heart was at peace when I thought of the little girl. Rickard was another matter. I fought with my heart over my feelings for him. On one hand, he assured me he was the same man I had met at the rectory, but who was he then? Was he really looking out for Father Julian, or was his warning a ploy to gain trust so he could root out dissension? Rickard was so kind to the children at the castle, and then he had Heidi whisked away to a safe house. Was this action on the monks' order, or did he act alone? Worse, did the SS direct him? He had warned me of Gestapo infiltration in church, yet he had given me no warning and no indication of what to expect tonight. Then he had kissed me, publicly. Rickard had suggested I come to this party. No, he had *insisted* I would be coming to this party. He had been so adamant, I had feared saying no. Was this his show of strength? A fair warning of what I would be up against if I crossed him? Why had he brought me here? I felt outclassed, like a little girl playing dress-up among high society ladies.

"Did you go to the university?" Rittenour's voice held a warm tone.

"Oh, no. I received nurse training at a diploma

school. I was eager to get a job helping people," I responded.

"Well, your skills will be useful. Nursing is such a noble profession." He smiled.

"Thank you." I averted my eyes.

"*Meine Damen und Herren*, ladies and gentlemen, my apologies for interrupting the dance, but our guest of honor has arrived. May I present Herr Christian Wirth?"

I applauded politely at the introduction. The name sounded vaguely familiar, but at the moment I could not recall its significance.

"Wirth was police chief here in Marburg before joining the SS," my companion whispered to me.

The man on stage did nothing to inspire warmth. His voice cut through the air like cold steel. He was a diminutive man, compact and muscular, who wore elevated shoes to enhance his height. His hawklike eyes looked through a person when he spoke. He was bald and, like the Führer, had a small, ugly mustache just under his nose. I hated the look of it. If a man chose to have a mustache, then he should have a mustache, not some half effort that looked like a centipede stuck beneath his nostrils. A mental image was conjured, and I stifled a giggle that refused to tone down.

"Are you all right, dear girl?" he asked.

"Oh, yes, I am fine, *danke*," I answered. "Perhaps we should find our seats."

Christian Wirth sat in the place of honor at the head of the table. To look at him gave me a chill, making me grateful to be sitting several seats away from him.

"How are proceedings at Grafeneck?" Wirth addressed Rickard.

"Well, sir. The occupants are being relocated. Renovations have begun. We predict completion of the project in two months' time." Rickard seemed unaffected in his response.

"Good. The retarded will be sent for euthanasia to Grafeneck. Transportation will be provided from surrounding areas. You may hire staff as you see fit. The monks have been disbanded. The state owns Grafeneck now," Wirth stated.

"Sir, the children currently living in the castle? Will they stay until renovations are complete?" I asked.

"They will be relocated, *Fräulein*. What, may I ask, is your interest in Grafeneck?" No smile played across Wirth's lips. There was no light in his eyes, only a stone-faced response to my question.

"I took internship there, and I live there. The children are under my care. The castle has an interesting history, and wonderful homemade candy is sold at Christmas," I replied.

"Perhaps plans should be made to purchase the sweets elsewhere," Wirth stated in a cool drawl.

"Pity. I was fond of the sweets." I forced a pleasant smile. Wirth's face was a blank.

"A woman's understanding of politics, sir," Rittenour joked.

Wirth disregarded me and turned his attention to Rittenour. "Use of Aktion Four will be put into effect in this facility. Grafeneck will act as the prototype, and other hospitals will be forged in her image."

"We will make reports on a regular basis, sir." Rickard maintained a professional manner as he spoke.

"You are a credit to your squadron," Wirth intoned.

"Death's Head Squadron," Rittenour whispered to me. My stomach lurched, and I took a sip of water. Death's Head Squadron would run the treatment centers. I tried to reason how Rickard fitted into all of this. What could I trust? Was Heidi safe, or was she a means to insure my cooperation? I had to find this out, so I could understand.

"Let's not bore the ladies with business. This is a party!" Rittenour lifted a glass in toast. "To Herr Wirth. His dedication to the welfare of Germany is an inspiration to be admired." Rittenour's warm voice was well received. All glasses were raised in a toast.

"To the welfare of Germany." I raised my glass with the rest and smiled through gritted teeth. I had the truth. This was what Rickard wanted me to understand. The reason for the secrecy was that Grafeneck would not be used as a hospital at all. It would become one of six killing centers. My fortress would be transformed into a disgusting house of horror.

As dinner ended, Rickard excused himself to speak with others in uniform. Dishes were cleared, and guests began to mingle. What had started as a pleasant introduction became a grating experience when it grew evident Rittenour had no plans to do anything but stick to me like glue. I had gone out onto the porch alone. Soft lights twinkled in the trees. Beyond the trees were well-manicured lawns. The cool air offered escape from the people and music. I had hoped Rickard would join me, although at some point I had lost him. The sky was smattered with stars, the perfect canopy for a lovers' meeting. Under any other circumstance, Rickard would have made me melt. I waited breathlessly for him to come out to me. His strong baritone would caress my senses and wrap me in warmth like a favorite quilt. I pondered his kiss, which still confused me. Was he simply keeping me from the other wolves in the pack, or was he interested? If he was interested, where was he? Why not introduce me as a cousin, if his only concern was to keep suitors at bay? I closed my eyes and remembered the beauty of that kiss.

Strength, warmth and gentleness had been expressed in one moment. Had it been a lie?

"Rickard was telling me about your job at Grafeneck." Rittenour came up behind me, his voice a casual whisper.

Scheisse. I kept from saying it aloud. His voice grated like nails on a chalkboard, but I forced a smile before steeling myself to turn around. "He must bore you terribly if he resorts to me as a topic of conversation." I folded my arms and glanced over his shoulder, in hopes of finding Rickard inside.

"Not at all. The SS are trying to incorporate more nurses to work in treatment facilities."

"Treatment? Do you mean euthanasia?" I did not smile, but I was interested.

"Disinfections. Treatments. Euthanasia. It is all the same." The jocular tone never left his voice, though I knew he watched me for signs of disapproval.

"Disinfections would include what?" I asked.

"The termination of genetic illnesses will be the cornerstone of the Aryan nation. No child will ever suffer the burden of handicap, mental or physical." I glanced at his hand on my shoulder. With his other arm outstretched, it looked as though he presented an artwork or revealed an image of a perfect world, an image I did not share.

"No child would suffer the burden of being sick or handicapped," I regurgitated the words Gregor had used.

"Exactly! You are a clever one! Rickard is a fool if he lets you go! Separating the grain from the chaff. The money spent on useless eaters is better utilized by aiding the citizenry that contributes, but let us not dwell on the tedium of economics. Ah! There is the prodigal now." He grinned as Rickard approached.

"Herr Rittenour has been telling me of the vision

he has for Germany." I smiled warmly, but inside I wanted to scream. Rickard took my hand.

"Erika is an asset to the Reich. I think she would make a fine addition to your staff." Rittenour seemed pleased with himself at this assessment.

"I hoped to soften her up and ask her about that tonight," Rickard answered. I purposely leaned against him as he held me close, hoping to be rid of Rittenour's apparent pursuit of my attention.

"Herr Rittenour has told me his vision. A world free of disease and handicap. Weeding out genetic illnesses to create a nation of healthier people." I looked to the man for agreement, as though I wanted his approval for understanding his revelation, the plans for a master race.

"It is an ambitious schedule, I admit. Future generations will be the better for it." His hands were now held behind his back, making me wonder if he concealed more information than he revealed.

"Everyone wants what is best for their children. They are the future." I could understand the desire to end the suffering of illness. I could understand wanting to find cures for disease and an end to the hardship of being handicapped. I could not understand killing a child. Cures were found through research, not through murder. Rittenour's friendliness reminded me of a viper. He maintained an illusion of kindness but no doubt would strike if the situation called for it. I would watch what I said.

"I know it seems harsh, the euthanasia of children. It seems simply sterilizing them should be enough." The viper looked into my eyes for a response, ready to measure my reaction, watching for a weakness.

Rickard knew the strategy and, before I could respond, let out a mirthful laugh. "Don't let Wirth hear you say that. He has little patience for those who coddle useless mouths." Rickard seemed to ponder a moment. "I believe his exact words went something like, 'The sentimental slobbering over such people makes me puke.'"

Rickard had sprung the trap before I could step into it. I could imagine steel teeth clamping around either side of my calf, pinning me in a belief running counter to those in this wolf den. Recapturing my poise, I managed a titter of laughter at Rickard's response. "He has an admirable devotion to duty. I can only imagine a country modeled after his values."

I looped an arm through Rickard's. Eager to leave, I could indeed envision a country run by the Christian Wirths of the world, and it made me shudder.

"It is an exciting venture. History will be made with the rise of a master race. Amazing." Rickard spoke proudly. "I have to take my leave, however. I have business to attend, and I don't want to disappoint Herr Wirth."

"It has indeed been a pleasure, sir." I extended my hand for Rittenour to shake, so grateful for the graceful exit Rickard provided.

"*Guten Abend*, and be well." Karl waved farewell as we left. I hoped he didn't see my shiver of disgust as we went back inside.

Chapter 16

Eager to leave the party, I slammed the car door as I got in but took a last look at the guests milling about the mansion. Beautiful women decorated the courtyard, laughing and talking with uniformed officers. I noted the elegant dresses and the expensive jewels they wore. Did they realize we were destroying our country's most precious gems? Germany's children were treasures that could not be replaced.

"Bastards!" I spat the word as I stared back at the grand building, wishing I had the power to raze it to cinders with a glare.

"Well, that's graceful. You did not care for my friend Karl's company?" Rickard smiled with his innocent query.

"I thought *you* were my date for the evening," I hissed through clenched teeth.

"Ah, but the two of you were getting along so well." He grinned.

I fumed. Jealousy? Is that why he played these games?

"I extended courtesy to your friend, and that is all," I protested. My head had a dull ache.

"Looked like flirting to me," Rickard stated simply.

"Flirting! I was being friendly, you dolt, and where did you run off to?"

"As you wish, but the last time I met a girl that friendly, she wanted fifty francs up front," he said with a chuckle.

I gasped at the insult. His retort burned like a

slap in the face. "How dare you! Stop the car. I will walk home! Let me out!"

"I am not going to stop the car." Rickard turned serious.

Anger drove me to pull violently on the handle, but when I moved to jump from the car, he pulled me back onto the seat.

"What do you think you are doing? Quit acting like a child, and calm down."

His words inflamed my fear and my anger. I wanted out and away from him. Rolling down the window, I began to shout, "*Hilfe!* Help, police! *Polizei!*"

He pulled me toward him, his voice now a menacing snarl, "Don't you suppose people are accustomed to midnight arrests by now?"

Rickard's viselike grip bit into my shoulder. The cold air from the open window crept into my bones. I rolled up the car window and slumped back against the seat. The grip on my shoulder loosened, and his hand trailed along my arm. He took hold of my hand.

"I am not a whore." I yanked my hand from his. My temper smoldered as I calmed myself.

"Most definitely not." His tone softened, and he placed his hand over mine.

"Does the radio work?" I said suddenly. My anger began to subside.

"Yes." He glanced my way.

I ran my hands across the dashboard and along the radio casing. I had no idea what I looked for. If I had found something unusual I would not realize it. "Any extra stations?"

"No listening devices in the car. Speak freely."

"Fine," I responded calmly, and then turned on him. "What in the hell were you doing at the party? Where were you?"

Rickard grimaced. "Not nice language."

"Humph!" I shifted my weight and tried to pull

my hand away from his, but he held fast.

"I am going to pull over. You stay put," He warned, as he parked the car in a playground a few blocks from my house.

"Like a good girl." My voice dripped sarcasm.

"You needed answers." Rickard shifted his body toward me. "I needed answers."

"Oh, very enlightening, thank you." I seethed, which made Rickard chuckle, and that angered me all the more. Frustrated, I hit my fist against the dashboard with a loud smack. "Tell me where you stand! Where is Heidi, and what will happen to the residents of Grafeneck?" I clutched his sleeve. "I endured that social parasite, and now I want you to talk to me."

"I stand at six feet tall."

I glared at him, the joke unappreciated.

His tone softened. "Heidi is staying with friends of mine, and the children of Grafeneck will be relocated to a treatment center. I'm sorry."

My heart stopped, and icy fingers of dread crept under my skin. "Oh, God, oh, God, no!"

I rocked back and forth, and tears poured down my cheeks. I had lost the battle to fight them back. I felt Rickard's arms about my shoulders folding me into a comforting embrace.

"Erika, I hate to see the pain in your eyes."

I slapped at his hands. "Don't touch me, you son of a bitch!" My hand came across his face in a strike so hard his teeth rattled.

"Ouch." He rubbed the assaulted cheek. "I really wish you would get out of the habit of doing that."

"I wondered, but I should have known, from the day we went to the hospital. You told the nurse you were with the Reich Health Ministry, but you told my parents you worked with property appraisal. I assume Death's Head Squadron is finding locations to be used for treatment centers, and it's all sanctioned by the Reich Health Ministry?"

Rickard nodded.

"Yet I'm supposed to believe you're Resistance?"

"Yes."

I refused to meet his eyes. "No. I'm tired of this. I have been in the dark long enough." I had steeled myself to have this conversation. "Gregor is easy to understand. He believes he's God, and the world revolves around him."

Rickard laughed. A genuine smile brightened his eyes, lifting the veil from his handsome features.

"But you, Rickard. You make no sense. Do you even like me?" I stole a glance and saw his eyes soften.

"Sure." He shrugged.

"You had to know the hospitals were..." I drew in a breath. The thought kicked me in the gut, but it had to be voiced. Voiced or forgotten. "You knew certain patients would meet their end."

"Yes."

"If you consider me a friend, then tell me the truth." I finally turned to look at him. "Please."

Rickard took in a big breath. His eyes glazed, unfocused, as though he garnered memories, so he could order his thoughts before putting them into words. "I met Father Julian at the university. He was a guest speaker in a comparative religion class. He was a friend to my favorite teacher, the teacher who was later arrested."

I didn't expect him to mention the priest, but I knew he was telling the truth. "How did you meet Rittenour?"

"As he said, at the university."

"He said there was a problem at the university involving students and radical ideas." I searched his face for any signs of deception.

Rickard snorted. "I was one of those students."

"You? But you were one of his finest, he said." I

was taken aback by his answer. His response only created more questions. How did Father Julian, Rick and the Hitler Youth tie together?

"Yes, but that was after." He paused. "Let me start at the beginning." I nodded, eager to hear what he had to say, hoping to learn a bit more about him. "I was able to attend university after a six-month tour of duty with the Labor Corps. I met my best friends at Munich University. Hans, Michael, and Gregor." He gripped the steering wheel of the car as he spoke.

"Michael sounds like an English name."

"It is, and so is he. The three of them all came from money, but the new order saw us as equals. England's economy was still in the toilet after the depression, and initially Michael was impressed with how the Germans were able to bounce back. He studied economics, and he hoped to learn more about how the Führer worked his magic." Rickard laughed. "Economics? Deadly dull subject."

"You said initially?" I queried.

"Yes, initially, we saw Hitler as a force for good. Then we realized civil rights were being violated. Considering ourselves free thinkers, we started meeting to talk about politics, philosophy and current events. We met at Hans' house and listened to some forbidden jazz from America." His eyes clouded over, and his features darkened. "Hans' father was in politics, a Burgermeister. He encouraged our meetings, and we began to talk about using non-violence to protest the Nazis." He paused as though fighting to say the next words. "Then the Gestapo arrived at the house. Hans' father was arrested."

Rickard's eyes began to puddle, and a tear threatened to slip over the brim. I said, "I'm so sorry. What happened next?"

Rickard snorted. "We were invited to come to the

police station for questioning." His lip contorted in a silent snarl. "During the interrogation, they kept us apart so we could not corroborate our stories. I insisted we were merely students discussing courses and meeting socially. The inquisitors were able to repeat snippets of conversation. They knew about our plans to protest. One of my friends had reported us to the Gestapo."

I was shocked at what I heard. For the first time, I was seeing a true side to Rickard and the depths of his hurt at a friend's betrayal. He'd kept the rage bottled inside him. I was honored he could trust me to share his pain. I reached for his hand before I finally found the words. "Why weren't you arrested, too?"

I wasn't prepared for the look in his eyes. It was as though I had sucker-punched him. A tear escaped, falling onto his cheek.

"I sold myself out. I let a good man go to jail and saved my own ass," he spat the words while he avoided my gaze and looked beyond me, as though avoiding my scorn.

"What options were there?" I wasn't prepared for this reaction. I put myself in his place, and I wouldn't have known what to do myself.

"Options? Choices?" He choked on the words. "I could have denied it. I could have said, 'No, sir, that is out of context. We are students and we merely explored the what-ifs.'"

"Yes, but Michael, and even Gregor, would have known what the Burgermeister said when you weren't there." I played the scene in my mind. Rickard could only have told what he knew. Was he testing me? Was he luring me into a false comfort by confiding in me?

His reddened eyes stared at me. "I could have taken the blame off Hans' father. I could have denied he had anything to do with our talks."

"What happened to the others?"

He looked wounded. His brow furrowed as though in pain, his sad eyes looked into mine.

"I'm sorry. I don't mean to hurt you."

"When I realized it was one of my friends who turned us in, I had to fend for myself. We were guilty regardless of what we said, but we were offered a choice." His lips trembled in anger.

"What happened next?"

"Michael opted to stay in England after the semester. Hans finished his course load and now works in the mayor's office, for the new mayor. We have had no word of his father in three years."

"Gregor?" I was sure I knew the answer, but I wanted Rickard to explain.

"Gregor introduced me to Herr Rittenour. He usually recruited the Hitler Youth into the SS, but he trolled the college campuses, as well. I told myself if I joined the SS I could find out where Hans' father and my teacher were being held. I could win their freedom."

"You joined the SS to prove loyalty?"

"I couldn't join right away. There were two things held against me. The professor and my group of friends."

"The professor? Father Julian's friend?"

"After the arrest, I sought advice. My teacher had disappeared, so I called on Julian. He told me if I wanted to save my life, I was to agree to retraining and to keep in touch with him."

"Retraining? What is that?"

"A chance to redeem myself through re-education and serving the Reich, which I chose instead of prison."

"What kind of re-education?"

"Teutonic history, eugenics and the theories of Darwin. My mind would be molded. There was also the physical training, of course. I liked it. Pain made me feel alive. I ran until I ached, and then I did sit-ups and push-ups until my muscles screamed. When the SS deemed me fit, I was sent out to scout locations for treatment centers. Death's Head Squadron will do the rest."

"Father Julian wanted this for you?"

"He needed someone for inside information. I wanted a chance to help Hans' father, a chance to make up for the arrest."

It made sense: hurting over the mistreatment of a professor and Hans' father, Rickard provided information to someone who wanted to help. I could see myself doing the same.

"How do I know I can trust you?" I looked into his eyes. I'd always heard a liar couldn't look a person in the eye. Rickard's gaze met mine. "I'm telling the truth. I told you a while back to trust no one. Erika, it's as though I have two separate personalities fighting for dominance, and I need someone I can trust." This time I wrapped my arms around him. He nuzzled my shoulder as he spoke. "Karl Rittenour is good at what he does. He tells people they can be more than what they are, and they can achieve excellence. He makes it look as though they have more freedom or privilege than they would outside the Reich."

"To a teenager escaping poverty, a bad home life or suffering general tedium, that can be very appealing," I agreed. "I understand the allure behind the Hitler Youth."

"When Karl gave me the chance to better myself, I took it."

A cold wave of mind-numbing fear washed over me. I realized I had been in more danger with Herr Rittenour than with Christian Wirth. Wirth was cold, but Rittenour would snare a person into his ranks with an offer of friendship. "So you became a good Nazi?"

Rickard laughed again. "A good Nazi? No. A good Nazi would have turned you in. A good Nazi would not let a pretty girl sway him from following orders. A good Nazi wouldn't fall in love with a traitor."

"What?" I couldn't have heard him right. He folded me into his arms and kissed me. Startled, I pulled away a moment, only to be lulled by the gentle caress of his hands along my back. I leaned into him, softening my lips against his as he gently dueled his tongue with mine, deepening the kiss. I felt as though I floated, only to jump when I heard a tapping on the window. Placing a hand to my chest, I tried to calm my thundering heartbeat. Rickard rolled down the fogged window.

"Evening," he quipped cheerfully.

"You are in violation of curfew. Explain." The young man's voice was vaguely familiar, but his flashlight kept me from seeing him as it shone inside the car. I made no move to hide my face, despite the irritating glare of the light. I didn't want the curfew officer to think I hid something.

"We have come from a party for a fellow SS officer. Do you need to see papers?" Rickard maintained a friendly tone of voice.

"Yes, sir. Thank you, sir." The officer seemed to visibly relax when he had confirmed Rickard's identity.

"Dirk?" I smiled in relief when I recognized my friend. He gave me a wink and handed Rickard his papers.

"Thank you, sir. All seems to be in order." Dirk turned from us.

Rickard started the car, saying, "I suppose, under the circumstances, I will not reprimand him for forgetting to say Heil Hitler."

Chapter 17

Rickard had promised me answers last night, and I had gotten them. His confirmation of my worst fears spurred me toward my office in a rush. I needed to think in the quiet of my workplace. Opening my office door, I stopped in my tracks at the sight of Gregor sitting at my desk. He smirked when I walked in, obviously pleased to see me surprised. Leaning back in the chair, he acted as if he owned the very air around him. When I took a moment to survey my office, I thought maybe he did own it, because my small vase of flowers had been replaced with a pen set and a small swastika flag. My file organizer had been removed from the desktop. My "to do" piles were conspicuously absent from the desk. The pictures the children had drawn for me had all been removed from the walls.

"Gregor, this is my office. May I ask what you are doing here?" I swallowed the anger rising from my middle like a storm.

"Come in, and make yourself at home. We will be working closely for the next couple of months. In the interest of convenience, I decided we could share a space." I seethed over the invasion. This was his way of cowing me, I was certain. "Close the door. I have something of interest to show you."

The edge of his mouth curled upward. His poisonous courtesy made me wonder if this was a command or a request, but I did what he asked. When the latch clicked closed, his outstretched arm pointed toward the lamp on the desk where a sheet of oversized paper lay in a roll.

"Blueprints?" I queried, unrolling the parchment.

"Building plans for the renovations. You'll note the two new buildings in the front courtyard."

"I really don't know much about reading blueprints," I told Gregor honestly.

He rose to stand next to me as I looked over the papers on the desk. I took note of the renovations on each page. A fence would surround the perimeter. There would be a parking area and a long circular driveway. A front office would replace the store. Two new buildings would sit away from the rest of the castle toward the entrance. I caught the words 'Aktion 4' before Gregor rolled the parchments up and placed them neatly on the edge of the desk. He leaned into me and spoke with malignant softness. "Have you been in a hospital for the terminally ill? People lie comatose, paralyzed in their own dirt, until someone has the time to clean them up. Would you want to live that way? As for the children, why would you force a child to be tied to a wheel chair for the rest of his life? All he can do is watch the others play while he sits. No friends, an object of pity, at best. What kind of a monster are you?"

I might have blinked if my face hadn't felt frozen. Gregor mimicked my shocked expression while he awaited an answer.

"What kind of monster...am I?" I couldn't hide my disbelief at this statement. He was baiting me. He wanted me to say the wrong thing, perhaps give him a reason to have me detained.

"If you really care about children, you don't force them to live as freaks, as though they are some sideshow at the circus. Don't you see how cruel that is?"

I nodded my understanding. I wouldn't argue with him. "Some say God gave us life. Only God can take a life."

"Then let the children go back to Heaven where they belong, rather than living a half life."

"Gregor, your logic is like nothing I've ever heard." He was all control, a brainwashed, unabashed current of controlled energy. I looked away, realizing my friendly predator had established dominance, just as he was trained to do. By moving my things and invading my space, he'd attempted to establish his authority. It nearly worked, but not quite.

I laughed, holding mirth like a shield to ban the fear stirring deep inside of me. It hadn't occurred to me until this moment he was one person I hadn't seen at the gala, which now seemed odd. Wouldn't the gala have been important to him? "I missed you at the gala."

He hesitated a moment as if caught unaware by my statement. "I was on an errand. You and Rickard seem to be getting along nicely."

"He needed an escort, and I was available. Not much more to it than that." He knew I was sympathetic to the children. Now it seemed he wanted to know if I was an influence on Rickard. I shrugged a shoulder at his suggestion.

"Do you understand why I am talking to you?" His sharp features studied me as he spoke. *Oh, yes, please, explain why you deem me worthy of your attention. Oh, please.* I couldn't stop the flow of sarcasm coming from somewhere in the back of my mind as Gregor continued to speak. "Rickard does not come from a privileged background. His father was wounded in the war, which made it difficult to find a job. His mother became overprotective of her only child, and she called him her treasure."

"That's sweet," I replied, keeping a neutral tone. Suspecting there was a reason he said all this, I listened.

"Thanks to the Reich, men like Rickard have a

chance to rise above their circumstances. He went to the University of Munich, a privilege denied members of his class prior to the Führer's rise to power."

"His class?" Maybe it was masochistic, but I was curious to get a glimpse of how Gregor's mind worked.

"Yes, his class. He can rise from poverty and become a member of the bourgeoisie. Rising through the ranks would give him not just status but a livable income and means to care for his parents in their old age."

It made sense. I didn't want it to, but it did. I thought of how kind Rickard was to the children, helping them with their coats and buttoning them up so they would stay warm. I could easily picture him caring for his parents. "That is a respectable goal. He works for his paycheck. He should be duly compensated."

Even though I agreed with Gregor, I wondered when he would quit circling and move in for the kill.

"He has much to lose and nothing to gain by falling in with the wrong people, or person." The steely gray eyes scoured my face for a response.

"I would assume he associates with whom he chooses. He has no reason to consult me."

"He associates with whom he chooses, yes, but I worry his choice may cloud his reason."

Suddenly I realized he was talking about me. "He's an adult. He is not some child who needs a nanny, and I assure you I do nothing to 'cloud his reason' as you put it. If you have something to say to me, Gregor, be man enough to say it."

"Very well. I have seen Rickard rise in the ranks. He is an SS officer now, and he doesn't need your kind keeping him from bigger and better things." He stood nose to nose with me.

"My kind?" I whispered. "What kind is that?

165

Poor? Catholic?"

"The kind who—due to an outdated religious belief—might gain his sympathy long enough for him to damage his career."

"I would never do anything to hurt Rickard. I doubt I have any influence on him, so don't worry."

"Erika. You need to understand me." He pulled me close enough that I felt his hot breath with every word he snarled. The buttons of his uniform mashed against my fingers; the rough material ground against my skin.

"You will carry out your duties for the remainder of your time here. You will not add to or detract from your expected tasks. You will not stray from any directives given to you, and you will not involve Rickard in anything running counter to his duties as an officer. I would hate for you to run into problems due to a misunderstanding."

I wasn't sure how to respond.

Gregor seemed satisfied he'd won this round. The arrogant smirk was followed by a slight tilt of his head when he finished.

Having had enough of this conversation, I turned toward the door, but Gregor took my hand, holding my curved fingers close to him. His gray eyes hardened. He stood too close for me to draw my own breath untainted by his. "If you cross me, there will be consequences."

Without warning, he bent my wrist forward, touching my fingertips to my inner wrist. Pain exploded across my arm as I fell to my knees. I must have screamed as I threw my head back. The next thing I remember is hearing Rickard's voice, demanding to know what was happening as he barreled through the door and jumped Gregor, a hand to his throat. A snarling glare locked onto Gregor's face, and a rabid growl came from his grasped throat.

"What is the problem?" Rickard's eyes never left Gregor.

"We were discussing Erika's duties to the castle. I wanted to make it clear what was expected of her." The cool words rolled off Gregor's tongue with ease.

"Gregor has decided to work closely with me. He even moved into my office to be sure he is at my beck and call at all times." I tried to smile, knowing Rickard would read between the lines easily enough.

"I made it clear her duties to the castle would be SS-approved. She is not to stray beyond SS guidelines."

"Good." Rickard maintained his steady tone. His face betrayed no emotion, but he loosed his hold on Gregor's throat and leaned toward him, lowering his voice into a menacing growl. "Let me make it clear any unauthorized harassment of any resident in this castle will be dealt with by me personally. Am I understood?"

They glared each other down, the challenge hanging with menace over the duo like a heavy storm cloud.

"By the way, there was another Resistance problem." Gregor broke his stare. Rising to his full height, he regained his calm exterior. Rickard followed suit.

"Really? What happened?" Rickard visibly relaxed.

"There was an escape the night of the gala." Gregor looked at me with suspicion as he spoke.

"Let's talk about this escape. Were you there?" Rickard spoke evenly, as though placating a spoiled child.

"I drove the car. My prisoner, a priest, was being held in protective custody. I was given orders to drive him to a detention center. We were coming around a bend in the road when we had to screech to a stop. A tree lay across the street. I was turning the car around when out of the bushes came hooded men, six of them. They were all armed, and they surrounded the vehicle. My partner, Wagner, and I never had time to get out of the car. Before we could do anything, they were in the car, holding a gun to Wagner and me. I had no choice but to surrender. Our uniform jackets were stolen, as were our guns. We were cuffed with our hands behind our backs, and they left us standing beside the road. They took off with the car, with the priest in the back. They just left Wagner and me in the street! That was very embarrassing for me to report to my commander, you may be sure. I may lose my rank of command, and *she* may have something to do with it all." Gregor shot me a hateful glare.

"Me?" I didn't have to feign surprise. This accusation was out of the blue.

"You think Erika has something to do with this? Did you recognize any of them?" Rickard asked.

"They wore ski masks. They were armed, some with pistols. It looked like at least one had a rifle. When we were questioned, the SS interrogators doubted me. Me!" Gregor spat the angry words. "They wondered if I worked with the Edelweiss Pirates. As if I would relate to that scum."

"Do the police have any leads?" Rickard seemed neutral, neither interested nor disinterested.

"It was the Resistance. Probably the same group that caused the incident at the New Year's dance."

"If you will excuse me, I have to tend the children." I glanced at Rickard. He nodded.

The day finally ended, but Gregor's warning was seared into my memory. I was not to sway Rickard with misguided morals or feminine wiles. His arrogance and condescension made me sick, and his assumptions were ridiculous. I tripped over my own tongue constantly, making me doubt I could tempt a kitten toward milk, let alone seduce Rickard. Gregor had nothing to fear.

What was left for me to do? The letters I had tried to write had been my best idea. Notifying the parents had seemed the easiest course, until the flames consumed any hope of the children escaping the castle. They were doomed, with no one to come to their rescue. The promise was clear. Any attempt to notify the parents would be censored. Any protest would be silenced, and any breach of confidentiality could be met with arrest. I may as well be shackled. I pushed aside the pile of charts in frustration. Grafeneck would be one of six treatment centers for the handicapped and mentally insufficient.

I looked at the blueprints again. The large fence would surround the perimeter at least as far as the forest. A paved driveway leading from the road to the castle would be constructed, as well as a parking area for staff cars. As a person drove through the front gates along a newly paved road, they would pass two newly constructed buildings. One would be a crematorium, and the other looked like shower stalls. There were drains and a water source, but the pipes on the blueprints led to what looked like canisters. I remembered overhearing a description at the gala of how Aktion 4 could be compressed into pellets that were harmless until activated to become an airborne gas. "Aktion 4 kills vermin," the unseen speaker had said with a laugh. So, I realized, pellets would be dropped into the canisters, and from these canisters would filter gas instead of water through the pipe system. The patients would inhale the poisonous gas and die.

The contents of my stomach fought to stay put, but bile burned its way up my throat. I wanted to tell someone, but whom?

Sitting at my desk, I came to the sickening conclusion the children were doomed. On sight, they would be singled out. Elimination of genetic diseases would be rooted out with the elimination of those born with the defects. Josef's mongolism, Lara's shriveled arm, and Wilhelm's leg braces all carried a death sentence. Heidi alone would pass scrutiny, providing she never had a seizure. To simply look at her, no one would know she was epileptic. She could slip under the radar. I could get her on board the Kindertransport. There was a shred of hope for Heidi.

The gala had given Rickard an excuse to remove Heidi while the other SS were gone from the castle. Part of me was glad, yet part of me feared Rickard could not be trusted. When I'd asked where she had been taken, he'd blithely answered, "To a safe house." Did he have a reason to lie? Did it benefit him to save Heidi? No. Did it benefit him to defy the SS? Double no.

As far as I know, please Lord, Heidi is safe. What about the others?

Murder is wrong. Is mercy killing right? Veterans spoke of the effects of mustard gas. If this were similar, a victim would feel burning eyes and a tightening of the chest as the lungs begged for a breath of clean air. It was painful. Each breath would be worse than the last, until, finally, the body succumbed to the poison rushing through the system, running its toxicity through the heart and depriving the lungs of needed oxygen.

I squeezed my eyes closed. The tears stung, and my own breaths seemed painful as I tried to reason with my conscience. Death by a loving hand had to be better than to be left at the mercy of a crazed, mindless government. There was one alternative. *God help me.* This was not a decision I wanted to make. I had the choice of using my own poisons, locked away in my medicine cabinet.

My hands shook as I filled a syringe with morphine. Could innocent blood ever be washed away? Would my hands ever be clean again if I continued on this course? The gas would make them choke, gasping for breath as their life was strangled to nothingness. Morphine would make them euphoric, and an overdose would put them to sleep, peacefully, with no pain. A sleep from which they would not wake, but they would be safe from the evil that awaited them otherwise.

I filled the second syringe. I thought of each child as I punctured the rubber stopper, the needle sucking up the lethal fluid filling the tube. *Little Wilhelm*. My treasured leader of the pack. The braces on his legs never stopped his imagination from soaring. *Lara*. An artist's soul expressed with the one good hand she had. Art was reflective of the beauty living in her heart. *The twins*. Isn't intelligence measured with creativity? I would sorely miss their energy.

My hand slipped, and the needle grazed the knuckle of my thumb. I swore and bit my lip. *Perfect. I'll kill myself before I get a chance to euthanize my children. Then, after I enter Heaven's gates, if He lets me inside them, God can tell me I am an idiot and a murderer.* I rubbed my shoulders. They hunched with an invisible weight that made my back ache.

One by one I loaded the deadly hypodermic cylinders. I filled the last syringe. Six. Six vials of death to be served up at bedtime.

Be sure to say your prayers, children, and ask God to forgive me.

I choked back a sob as I walked down the hall with a tray of syringes in my hands. I walked into Josef's room. He threw the covers over his head and giggled. He could never pretend to be asleep. He would lie still until laughter overtook him, and he could no longer fool me into believing him to be slumbering. I sat on the bed. He removed the covers from his head and giggled, saying, "Boo."

I rubbed his shoulder and held him close. His arms came around me. Is evil ever remorseful? Would a murderess care so much? I leaned in to kiss him one last time. A voice came into my head. *"You betray with a kiss?"*

The thought froze me to my core. I shivered.

Please, Lord. I can't let him die like he doesn't matter, my thoughts begged.

I caressed Josef's cheek. *"Kindlein,* I have something to help you sleep."

I swallowed hard. The words were like ash in my mouth. Josef spied the tray and shook his head. "I hate shots. I'll go to sleep now. See."

He laid his head on the pillow and pretended to snore.

"It won't hurt. I promise. It will just be a little prick, like a bee sting."

"Don't like bees!" he protested, holding the covers like a shield against his body.

I wanted to cry. His hand was on mine. For a moment my heart sank. Was murder by my hand truly a kinder alternative? I ran my thumb toward the crook of his elbow feeling for the spongy softness of an awaiting vein. When I went before the Almighty on Judgment Day could I say with a clear conscience, "I killed out of love?" Was such a statement a form of blasphemy? I had steeled myself to do the deed, certain I would rather do it myself than to have them cold and afraid in the dank barracks, waiting to die with no one around who cared.

Needle poised over its target, I steeled myself to hit the mark. Who would make the excuses to God? Would he understand my reasoning? Would the soul of this child?

Suddenly my wrist was firmly grabbed and held, until I relinquished the vial.

"Maybe a glass of warm milk?" Rickard

suggested.

A gasp of air forced its way from my lungs.

"No need for shots tonight," he said to Josef. He turned and looked at me. "Plans can change."

I would always be grateful Rickard stayed my hand and never left my side that night. The loss of innocent blood would not be mine to claim. Relief flooded my being.

Rickard did not speak of the incident. Thank God. How could I explain what I'd been about to do?

Later, Josef sipped the hot cocoa, leaving a chocolate mustache. I had to smile, my heart wrapped in warmth, at the little boy who would never outgrow his innocence and could forgive anything with a hug and a kind word. He was a wonderful child, and he harbored ill will toward no one. For this he was dubbed an expendable life.

My throat closed up. Josef smiled as his little hand wiped a tear from my cheek.

"Are we going away?" Josef asked with great concern. His little eyes glittered like black marbles.

"Would you like to go away?" Rickard asked casually, sipping his cocoa.

"Where did you hear that?" I asked. *Mother of mercy, what do I say? Help me, Lord. I don't know myself when or where they are going.*

"Heard guys talking," Josef stated.

Rickard leaned toward Josef, and his eyes softened as he spoke. "You all are leaving. The monks and Erika will go, too, before September."

He focused more on Josef than on me. I could only guess what he must think. Rickard now had two reasons to have me arrested. I was glad he hadn't asked for an explanation. I could not have given one.

"Will that be when the leaves change?" Josef asked.

"That's right." Rickard winked.

The thought of the forest dropping leaves from the trees gave me a chill. I could see the barren branches reaching lifelessly toward an uncaring sky while dried leaves blew about the forest floor.

"It's still a month or so before the leaves change." My voice sounded far away. I wished for summer to last all year.

Ruffling Josef's hair, Rickard asked, "Would you like a story before bed?

The Nazis are good at telling stories, I said to myself. *Stories of glory. Stories of honor. Stories to keep the populace happy while they tie our hands and gag our mouths, telling us the whole time it is for our own good.*

Mother of Mercy, pray for us.

Chapter 18

I was staying in the castle to be with the children. I lay in bed until nearly sunrise. The cool of early morning would give way to the late August heat.

There were constant rumors of war, reaching us even in our secluded castle. People collectively held their breath, waiting for the hammer to fall. Treaties were made. Words were spoken. Treaties were broken, and lies were spread.

I punched my pillow and tried to get comfortable. A hand on my shoulder made me jump. A silhouette leaned over me, a dark figure against a gray backdrop.

"Brother?" The word was a fervent wish.

The baritone voice that made my heart jump did not belong to monk or child. "No. It's Rickard."

Cold dread pierced me through the darkness. "The children. Are they all right?"

Startled, I sat up quickly, tearing the covers from my body, but he quickly calmed my fear. "They're fine. Be quiet. The transport is here."

"Transport?" I sprang to my feet. "No one told me about a transport."

"We must be quiet. Gather the children. They leave now."

I grabbed the robe from the foot of the bed. My heart raced. My mind fought the sleepy haze and sprang into reality. I grabbed Rickard by the shoulder. "They're being taken away. Oh, God! Don't take them away yet. Not now." I scrambled for what to do. There had to be something. A way to protect them. "Please. Can we do something?"

"There is nothing to do. They leave now."

I fell to my knees, clutching Rickard around his knees. "No! Wait. Please. Please. They can't go."

"Get up."

I fought the tears. The sweet, innocent children would die like Helga had died, in a mysterious facility from an illness they didn't have. "Rickard! I'll do anything! Please! There has to be another way!"

He grabbed my arm and pulled me roughly to my feet, hissing through clenched teeth. "Never, and I mean *never*, flaunt weakness that way again! Now move."

He gave me a push toward the door. The stone floor was cold under my feet. I wanted to vomit. My stomach cramped painfully. I went to each room to wake the children.

One child, then another and another. One small duffle bag per child.

Rickard led them outside. I followed at the back of the line. A gray van with smoky windows idled by the door. I stifled a sob. They were going to their deaths, and there was nothing I could do about it. The ache of realization burned. Rickard picked up Wilhelm and opened the back of the van.

I neared the driver's door. A full-bearded man wearing a laborer's cap sat at the wheel, his long sleeves reaching nearly to his knuckles. I held the door handle for balance. "Hey, lady. You sick?"

The driver was a burly man. Large hands gripped the wheel, and his face turned to me.

"Yes. I think I am." Feeling faint, I tried to focus, but my voice wavered. My energy ebbed as the children boarded the van that was taking them to meet their end.

"Chin up, girl. The sun rules the day." The sudden softness of the voice startled me.

"What?" His eyes met mine. The lush silver

beard disguised his noble features. It was Father Julian. My mouth fell open in a silent shriek. He gave me a wink.

"We'd best say *auf Wiedersehen*."

"Father!" I whispered. I wanted to hug him. I gave his arm a squeeze. Tears fell freely down my cheek. I ran to the back of the van. The children sat comfortably on either side of the vehicle.

"*Auf Wiedersehen!* Goodbye! I love you. You are in the hands of the Lord's helper." Indeed they were. There was a God, and he sported a silver beard and drove this transport.

The van would make its way south. A new day had broken. A new hope.

"Let's go." Rickard took my hand and led me back inside.

"The monks are at a five a.m. mass. We need to be out of here by six. Grab what you need. You have ten minutes."

With a lighter heart, I sprinted up the stairs, dumped my clothes into a suitcase and threw on a dress. I had a little money in my purse. I hoped to get breakfast later.

"No suitcase." Rickard stopped me. "Take what you need in a pillow case. Without questioning, I shoved the case under the cot. I had few belongings, and I stuffed what I could into the pillowcase. When I was done, Rickard nodded. "It has to look as though you may come back."

"As though I may...?" I readily obeyed, though I wasn't sure what was going on.

We ran to the forest. My feet became dew-soaked while patches of early morning sun peeked through the trees. I felt my knees weaken, and I stumbled. "The SS will wonder where the children are. The monks have the prayer service as an alibi. You don't."

"The children escaped, leaving me suspect with

the SS. Yes, I see."

I kept pace as we hurried along the trail. The horses, Sugar and Spice, were tethered to a tree and snorted a greeting as we approached.

"Hey, pretty girl," Rickard crooned to the white mare. "They were in the stable. I brought them out before Julian arrived."

Rickard climbed onto Sugar's back. I tethered the pillowcase to Spice's saddle and followed Rickard through the forest. The forest path ended near a dirt road, where a white Volkswagen sat on the roadside. A sweet-faced middle-aged woman held out a road map as she waved us inside. Sugar gave a whinny when we left her. The woman smiled as she folded the map and tossed it through the window. She had the face of an angel.

"Good morning." Her cheerful voice was insanely out of place. "Crazy horses always get loose and find their way home. These are special horses, bred for strength and gentleness."

"Just like you." Rickard kissed her cheek.

"Get out." The woman waved him away.

"I'll keep the horses at the farm. The three of you better get moving."

"Three?" At that moment I saw two little arms waving to me from the window.

"Heidi is in the car," Rickard explained.

"Oh, thank you!" I gushed relief as I hugged the woman. She motioned me into the car and handed Rickard the keys. I smiled at Heidi, who sat happily in the back seat.

"Miss Krystal is really nice. Are we going to see the horses again?" Heidi asked, unaware of the gravity of the situation.

"Is that where you were the whole time, darling?"

"Heidi, no names," Rickard interrupted. "Yes, she was in a safe house, as I said. We are making good time, and I hope to be in Hanover by noon."

"Hanover? We're going to Hanover?" I thought for a moment. From there, the Kindertransport would leave for the safety of the Netherlands. I supposed we would pass through Hanover en route. "I wanted to stop home first."

"No," Rickard's one-word answer was adamant.

"My parents will be worried sick," I protested.

"Better for them to be worried. The Gestapo will look for you there. I am sorry, but they cannot tell what they don't know, no matter how enthusiastic the questioning." His words hit like a bucket of ice water.

Enthusiastic questioning?

Liebe Gott. What have I done? I could see the SS showing up at my parents' door, explaining I was the last person to be with the children before their disappearance. Children under Reich care.

I am now branded as an outlaw.

My head battled with my stomach over the decision to pass out or vomit. I was glad I hadn't had breakfast. Forever, hereafter, I would be wanted by the SS and hunted by the Gestapo. Authorities would, of course, question my parents, my friends, and anyone who might have knowledge of my whereabouts. The monks would have the alibi of a five a.m. prayer service. As far as anyone knew, I had been alone in the castle with the children.

"I'm a decoy." Realization hit like a brick. "At the very least, you could have told me."

"In this war, everything has double meanings. It was necessary. Father Julian will flee to the south. Hopefully, they will make the Swiss border by the time we get to Hanover. The children will be put in safe houses there."

"You couldn't mastermind this without putting me in the line of fire. I assume the SS will suspect me of kidnapping."

"I didn't leave a note to the contrary, no." He smiled. "The monks will not report the children missing unless they have to. That will buy us time. The Gestapo will visit your parents. It would be better for them if they were to report you missing first. That way it will look as though they know nothing of your whereabouts."

"But they *don't* know anything about my whereabouts!" I held my stomach. "How long before they come looking for me?"

"No way to tell. I am hoping not for a couple of days. The SS doesn't have much business in the castle before the relocation. Three days, if we are lucky."

I leaned away from the window. "Three days." I hoped to draw confidence with my next breath. "Three days. We can do this."

"Everyone knows you are attached to the children. You might have thwarted the move, had you known. My guess is that Gregor will miss you." A note of mischief rang in his voice.

"On the up side, he gets his own office." I paused. "What about you? Does this reflect on you?" I was curious to know if I was alone or if he was under the gun, as well.

"Not yet. I am on leave until further notice. There will be a lull in activity until January when Grafeneck will be..." He stopped himself. He licked his lips as he shifted the car.

I knew what he would say so I said it for him. "January will start the neutralizations, the gassing of children."

A wave of nausea threatened to overwhelm me once again. I had condemned my sister to death when I encouraged my father to put her into the clinic. *God, forgive me. I thought she was getting help.* Now, I had in my care the last child of Grafeneck Castle. If I could save her, get her on

180

board the Kindertransport, was that enough to redeem my guilt?

I leaned my head against the car window. Marburg was my home, and now I was leaving. How far could I run before the Gestapo escorted me inside a black Mercedes with tinted windows, a deadly leviathan, whisking me away to an unknown end? I held my stomach. The end was not unknown anymore.

"What are we going to do in Hanover?" I managed a sentence through the dizziness of my thoughts.

"Get married," Rickard responded.

Chapter 19

"Married? Are you crazy?" I was stunned. With so much happening, I wondered if I had heard wrong.

"It's within the realm of possibility," Rickard answered with a grin.

I was the last person I would call a political dissident, yet my friendship with Gretchen and Father Julian made me suspect. I had been present at a dance where a Resistance demonstration had taken place, and now five children had mysteriously disappeared while under my care. Even if I wanted to be active in the Resistance, I was compromised and would be of no use to them.

Rickard placed a hand on my knee. The unexpected action made me jump, though the warmth of his touch calmed me. He was trying to reassure me, I realized, but there was little comfort to be had when the Gestapo showed up at your door. "Is there a way to warn my parents?"

"Your parents won't be able to tell them anything. Giving them warning would endanger both you and them. Genuine concern and lack of knowledge is their best chance to get through the interview." His brow creased. "We have to get out of Marburg. The SS won't get wind of your disappearance for a while. We have to make the best use of time before they conduct a search for you."

I rubbed my belly, hoping to ease the cramping the way a mechanic might buff scratches off a car. "Rickard, why get married? It makes little sense to marry a fugitive. That would implicate you, as well."

"A sad story. A brokenhearted newlywed jilted shortly after his honeymoon when his new bride ran away. I had hopes of changing you after the wedding. I was certain marriage and motherhood would tame your crazy ideas. Alas, I was abandoned."

Heidi giggled. I could only stare in disbelief.

"The SS will believe that?"

"I need to get you out of the country. Heidi needs an escort. It works out."

"Leave Germany? It's my home." I couldn't imagine being away from Marburg, let alone away from Germany altogether.

"Erika, if you stay, eventually you will get caught. If you marry, you get a name change. It will take time for the SS to get a message to look for you, and even then the logical assumption is that you would continue south toward Switzerland."

"That's where Julian is going."

"Right. But the SS isn't looking for a man, much less a man in a State van."

Another cramp kicked. I massaged my side, willing away the pain. "What if he is caught?"

"The SS will quit looking for you. As far as they would know at that point, the children were taken, and so you left, perhaps fearing a false accusation."

Was my life a fair exchange for six innocent people? I thought of my sister. Had I not recommended therapy, she might have stayed home. If she had stayed home, she could have been kept safe. My bowels turned to water as my insides began to twist. My life in trade for the Grafeneck children. It was fair.

"Are you all right?" Rickard caressed my thigh.

"I'm a bit queasy," I responded, unsure how to react to his touch.

"We will stop and eat in Hanover. There is a basket in the back seat. Help yourself."

I munched a piece of bread, taking tiny bites and chewing thoroughly. *Ignore the emotional and focus on the logical.* I hoped diverting my mind would calm my body.

"In addition to changing my name, you are looking to get a marriage loan, aren't you?" I asked.

"Yes. The SS are encouraged to marry. Are there any embarrassments in your family?"

"Just an uncle who gets loud when he drinks."

"I think you know what I mean." Rickard's tone turned serious.

"Yes. My grandmother is Swedish. My father's side is all German. No Jewish or Gypsy blood."

"You can pass a physical, I assume?"

"I don't see why not. Maybe we shouldn't do this. Marriage is a sacrament. A contract we make with God. I can't take it lightly."

"This coming from the woman who ripped my still-beating heart from my chest and mercilessly stomped on it."

"Seriously."

"We will contract with God for this. We use the marriage loan to fund a trip to England. I intend to bring proof of what Europe fears most. Hitler is preparing for war."

"What about the treaty with Chamberlain? The peace talks?"

"I think you know the Nazis are capable of lying."

"What of the Kindertransport?"

"We aren't going to the Netherlands. We will be leaving via Hamburg."

"Hamburg? As in The Gateway to the World, Hamburg? As in the most important dock in Europe, the one that will be covered in security? That Hamburg?"

"That Hamburg," he affirmed.

"Now I know you are out of your mind."

"A little sightseeing before you go."

Heidi perked up. "Are we going on a boat? I've never been on a boat before."

"Yes, baby, but first we are going to visit friends. Would you like that?"

"After that we can go on a boat?" Heidi perked up. I envied her. As far as she knew, she was on an adventure with friends, and she was unaware of any peril.

"We sure can," Rickard promised.

"The money from the marriage loan is funding this expedition?" I twirled a piece of hair around my finger, while new worry rippled my pools of thought.

"Yes. We get our marriage license, sign up and receive a check. We will cash it in Hamburg and have your new papers drawn up."

"Very easy for you to say. Are you going to help me pay it back? How will I pay anything if I'm a fugitive, living in England with only rudimentary skill with the language? I'll be lucky if I can order a ham sandwich, much less find work."

"Twenty-five percent of the loan is paid off with the birth of each child. If you have four children, the loan is paid in full."

"Brilliant. I assume you have never seen the birth of a baby! It isn't like making gravy. A lot of work goes into it. Typical male arrogance—all the grandiose plans eventually fall to the woman for fruition."

"If I'm so arrogant, why did you agree to marry me?"

I began to sputter a protest when Heidi giggled. It was good to hear her laugh. I turned to look with a smile at the little girl. "Don't encourage him!"

I hated to base the most important decision of my life on something as cold as money. It did stand to reason I couldn't get married from prison, either. When God wrote the blueprints for marriage, the SS hadn't been considered. The state had requirements for valid marriage, and the church did, too. I exhaled. "I can do this. God would honor the greater good. A marriage is valid only if consummated. I simply say you're impotent, and we can have it annulled."

Rickard let out a disbelieving laugh, and his face broke out in a half smile. "No, no, no. I see no reason to lie to the Almighty. He knows everything works."

"Well, obviously we will resolve this when we get to England. I am sure they will understand."

"It isn't the usual circumstance."

"No. It certainly isn't," I muttered.

Rickard was silent. I could feel the air grow heavy as an invisible wall divided us.

****

The café was at the end of a quiet street. It was Sunday morning, and shops were closed. There was little traffic, but the delicate chiming of church bells could be heard in the distance. I walked hand in hand with Rickard, Heidi on his other side, as we rounded the back of the café. He knocked three times on the door, and to my amazement my friend Johanna answered and let us in. I hadn't seen her since the dance, and I wondered why she was here. I took a seat at the small table, and Heidi took a seat next to me.

"Only one child?" Johanna asked. My eyes darted from Johanna to Rickard. Would she know about Julian, or, like me, had she been uninformed until the last minute?

Rickard gave a curt nod, but offered no explanation. He stood facing Johanna while she crossed the room to where her pocketbook lay on the drain board.

"What did you do with the other children?" The casual lilt in her voice sounded forced to me.

"The passports, please," came Rickard's reply.

Johanna turned, a gun poised at Rick. I could only stare in disbelief. Even if Johanna was a believer in Nazism, she had been never the type to watch another person get into trouble, yet here she was, the bait in a trap that sprang all around me, around *us*.

I feared looking at Rickard. I needed to trust him. I couldn't bear the thought of having been led along doom's highway with an innocent child in tow. *Would I be able to face the Nazis with quiet dignity, as Gretchen had, or with the courage of Father Julian?*

There were footsteps coming up the cellar stairs. I knew, before the door opened, that it was Gregor who would walk through it. The steps drew closer. I sat still and quiet, so I would not tempt the viper to strike.

The physical warmth of his body assaulted my back, sending a trickle of cold sweat between my shoulder blades. He leaned over my shoulder, his breath hot against the shell of my ear.

"You disappoint me, Erika." Gregor's voice was a poisoned whisper. My heart stopped. I fought to stop myself from rubbing my arms. I flinched. The sound of his voice drenched me with cold dread.

"The transport is legal." I kept my tone low.

"Removing children from Grafeneck Castle is not." Gregor's lips contorted into a malicious grin. I had to think fast. If they were after me, then Father Julian had more time to escape. It hurt to know Heidi would go down with me. Perhaps I should have gone through with the overdose. I hated the thought of her choking her last breath before death took her.

Rickard seemed unflustered, almost bored with the scenario. I was determined to show no fear, despite the fact my tongue swelled and melded itself to the roof of my mouth. "I really don't know what you're talking about. Have the children been moved?"

"You were the last to see them." Gregor maintained a conspiratorial whisper.

"The last time I saw them they were snug in their beds."

"We assume they went missing between midnight and 6 a.m." Gregor continued.

"I was snug in bed during that time myself."

"You slept while six children were taken from under your nose? Unlikely," Gregor sneered.

"I'm a heavy sleeper."

"Of course. They were simply whisked away while you were snug in your bed."

"If what you say is true."

"If what I say is true! Are you calling me a liar?"

"I can neither verify nor disclaim what you say." Blood coursed through my ears, almost deafening me. If I kept it circular and tried to keep the questions redirected to me, I could keep from giving anything away. Maybe, at least, Father Julian would get the other children to safety.

"Let's recap your day, shall we?" He paced, and Rickard sat opposite me, shrugging his shoulders in a casual manner as though indulging an old man retelling the same tired story he had told many times before. I sat patiently, waiting for Gregor to speak. "You spend all day with the cretins, medicate them, put them to bed around nine p.m., and then do what?"

"Charting. Clean up a bit, personal grooming, and then I generally read until I get tired and fall asleep."

Rickard cleared his throat. Gregor paused, giving the other man his attention.

"I believe Erika was ready to relinquish her post at the castle. I caught her with a hypodermic needle. She was going to give the children an overdose,"

Rickard explained. His voice was calm, like cool water standing in a lake, unsettled. The room was silent. I hazarded a glance toward Johanna. She looked shocked. Did she know the fate the children faced? My guess was that she did not.

I remained quiet. I was tempted to say, "Thank me for making your job easier," but I stared over a precipice, and the wrong word, I was certain, would push me over the edge. The silence stretched across oceans of minutes.

Gregor stroked my cheek, and I flinched. I could force myself to stare into his eyes. I could keep from throwing up at the sound of his voice, and I could muster the courage to keep my answers to a bare minimum, but the touch was too much. Static electricity shocked me. My bare cheek twitched at the unwelcome attention.

"Overdose. You are certain?" Gregor seemed surprised. Should I confess? Should I tell them I had figured out what Aktion 4 was to be used for? Should I play ignorant? What should I say, and how much would be too much? I silently prayed for guidance.

He leaned against the table next to me. The silver adornments against the black uniform were obscenely bright. Was black slimming? He looked broad and muscular under the coat, where the leather band crossing his chest held a dagger in a holster opposite his gun.

Invasion of my space: I realized this was a common tactic of his. First, at the dance, when he had taken me to the floor, and then the takeover at my office, and now my hand was mere inches away from his suit jacket. I could have felt the material against the back of my hand if I'd moved at all. I held my head high and remained still, though my hands trembled.

He looked down on me, another intimidation tactic, I realized. He wanted me to know he had the upper hand, and he was quite satisfied because of it. I quirked my shoulder a bit, in response to Rickard's statement, as if I didn't deem the matter worthy of note.

Gregor leaned toward me. His arms supported his weight, and the material now brushed against my bare arm. I flinched again. Damn it! I smelled my own fear. My armpits were drenched as I met his eyes with mine.

The skull resting on top of crossbones, the symbol of the Death's Head Squadron, was displayed prominently on his hat.

"What was in the syringe?"

"Morphine," I answered simply. I could not feign ignorance. Rickard had delivered me. My word would never stand against his. Gregor quirked a brow, his face now inches from mine. "You did this to defy the Reich."

"I didn't think you'd mind." His gaze bore into me. For a crazy moment I thought of a seagull dropping a crab against a rock, waiting for the shell to crack. This was what Gregor tried with me.

Rickard laughed. We unlocked our gazes and directed our attention toward the laughter. "She thought to defy me. I'm sorry. No one clued you in, partner. The children were indeed moved. To make Erika cooperate, I promised her the children would be put on the Kindertransport, and they will, once they are infected with tuberculosis." Rickard's cool tone froze the blood in my veins.

"Go on." Gregor straightened, and I was relieved to have my breathing space again. I stared at the tabletop. For many years I would remember the grain of the wooden table, where the natural wood made its own design across the surface. I couldn't look at Heidi. I hoped she didn't understand what we said. *Please, Lord. Don't let her think I would betray her. Let her realize I tried. I wanted to save her.*

"The purpose behind infection?" Gregor motioned his friend to continue.

"Well, it is apparent the British are failing to see reason. Eventually, they will come against us and bring their Yank friends along for the ride. Despite America's protests, Chamberlain's lap dogs will jump at the chance to defend England." Gregor twisted his hand in a circular motion as though impatient to hear what Rickard had to say. "So we infect the transport. Sick children are sent to England, and the disease spreads. It's a start at weakening her from within."

"Brilliant. How do you keep it from affecting our people en route?" Gregor crossed his arms across his chest.

"We inoculate them just before sending them off. Once in the body, the virus takes time to incubate before symptoms of any sickness become evident."

"Has this been going on all along?" Gregor seemed curious.

"Ten thousand infected children would make an impact." That was neither a yes nor a no. Truth and lies lay so close together lately, it was difficult to see where one began and the other ended.

"It would," Gregor agreed. "Now explain one child and six passports."

I remained silent. Bile erupted from my stomach and burned my throat. I couldn't stand to look at Rickard, so I closed my eyes and listened. "I suspected Erika was easily misled, when I realized she was a local girl. The Catholics have an annoying habit of assuming a faith in religion should come before a faith in the Fatherland. It was easy enough to make her agree to cooperate with me, once I promised her the children would be put on the Kindertransport. Obviously, I don't want to put them all on the same train. That might make it too easy to isolate the cause of the infection. We take them to different towns and have them leave the country at different times. The added bonus, of course, is meeting another of the Resistance, but I see she's yours."

Gregor smirked. I felt nauseous. He had explained it. The passports, my assistance, and the fact we had only one child in custody. He had pulled it off, leaving me with nothing but faith it was Gregor, not me, who was being deceived. I knew no one in the Resistance. I knew I had not contacted anyone about passports, and if he wanted me arrested, he could have done it long ago, unless I was taking the fall for any number of things I did not know about.

Johanna's brow furrowed. Was she wondering about the connection? She had been misinformed about the passports. We only needed one, unless Rickard lied about the other children. Trying to unravel the truth along with suppressing my fears wore me down.

"Erika was going to overdose the children in order to prevent transfer?" Gregor verified my motive, and all I wanted to do was throw up. I had forgotten about Heidi. She sat next to Rickard, her trusting eyes trying for comprehension of what she heard. I hoped she still did not understand. I couldn't bear that innocent face looking at me with pained eyes, unable to comprehend my actions.

"That is the way it looked to me, yes." Rickard's tone was unwavering. The steady timbre would be my undoing, would allow me no escape. The café was on a cul de sac. I would have to grab Heidi from Rickard, assuming I could flee from Gregor, and make it out the door, where I was sure more SS waited. Any attempt would result in my being shot. I was trapped. Heidi was doomed.

"You had authority to do this?" Gregor refocused his attention onto Rickard. Perhaps he didn't trust either one of us.

Rickard simply looked bored. "We are Death's Head Squadron, are we not? Eliminating life unworthy of life is our primary function."

Again he didn't specifically answer yes or no. Heidi had slipped off the seat of the chair to stand closer to Rickard, seeking comfort, perhaps even protection. Had she sensed I had betrayed her? Was she frightened I might? I wished I could console her. I wanted to tell her I would never hurt her, but how could I explain to a seven-year-old what most adults could not understand. I didn't dare say anything. The two men stared each other down, observing one another for weakness and untruth.

I folded my hands in my lap and kept them under the table, certain Gregor would note how they trembled, otherwise. I was the type who fought nerves by keeping busy. I hated the silence. I hated the inactivity even more.

I could only assume what went on in Gregor's mind. Was Rickard acting independently or on orders?

Heidi remained at Rickard's side. From across the table, I finally got the courage to look into her dark eyes. *Please, please, don't believe I would ever hurt you, I begged silently.*

"You do, of course, realize I can verify what you say." Gregor studied his friend.

The corner of Rickard's mouth quirked upward. "Of course. Johanna, the passports, please."

She rose from her chair and retrieved the pocket book from the counter. My stomach clenched. For one insane moment, I expected her to again pull the gun. We could be shot down, our bodies tossed in the trunk of a nearby car and blood cleaned from the tile floor in time for the café to open for business in an hour. Instead, she pulled out six leather-bound passports and handed them to Rickard. He flipped through each one and stuck them in his pants pocket with a word of thanks as he rose to leave. Heidi held tight to his belt loop.

"I have one concern," Gregor stated. Rickard tilted his head slightly to urge the man to continue. "If Erika tried to foil your plans once before, how is it you trust her now?"

Rickard quirked his lips into a playful smile.

"Everyone she loves is in Marburg. This assures me of her cooperation."

He turned his gaze to me, and I looked away. Then Gregor pulled my chair out for me so I could rise from the table. The act of courtesy seemed vulgar under the circumstances. I barely acknowledged the man behind me as I went to the door. I wanted to hold Heidi and assure her she was safe, but she held close to Rickard, placing him between her and me.

As I suspected, there was an SS car out front, and the Reich banner fluttered on either side of the hood. We turned away from the car and made our way toward the white Volkswagen.

"Say nothing," Rickard whispered. It was an easy instruction to follow. I had no words.

Once in the car, we pulled away toward the autobahn. Rickard adjusted the rearview mirror for the third time. "It does not appear we are being followed. Regardless, Gregor knows what I am driving. I need to call a friend and ask him to meet us in Hanover. You did well back there."

"I sat like a stone—hardly a star performance."

"He expected you to defend yourself, protest your innocence. Once he got you talking, he would use your words against you. Silence was your best strategy."

"If by strategy you mean scared witless, I agree." I had to look back. The road behind us was sparsely dotted with cars. "Are you all right, sweetheart?" I took in the look of Heidi's face. Wide, innocent brown eyes regarded me, and I wondered what she thought had just happened. Had she realized how much danger we were in or how close we had come to being arrested?

"I'm all right. Are we going on the train soon?"

"Not just yet, *Kindlein*. There is cheese and crackers in the basket. Let's eat something on the way."

"Are the passports legitimate?" I asked.

"Yes, they are."

"Good. We have too many, but we can put Heidi on the transport with no problem now." I found myself smiling. I reached for Heidi's hand, and blessed relief poured over me when she took it, returning my smile with her jack-o-lantern grin.

Chapter 20

"Am I being paranoid, or was that far too easy?" I asked as we entered Hanover. I couldn't help feeling we'd narrowly skirted disaster.

"Gregor will not risk the demotion he could face if I am telling the truth. What he will do is verify my story, make a report, and ask for instructions."

We drove to an apartment complex and parked. When Rickard rapped on the door, we waited for the bespectacled man who opened it to invite us in. He looked to be in his early thirties, with his hair unkempt and his suspenders hanging freely at his sides.

"Rick, come in."

I felt awkward, but Rickard tossed the man his car keys and plopped down on the couch. "We need papers and a different vehicle. There has been a change in plans."

"What happened?"

I noted there were no introductions made, and I was wondering if I should introduce myself when I remembered what Rickard had told Heidi about not using names. Rickard molded himself into the corner of the couch, arm outstretched along its back. "I've been compromised."

"*Scheisse*." The man ran a hand through his hair. He smiled weakly at Heidi. "Sorry, *Liebchen*. What happened?"

"Gregor is about to catch me in a lie," Rickard stated. The man swore, then nodded. He moved the kitchen table away from a plain white wall. Grabbing a camera off an old bookcase, he motioned

196

for Rick to stand against the wall. A few hours later, we held fake passports in our hands.

"You are now Anna and Maxwell Schmidt, with your daughter, Sophie. Keep your old papers in the false bottom of your traveling bag."

"Do you have the package?" Rickard asked. "I may as well hand deliver it. There will be nowhere to hide."

The man took a picture from the wall, pulling out the back of the portrait and revealing the hiding place of a plain envelope.

"I hope this is worthwhile. What's in it?" Rickard placed the envelope in his jacket pocket.

"Photos of airfields, factories, and a detention center." He took an old book of Bible stories off the shelf. "This is for you," he said, handing the book to Heidi. In the book was a silk ribbon with an old army medal pinned to it. I recognized the Edelweiss flower blazoned on the darkened bronze surface. "My father's war medal," the man explained when he saw me studying the piece.

"It's lovely." I tried to smile, but guilt weighed upon my shoulders. Rickard was valuable as an insider to the SS. It was my fault he was in danger. Now he was no longer of use to the Resistance.

Rickard hugged his friend, who then turned to hug Heidi and me before leading us all to the rear of the building. The men stared at the car. Rickard, sighing as though saying goodbye to a lover, stroked the rearview mirror gently.

"She was my first."

"You always remember your first. She's so beautiful."

"She is. A thousand black Volkswagens, and I had to pick a white one."

"Fine time to be original. I can have her painted." His friend placed a reassuring hand on Rick's shoulder.

Rickard grimaced. "Don't tell me. I'd like to remember her just as she is."

"Oh, would you stop it! It's only a car. Which one are we taking?"

The men both groaned, and Rickard held his hand to his chest as though it pained, while his friend pointed to a black Audi.

"Thank you." I hesitated and then hugged the stranger. "I hope we can repay you some day." I pulled the back door open and motioned Heidi to climb in. The two men shook hands. Rickard got in the driver's seat, and our friend disappeared back inside.

Darkness had fallen. We drove across Hanover, looking for a mid-priced hotel. Anything too fancy or too shabby might look suspicious. Rickard was determined that we look like a middle-class family on holiday. We pulled into the parking lot. Rickard snapped off the engine and turned to me. "You don't need to talk. Just look at me like you would your beloved husband."

I stretched my mouth into an exaggerated smile. Rickard rolled his eyes. "Practice."

Rickard signed the hotel register Erik Weiss. The room was adequate, with a settee large enough to sleep Heidi comfortably. We took turns in the shower, youngest to oldest. Heidi was ready for bed, so Rickard tucked her in and kissed her sweetly on the forehead. Heidi would be asleep in moments. Turning toward me, he motioned toward the bathroom. "Go shower. I will be here when you get back."

I noted the dark circles under his eyes. He wasn't someone who wanted to run, but thanks to me he had no other choice. Was I wrong to put him in that position? Losing Rickard was a big loss to the Resistance. But what else could I have done? I didn't ask him to become involved.

As hot water ran down my back, I closed my eyes and let my thoughts run free. I could have been arrested without any playacting on the part of Rickard, yet the ease with which we'd left the café haunted me. What if Rickard was telling the truth about infecting the children with TB? Why would he ask for six passports if he only needed one?

How did I know whether he was only trying to gain my trust by having Gregor threaten us?

My head began to spin. I wasn't sure what made sense anymore. I knew no one in the Resistance, but he'd said he hoped I could lead the SS to more derelict personalities.

Lord, help me. I didn't want to be used, and I certainly did not want Heidi to suffer because I had trusted the wrong person.

I wrapped my hair in a towel and enfolded myself in a hotel robe. While Rickard took his turn in the bathroom, I dried my hair and put it back in a bun, glancing up when the bathroom door opened. Rickard stood there in his under shorts. I tried not to stare, but he had the most beautiful legs I had ever seen on a man. My eyes feasted on a buffet of muscular planes and angles. I'm not sure how long I stood mesmerized before I realized Rickard was snapping his fingers as though trying to free me from a daze.

"Are you all right?" The cool baritone broke my trance. "Yes. I-I'm fine," I stammered. I closed my eyes, but the image was burned into my mind: this man in his shorts, mussed hair tousled from being towel-dried, a rebel drop of water trickling along the corded neck toward a well-muscled chest. And, always, those piercing blue eyes that made my heart somersault. I rubbed my eyes.

"I must have soap in my eyes." I had to make some excuse.

"You're very brave. I respect that."

I uncovered an eye and looked at him. A compliment? It seemed a bizarre statement to fit this bizarre situation. "As you pointed out, there is a fine line between courage and stupidity. I have since endeavored not to cross it."

I commanded my gaze to stay focused on his eyes. Rickard laughed. "Brave and funny. You have many endearing qualities, Fräulein Lehmeier. Or should I say Frau Schmidt?"

My throat went dry again. We weren't married, and even if we were...

My eyes darted toward Heidi's sleeping form. Rickard's lips twitched in a half smile. "You think I am going to ravish you with a seven-year-old child in the room? Please. There are some things even the SS won't do."

My head snapped toward him. For a moment I had credited him with an occult sensitivity. Had my mind not been thrown into such a whirlpool of confused emotion, I would have seen it wasn't such a stretch to figure out.

He moved closer, or I think he did, as I could feel the heat from his body once more. My tongue tripped over the words my mind struggled to find.

"I...I wasn't sure." Why couldn't I verbalize a coherent thought? Maybe because my brain refused to focus on anything but the way he leaned toward me. I remembered the museum exhibit of a nude male form emblazoned across a bronze circle, titled "The Aryan Warrior." The perfect male physique had been openly displayed for admiration, and the sculpture had made my sister and me giggle until we'd been abruptly escorted out of the room by my morally outraged mother. I remembered her rant to the museum curator. "Exposing young girls to such vulgarity! Outrageous!"

Rickard wasn't vulgar. He was beautiful. He took my face in his hands. Gentle fingers caressed my jaw, making me sigh aloud. "You insist on wearing your hair back, don't you?"

"I..." My tongue knotted. Rickard smoothed the hair behind my ear, running a thumb along its shell toward the earlobe until he found the hair clips. In one fluid motion, my hair cascaded down my back. Rickard's eyes warmed as he played his fingers through the strands. I feared the rage of my heartbeat would wake Heidi. I closed my eyes.

"Erika." My stomach flipped at the sound of my name. I breathed in his scent, crisp and clean from a fresh shower. The warmth of his nearness enveloped me. I opened my eyes and started. He was closer now, brushing the tip of my nose with a gentle kiss. He whispered, "I told you I make no demands. If you choose to honor your marriage vows, it will be when you come to me."

A half smile crossed his lips. I shoved him away from me. "The arrogance! How dare you presume I had any motive other than Heidi's safety? I should slap you. That is what a proper lady would do."

My hand jerked as if in spasm. Ignoring my outrage, Rickard leaned in, caressing my cheek as his lips brushed against mine. My eyelids fluttered shut while my breath hitched. The kiss deepened, and his gentle fingers slid along my jaw, and then caressed my hair. I felt like I was falling. My body melded into his, and my lips parted slightly. His arms came around me in a protective circle. It was strange how he could be so strong yet so soft at the same time. My senses filled with him.

He broke the kiss, leaving me panting for more. In one smooth motion, I was in his arms as he carried me to the bed. He lay beside me, encircling his arms about my torso to pull me close. I felt myself relax as I nuzzled my cheek against his warm chest. "Erika, we need to talk."

"Talk?" The word came out in a rush of relief. He

would keep his word and remain a gentleman in this awkward situation.

"We need to take the Nazis seriously."

I laughed. "I really don't think anyone takes the Nazis lightly." My voice was softened so I wouldn't wake Heidi. She slept peacefully on the settee. For her, this was an adventure, just an outing with friends. I envied her that.

"In my bag is a false bottom, where the envelope with pictures is hidden. There's proof of Germany's intent to go to war."

"War?" The word filled me with horror. I remembered stories the men at church had told of the trenches, the mustard gas, and injuries so severe it seemed more merciful to die than to endure the pain.

"I have to get these photos to England."

"We will go with Heidi on the Kindertransport."

"We can't."

"What?" I pulled back to look him in the eye. "We have the passports. We simply board the transport. You have your SS uniform, so no one will question you."

"I have been compromised." Rickard was patient with his explanation. "Gregor will check my story with his superiors. The only reason we weren't arrested at the café was my word that I was telling the truth."

"Were you?" The thought of deliberately infecting children with TB shook me to the core.

"No! The Reich has some honor, twisted and convoluted though it may be, but it's honor all the same. The transport has been sanctioned by the Führer. It is a goodwill measure on his part, and there would be serious repercussions for anyone tampering with that."

"He wants to keep a decent reputation with other countries," I added.

"Exactly. One doesn't become *Time Magazine*'s Man of the Year with a sloppy performance. But these pictures will show Hitler's true intent—at least, that is what I am hoping."

"What is the plan?" I firmed my resolve. We'd brought Heidi this far, and I would go with her to England.

"I have painted you into a corner, and I am sorry. There is no backing out now. If the SS has taught me anything, it is to be strong. You need your allies at your back. You can't be my ally if you don't trust me."

"Rick, I want to trust you." His deep blue eyes stared unblinking into mine. Realization hit me. Father Julian had defied Reich policy directly, whereas Rickard had attempted to undermine them from within. Looking into those sky blue depths, I wanted to know who he really was. "Were you ever a true Nazi?"

"Erika, politics is simplified so the populace can ingest an ideal. Hitler is smart enough to know a man serves his best interest. If he is comfortable, and he is valued, he is loyal. If a man is denied basic needs, he questions and becomes a dissident."

"When did you begin to question?"

He held me closer in response before he began to speak. "I was part of the free German Youth before it was disbanded, and then I went into the Labor Corps. We worked, and we did drills in the field. The drills were done with shovels. I began to think the drills were similar to military drills with rifles. When I finally got a rifle, I realized both it and the shovel I'd used were weighted the same. They were already preparing teens with paramilitary training. The sterilization laws and the marriage laws never concerned me, so I disregarded them."

"Until your teacher was arrested." I began to put the pieces together.

"He was part of our talks for a while. One point he brought up was the status of injured veterans if our euthanasia policies continued."

"I know people in our church were wondering what would become of those injured on the job."

"Right. My father was injured in the war. I began to wonder if somehow I worked to ultimately hurt him."

"Then you joined the SS?"

"Yes. A government who turns on its own people will not last. A house divided, Lincoln said."

"Jesus said it first," I corrected. "Where does this leave us?"

"We get married tomorrow, using the IDs our contact gave us. Then we leave Germany."

"Before Gregor realizes what has happened."

Lord, watch over us, I prayed. *If we save Heidi, the greater good is served.*

Chapter 21

We had no difficulty getting our marriage loan. There was no wedding, just a civil ceremony and a questionnaire that made me laugh. It was made up of twenty questions designed to measure our suitability to be proper German parents. When I got to the question: "Do you believe in putting children first?" I answered with an emphatic yes. I was encouraged to attend a bride's class on how to manage a household and care for children. It hurt to think there was so much emphasis on the proper care of certain children and such disregard for others. I left Hanover as Frau Schmidt. By noon the three of us were back in the car and headed north. The roads were busier during the day. Despite numerous businesses in the city, parks were abundant, I noted. I thought of home.

"I've never been outside Marburg," I told Rickard as we drove onto the autobahn headed for Hamburg. "How long will it take to get there?"

"A couple of hours. I don't plan to hurry. We are on holiday, after all." He smiled. He'd left his uniform neatly packed away; now he sported trousers and a button-down cotton shirt. Without his uniform, Rickard looked like a typical college student.

The engine purred as the miles went by toward the northern port city. I dreaded the security that would line the gateway to the world. Rickard had to be crazy if he thought we would simply waltz away without a problem.

Once in Hamburg, it was clear Rickard was

driving through the poor side of town. The neighborhoods began to look dismal and bleak. My temples throbbed with a dull, pulsing beat against my fingertip as I surveyed the rundown villas. Moving to push the lock on the door, I glanced nervously into the rearview mirror. Despite the Nazis' assurance crime was at an all-time low, the impoverished surroundings made me leery. Heidi looked on with interest at the sight of unkempt children playing in the yards. Finally, Rickard parked alongside a garbage-strewn alley. I closed my eyes and tried to banish the dread threatening to overtake me, to suck me into some bottomless dark.

"*Wir sind spatzierengehen*. We take a walk from here." Rickard seemed unaffected by the seedy area.

"Here?" There was no containing my shock, and Heidi was startled at the sound of my voice. "What if there are robbers?" Rickard's even tone failed to soothe as I took in the dilapidated area.

"It's a short walk." Rickard assured. "We each take a bag, walk through this alley and down to the corner."

"Rickard! I really don't think this is the best neighborhood to be walking around in."

My wordless plea went ignored.

He winked. "Come, Heidi, let's go meet Olga." Rickard got out of the car and moved toward the trunk. My head fell against the window in surrender.

"Olga?" Heidi grinned broadly, her little pigtails bouncing happily as she got out of the car and trotted over to Rickard.

When Rickard opened the trunk, I steeled my courage and got out of the car also. Ignoring my fearfulness, I managed a charm school poise that would have made my mother proud as I joined the others.

"We're visiting Olga!" Heidi said with a smile.

"That's lovely." I smiled in return as I gave Rickard a querying look, hoping for an explanation.

"Olga is a housemother. A sweet little lady who lives around the corner." The deep blue eyes twinkled mischievously. There were few times when he simply enjoyed a moment. Normally, Rickard measured each word he spoke for weight and effect, and every motion seemed calculated and controlled. I remembered how he had bolted into the room the night Gregor threatened me. My heart warmed at the memory, though I doubted the friendship between Gregor and Rickard had been changed.

The alley reeked of urine and days of old lunches deposited by wandering drunks who had paused long enough to empty their stomachs when sobriety threatened to release them from past revelry. I took Heidi's hand in mine, eager to escape the stench of vomit and garbage. The child's nose wrinkled in disgust.

Once out of the foul-smelling passage, we made our way down a dead-end street. A stone fence stood on either side of a dirt driveway, and we stood a moment to gaze at the old house.

"Olga's place." Rickard smiled.

Olga's place was the grandest of hovels. The yard was clean, though there were no flowerbeds. The paint was worn and cracked on both the house and the weatherbeaten porch that ran the length of it. Dust danced around our feet as we made our way up the drive. The two-story home appeared larger as we neared it, only because overgrown trees and shrubs overshadowed the house.

The floor creaked as we approached the door. Rickard knocked, while Heidi skipped happily along the wooden porch. Standing on tiptoe, she peered into the draped windows, the dirty glass leaving a gray smudge on her nose.

"Heidi," I warned. "That's bad manners." Heidi

grinned, showing the mismatched teeth that seemed too big for her mouth. I thought warmly that this gangly, awkward girl would one day become a bright, fun-loving young woman. I would do all I could to protect her. My father's gun lay at the bottom of my travel bag, just in case.

The child's grin broadened when she heard the feminine voice from the other side of the door holler, "Keep your britches on!"

Rickard laughed. I thought I heard a muttered "for now" just before the door opened.

"Rick!" The woman at the door smiled in surprise as she gave Rickard a one-armed hug that he returned.

"Heidi, Erika, this is Olga. Friend, confidante and general pain in the..."

"Manners, boy." She gave Rickard a scolding look. Opening the door wider she motioned us to come inside.

Olga was an attractive woman in her late forties. The chestnut hair was decorated with delicate strands of silver.

"*Guten Tag!*" Heidi smiled up at the buxom older woman, who bent down to Heidi's eye level.

"*Guten Tag, mein Schatz!* I'm going to need you to go upstairs with Elsa while the adults talk. For now, let's have a bite to eat. Elsa?" I followed Olga's gaze as she called out. A girl about my age came through the swinging doors and walked into the parlor.

"Rick!" She smiled at Rick in genuine pleasure. "I'm Elsa." She gave a friendly wave to me.

"I'm Erika, this is Heidi, and you know Rickard."

"Sure do," Elsa replied.

"Elsa, would you mind fixing us a bit to eat?" Olga asked warmly, her glance moving from Elsa to Heidi in an unspoken request. Elsa nodded and took Heidi's hand in hers.

"Let's go into the kitchen." Elsa spoke sweetly to Heidi, and the little girl followed.

I glanced from Rickard to Olga. Separation was not in my game plan, but Rickard seemed relaxed. Olga led us into a large room with a fireplace against the back wall and chairs arranged about it in a semicircle. The wooden floors creaked and snapped as we entered. The dark paneled walls lent warmth to the room. It was difficult to tell whether this had been a home turned tavern or a tavern turned domicile.

Olga motioned us to sit by extending her arms toward the chairs by the fireplace. Sitting, I folded my hands neatly in my lap.

"They'll be right back. Don't worry." Olga smiled.

"*Naturlich*, of course," I added, glancing toward the doorway the girls had gone through. I could hear the gentle rattle of dishes as they moved about the kitchen.

"Elsa's a good girl," Rickard assured me.

They returned through the swinging door, Elsa carrying a tray while Heidi followed. The rail-thin brunette's pretty green eyes warmed when she smiled. She placed the tray on the coffee table and took a seat next to me. It was then I saw the fading green bruises on her upper arm. Below her right eye was a purple smudge, a bruise in later stages of healing.

"Tea and croissants," Elsa announced cheerily.

She seemed to be in a good mood despite past mistreatment. It made me wonder what had happened.

"It's good to see you, Elsa." Rickard grinned at her. Elsa tapped him on the shoulder playfully.

"It's been too long," she agreed.

Rickard studied her face. I was sure he saw the same marks I did. "You were hurt?" I saw real concern in Rickard's eyes. "Tell me what happened."

Else took a sip of tea, and I noticed her hands trembled as she spoke.

"I was walking home after dark. The Gestapo gave me a hard time. They slapped me around a little. Let me go, thank God."

I saw Rickard eyes darken at the news.

"Bastards. They know Elsa's legal," Olga snorted.

"Legal?" I felt lost.

"Before the Nazis came to power," Olga explained, "Brothel workers were independent. We are now under the control of the Gestapo."

I was stunned. Rickard had brought us to a brothel?

Olga continued to speak. "The Gestapo likes to remind the public how safe they keep them by limiting the health risk or—how do they put it?" The busty brunette glanced across the room a moment, as if to collect her thoughts. "Ah! 'Protect the populace from negative moral practices.'"

"We are allowed to live only in certain parts of town," Elsa continued. "We aren't allowed to travel, and we have to keep our health checkups up to date to prevent the spread of venereal disease."

"And what of Elsa's harassment?" Rickard's unruffled voice asked, though worry lines marred his face.

"No independent practicing. They accused her of streetwalking. Elsa told them she works for me but instead of confirming with me, the low life's roughed her up."

"Perhaps she brought it upon herself," I reasoned. "A woman who chooses this line of work could not reasonably expect to be treated with respect."

The room grew quiet. Not a sound was made until Olga's cup clanked loudly against the saucer she held. Reaching across the coffee table she took me by the chin. Long, lacquered nails bit into my skin.

"Let me explain the facts of life to you, little girl." Her voice turned to ice as her eyes bore into mine. "I have five girls working for me. I love them like my own. We've got nobody, so we band together so we have something. Not everybody has a papa they can cry to, Miss High-and-Mighty. Nobody bails us out but us, and if you to have to spend time on your back to stand on your feet, that is what you do." She turned my face roughly to the side when she released me.

"Olga, she doesn't understand," Rickard sought to explain.

"She's about to understand. She can look down her nose at us, but when our beloved Führer talks about a master race and the mother of a pure generation—who do you think gets pinned with the honor of making these babies, huh? Think about it, baby doll, and forget any handsome African boys. With your Nordic background, you get to breed with the best, right? Your ultimate duty to God and country is to crank out all the racially pure babies you can spew forth. Be a good little brood mare and Hitler gives you a medal. So tell me, when that's your highest merit, who's the whore now?" Gone was any friendliness in her voice.

I was too stunned to speak. Rickard tapped Olga gently on the shoulder and motioned toward the bags.

"Want to see upstairs?" Elsa took Heidi's hand, glad to escape the tense scene. The little girl sprang to her feet and then laughed as Elsa led her up a staircase hidden behind a closed door. I looked helplessly after them. Rickard and Olga rose to follow.

"We are open in ten minutes. You tend bar while

we are gone," Olga commanded. I stammered, helpless, as I responded.

"Wait. What do I do?" Having been chastised, I felt guilty for my careless statement and sorry Elsa and the others had no other choice but to work here.

"They ask for a beer. You give them one. Is that too complicated?" came Olga's sharp retort.

She looped her arm about Rickard's, and then the stairs creaked as their steps echoed up the stairwell. *He brought us to a bordello!* I shrieked mentally through a fog of dismay. *Mother would kill me!* was my second thought.

I laid my face in my hands, not hearing the soft close of the door. At the creak of the floor, however, I peered over my fingertips to watch the older man who had entered thumb through a box of colored envelopes, choosing the lone white one.

I froze.

"I'll have a beer," he stated cheerfully. "Is this your first day, *Liebling*?" He looked careworn, but his kindly manner seemed unreal to me at the moment. Unsure of what to say, I merely pulled myself off the settee with a chipper, "Certainly."

I looked along the short bar; chilled glasses were kept in a small cooling unit—odd, as most people I knew drank warm beer. I looked at the handles of the beer dispensers as I tried to figure out how they worked.

"The blue one, dear," came his helpful response. "My name is Fritz."

I chuckled to myself, shaking my head with a sigh as the foam overfilled the mug in a waterfall to the floor. The old man laughed.

"Tilt the glass so the beer doesn't head so much," he suggested. I shrugged and tried it. Bringing the filled mug to his place at the bar, I noted the white envelope next to his mug. What was I to make of that?

"Is Elsa all right?" The lined face showed genuine concern. My gut twanged with guilt.

"Some bruising. I think she will be all right." I could reply with honesty. It seemed the customers did care for the workers here.

"Good. Good, hard worker. With her father dead and her mom so ill, it is hard on the kid."

"I imagine." I whispered. I was an idiot for judging her. Fritz took me by the hand.

"We will get by in this world. I lived through a world war, and the depression that followed. We get by," he said with a wink.

I smiled sadly. "Thank you."

His grin turned devilish.

"I got to see my grandson last Christmas. He's a big boy now. Six."

"Such a cute age!" I agreed.

"You know, I told him, 'Be good. Santa is always watching. He sees everything. He knows when you sleep, and when you misbehave.' Know what he said to me?" His eyes twinkled.

I shook my head.

"He said, 'I thought that was the Gestapo's job.'" He snorted a laugh, and I gasped before I broke into a fit of giggles. It felt good to laugh. The older man made me feel at home. He had a mischievous warmth that reminded me of the silly uncle who played harmless pranks on my parents.

"I tried being good." Fritz hung his head in mock repentance. "But I gave it up for Lent."

I laughed again, shaking my head.

"Humor keeps you sane. A person laughs or he goes crazy." Fritz shrugged. I leaned against the bar. Fritz leaned forward to press his forehead against mine.

I closed my eyes. I wanted so much to confide in this kind man. Suddenly I stood bolt upright. Gestapo were even in the confessionals. Why not use a kindhearted old man to eavesdrop around town or in a place where people went to relax?

I smiled. "It is difficult not to like you."

He quirked his head to the side, and the gesture seemed familiar somehow. "I hope you're not fighting hard to dislike me."

"Not terribly," I answered.

Fritz kissed my hand "You are a nice girl. Olga will take care of you here."

Fritz left ten marks on top of the white envelope.

"Oh, the beer." I whacked myself on the forehead.

"The rest is yours, dear," the kindly voice responded. He turned at the sound of footsteps coming down the stairs, and Olga and Rickard strolled into the room.

"Fritz!" Olga took his hands in hers and kissed him sweetly on the lips.

"Olga, lovely as ever. Rickard, how are you?"

I suddenly felt myself to be the odd person out, like this club was members-only and I hadn't paid my dues.

Olga stepped aside as the two men shook hands and hugged. I thought I saw Fritz slip something to Rickard.

"You'll take my car," Fritz said to Rickard.

"Thank you." He nodded to the older man.

"Michael and I hoped to meet up again in two weeks," Rickard explained.

"Hoped?" Fritz queried.

Rickard sighed. "I have been compromised." Fritz nodded his understanding. Olga remained silent, though I could see the worry in her eyes.

"Let me drive you to Cuxhaven," Fritz offered. Rickard looked as though he were going to protest. I knew my geography, and the small town would put us well past the huge port of Hamburg. I felt a shiver run down my spine as I wondered who these people really were and who they might be if circumstances were different.

We drove Fritz's car west toward the town of Cuxhaven. We would avoid the large port altogether and make a break for the English Channel from there.

The black Porsche hummed along the decrepit streets. Rickard drove while Fritz took the back seat with Heidi. The car was expensive and didn't blend into the humbler parts of town.

"Are you all right?" Rickard asked me.

I felt the heat rise in my cheeks again. "Fine. Really. I'm just enjoying the scenery." Curiosity got the best of me, and I finally had to ask. "There is something I have to know. What was in the white envelope?"

The men laughed. It was Rickard who spoke up.

"Olga has color-coded envelopes to denote what service the customer is requesting. Money is put in the envelope, and then it is given to the girl before they go upstairs."

"Oh," I paused. "And the white one?"

This time Fritz spoke up. "Holding hands. It is the one Resistance uses when we want to speak with Olga. It isn't used often."

"I can imagine," I deadpanned.

"Olga's place is great for the Resistance. It is amazing the things the girls hear. No one expects Resistance to meet at a Gestapo-run establishment."

"I knew you were new and you didn't seem to know what it was, so I was glad Olga showed up when she did," Fritz added, before asking Rickard, "What of your meeting with Michael?"

"We were going to meet, and I was to give him pictures to take to England. Now, I am going to deliver them personally."

Guilt began to gnaw at my gut. "Rick, I'm sorry.

If it hadn't been for me you wouldn't have been discovered."

He took my hand. "I have the best chance for escape now."

"Everything happens for a reason," Fritz's kind voice stated.

Rickard pulled the car around the side of a sadly dilapidated building and parked.

"There's a stretch of beach before we get to the dock. The boat is berthed there," Fritz explained.

We got out of the car, taking our meager possessions with us. Fritz offered to carry Heidi's bag for her.

Once again, Rickard left the keys in the ignition. I worried about someone stealing Fritz's fancy car.

"Is this wise?" I pointed toward the keys. Rickard looked at me and shrugged.

"Everyone is afraid of the Gestapo. It's hard to get anyone to steal anything, anymore," Fritz explained with a good-natured chuckle.

"Pity. If you can't trust a thief, who can you trust?" Rickard replied.

We began to walk along the shore. The few businesses looked old and forgotten, as though it had been a while since anyone made their livelihood here. There were a few wooden paths that led to forgotten docks. We followed a small ramp up to a wooden dock. The boat was tied along its side.

"Rickard and the boys made this boat. We discovered an Italian-made engine, a beautiful thing, but putting it in this boat is like having a ruby in a tin setting," Fritz spoke as though we were doing nothing more than taking a pleasure cruise.

"She doesn't look like much, but she's fast." Rickard smiled, looking at the vessel with affection.

The two men were relaxed around each other, as though they had known each other for years, and I felt as though I were seeing Rickard for the first time—seeing the man he was without the SS, without the Resistance, just a young man having a day with someone who could be his grandfather. God brought us this far, surely he meant for us to get to England.

Rickard carried our bags along the dock to the boat and tossed them on board. The vessel looked like a hybrid between an old fishing boat and a sailboat. I could see what Fritz meant about a tin setting.

"We're not going in this," I pleaded.

"She's an old runabout. Fast, like I said. The boys gave her an engine you can't fault. There is a small hold below deck, and it should be comfortable enough to get across the Channel. And the weather promises to cooperate."

Rickard lowered himself onto the old fishing boat, which groaned with the unexpected weight.

"Come, *Liebchen*. Come aboard, and you can put the bags in the hold." Rickard extended a hand to me. I felt faint.

"Is it seaworthy?" I asked.

"Of course, unless you would rather swim across the Channel." Rickard seemed amused at my response.

"The flights were all booked," Fritz chimed.

I didn't know what I expected. I was hoping for something that wouldn't sink. I placed my hand in his, half expecting to fall through the bottom of the boat as he lifted me onto the deck.

"Don't be afraid. I've taken her out before."

"I've never seen the water!" Heidi was excited. "Can I go on?" Fritz laughed and picked the little girl up, groaning as he did so. She was passed over to Rickard, who lifted her with ease and placed her on the deck beside me.

"The North Sea is full of water; you'll love it." Rickard stated. "Take a look in the hold."

Heidi scurried to the edge to look at the water, causing the boat to sway. I crossed myself.

"Don't you think you are overreacting?" Rickard's eyes took on a deeper blue against the sea's backdrop.

"I've never been on a boat. What if it sinks?" I glanced about.

"Then we have a U-boat." Rickard answered with an amused tone.

"An underwater boat? Not funny." My stomach lurched. "What of U-boats? Will we be arrested?"

"A submarine will surface to arrest a fishing boat?" Fritz raised his eyebrows furrowing his forehead in horizontal lines. "More than likely they will simply bomb you." The two were having a grand time at my expense.

"*Dummkopf!*" I mumbled, annoyed.

"We will be sailing north. The waters are not so guarded. A small commercial boat will be of no notice," Rickard replied.

The small deck held nets and fishing equipment. It would indeed look like we were simply fishermen.

"The deck below has a sleeping compartment. You can stay out of the sun, if you wish." Fritz waved a hand in farewell.

I steadied my breath as I looked up to him.

"Thank you. We are really going." I smiled. Days of worry were finally over. I threw my arms around Rickard.

"Yes." Rick's eyes widened as I hugged him. "Take Heidi below, and get comfortable."

I squeezed his hand in response. I had been more afraid these past few days than ever before. I'd worried so much about Heidi's safety, and now I wondered what else would give my life meaning in the days ahead. Looking at Rickard, I knew loving him might be part of it.

I blew Fritz a kiss. "*Danke schön*. Thank you."

The simple words seemed so inadequate for the help he'd given us.

"*Bon Voyage*. We will see you again." Fritz made the motion of catching the kiss as he spoke. I looked back and waved just before going below deck.

In the hold, I helped Heidi explore and get comfortable. The boys would say their goodbyes and then we would set for England. I put an arm around Heidi. "It won't take long to cross the Channel. Once in England, you will be placed with a nice family." I wasn't sure how much I should tell her, when I wasn't sure myself what would happen. It looked as though the Germans were poised for war. Other countries, including England, watched the Fatherland with apprehension. The Germans themselves drew in fear with each breath. Fear for ourselves and fear for the future. I prayed for a return to sanity before disaster could strike.

And then there was a shot.

I recognized Gregor's voice. The sound of his jackboots on the wooden pier told me he was drawing closer to the boat.

I gasped and held Heidi close to me. The little girl buried her head in my shoulder. I bit my hand to stifle a scream.

"I've finally found you, Rickard." Gregor's voice made my blood run cold. I held Heidi tight against me.

"That was a warning. Come with me now, and I won't shoot again. Is that slut with you?" Gregor's tone was deadly.

Heidi shivered. I kissed the top of her head to try to calm her.

"Just me and Rickard." I sighed in relief to hear Fritz respond.

"You are aiding a felon. Rickard is under arrest, by the authority of the Third Reich. If you do not stand aside, you will be placed under arrest, as well."

"Gregor, listen to Opa." Fritz was trying to reason with him. *Opa*? Fritz was Gregor's grandfather?

"Don't make me shoot you." Gregor warned.

"Gregor, look at what you are doing. It's one thing to serve your country, but another to turn on a friend. Let Rickard go," Fritz urged.

"He lied to me. He knowingly aided a fugitive in the kidnapping of a child from a state institution and used his status as an SS officer to circumvent the law. Stand aside and let me apprehend Rickard," Gregor said.

I looked about for a place to hide Heidi. The padded seat lifted, and I motioned for Heidi to hide inside it. I scrambled for a plan.

"No!" It was the last word Fritz would utter, as another shot rang out.

Rickard screamed, "You son of a bitch! How will you explain his death to your father?"

"My father well knows the consequences for betraying the Reich. Grandfather did, too."

"Why did you come by yourself?" Rickard asked. I wondered if he was trying to tell me they were alone.

"This is your last chance. Turn in the traitor and bring the child back, and no one needs to know of your involvement. We are friends, Rick."

"I don't know where she is. We were on the way to the Kindertransport when she ditched me."

"Don't take me for a fool. You cannot betray the Reich. They have done everything for you. Given you an education, a job. You owe them everything."

"Without them I would be nothing," Rickard replied. I listened.

"Think of your mother. What will she do with you in jail? Disgraced and dishonored."

"It would hurt her more to know I did nothing."

"I would rather kill you myself than allow you to become a traitor to the Reich."

Gregor was mad. Heidi had been taken from under his nose, and his friend had lied to him. Gregor was not the kind to forgive such transgressions, especially when it meant losing face with his superiors.

"They will kill me anyway, as you noted. I have only one child in my custody," Rickard responded. He was buying me time.

My eyes rested on my bag.

I knew what I had to do.

"Don't throw away all you worked for. She isn't worth it," Gregor reasoned.

A shot and a trail of smoke from the end of Papa's revolver brought home what I had done. Gregor screamed as the bullet tore through his arm. He held the injured spot a moment before his hateful gaze met mine as Rick dived onto the deck and started the engine. "Erika, get down!" he commanded but my eyes stayed locked on Gregor. The gun that had killed his grandfather slipped from Gregor's hand and lay harmless on the dock.

"Oh, *mein Gott!* I shot him! We have to get him to a hospital!" I heard myself scream. Rickard swept his leg behind my knees, buckling them, and I fell forward as we raced to the open water.

Chapter 22

The August sun glistened off the smooth water, sunlight dancing in patterns marking a path toward England. Heidi would be safe there until the mania subsided. Rickard was so certain war was imminent. For now, it was just Rickard and I on the deck while he navigated the boat across an endless blue.

"Despite it all, I pity Gregor," I said as I looked out onto the open water.

"He tried to give me a chance right up to the end, but if you hadn't stepped in, I think he would have shot me," Rickard replied.

"I can't believe I did that. I don't want to be a murderer."

"The wound wasn't fatal. He will live."

"I'm sorry I shot him, but I just couldn't see any other way out." I nestled close to Rick, resting my cheek against the round of his shoulder.

"He wouldn't have given us another way. Had he arrested us, we would be on death row now."

"We won't be able to go back now, will we?" I looked back toward the distant shoreline we'd left. "I will miss home."

"Me, too." Rickard's cheerless response betrayed the sadness he felt, abandoning his homeland, our homeland. I ached for the familiar as we cruised toward the unknown, wondering when I would see Marburg again. His strong arm enfolded me, bringing me closer. We would be all that was familiar to each other in a nation of strangers.

We docked in the small village of Norfolk. The fishing docks looked similar to the ones we had left.

A few modest buildings acted as fish stores and bait shops, and workers went about the business of making a living. We disembarked to finally set foot in England.

"The air even smells different here." I inhaled a deep breath of salty air.

"That is the fish." Rickard's boyish grin lit his eyes. Heidi was fascinated. She seemed to take in all the sights and smells, cataloging them in her mind for later use. We walked away from the docks toward a small restaurant. I smiled pleasantly but allowed Rickard to speak. I spoke very little English and was not willing to draw attention to myself. He ordered fish and chips for the three of us, placing Heidi's book of Bible stories on the table, the Edelweiss medal sticking out from between the pages.

A few minutes later he stood to greet a young man who approached. The two shook hands and hugged like brothers. This had to be Rickard's English friend from the university. Michael was average height, muscular, in his early twenties, with blue eyes and dark brown hair.

"Hi there, princess, how was your trip?" He ruffled Heidi's hair playfully.

"Very good, thank you!" She beamed.

"Welcome to England," he quipped cheerfully. Turning to me he asked, "And you are?"

My English was not as good as Heidi's. I had to assume he followed the normal introductions, so I said, "Hello."

I looked about, relieved no one found me odd or out of place.

"*Guten Tag, Fräulein,*" Michael addressed me again, and I smiled, nervously glancing about, concerned about the reaction people might have to a German in the restaurant. Michael gave my hand a reassuring squeeze, and then turned his attention back to Rickard. The men switched from English to

German to English with the ease of flipping a switch. I nodded and laughed, to make it look as though I understood them. I wanted just to blend in. I held Heidi's hand more to comfort myself than out of worry for her.

Heidi greeted everyone she saw, staring wide-eyed at all the sights, trying to take it all in as Michael drove us into the country and down an unpaved road to a small cottage. The front door opened into a sitting room, with a kitchen off to the left and a bedroom in back. I cooed in delight. It was like something from a fairy tale.

"Settle in, and I will make tea." Michael tapped me gently on the shoulder and motioned for me to sit down. I took a seat on a rocking chair while Heidi rushed to help Michael in the kitchen. There was a saddened look in Rickard's eyes as his gaze met mine, but before I could ask what was wrong, Michael and Heidi came out with tea and sandwiches.

We could finally relax. The rocking motion was a comfort. I was grateful to have Heidi safe at last, though I was loath to be parted from her. However, had she boarded the Kindertransport, I would have had no knowledge of her whereabouts after she left Germany. This way, I might be able to see her once in a while. There was so little to remind me of home. A knock on the door made me jump in my seat. Hand to my chest, I commanded my heart to calm. The woman who entered had chestnut hair and dark eyes, and a family resemblance made me assume she was a sister to Michael. She knelt down next to Heidi.

"Hello, there. I am your Aunt Constance. You will come to stay with me at my house for a while." She smiled at the child, but I could not help feeling depressed. Heidi's parents thought she was dead. Could she ever go home again? Could we?

Heidi had been coloring a picture, and she smiled at the woman and spoke to her in English.

"Will Mama and Papa come?" she asked.

Constance sighed visibly and caressed Heidi's hair. "I am not sure, darling. I hope so, someday."

Rickard sat on the floor next to Heidi and took three crayons in hand. He drew a swastika on the inside cover of her coloring book.

"This is not Germany's flag," he explained in German, as he marked an X across the symbol. "This is a banner flown by someone we thought was good at first, but we found out he wasn't. Our real flag has three colors." Rickard took the black crayon and drew a line. "Did you know black is all colors mixed up?" He smiled at her, and Heidi laughed.

"Black is for the soil. Red is for courage and passion. Gold is prosperity. When this flag no longer flies," he said, pointing to the swastika, "It is time to go home."

He drew the colors of the German flag on the cover of her book. A stray tear ran down my cheek. We had made it. Heidi was safe with Constance, whom I hugged and told my thanks, although I wasn't sure how much German she knew.

What I was certain of was that Rickard and I had to find a way to adopt England as our new home. We couldn't go back.

In this small town, Michael said, we could move about freely, for the most part. I'd caught a glimpse of a small church nearby, and it made me yearn for a confessional. I had shot a man. It had been an act of violence that could have ended his life. I had to speak to a priest and unburden my soul, but first it was time to say goodbye to Heidi.

"*Liebchen*, I hope to see you again soon, but you will stay with Constance for a while. *Ich liebe dich.* I love you." I hugged her.

"We will come back to see Erika and Rick,"

Constance promised. Heidi seemed unsure, and I hated to see her go, although I waved cheerfully.

When they had gone, I went to the table where Rickard and Michael talked. "So I do what? Stay here and hide? I don't speak English, so how do I work?" I waited for answers.

"If we go to war, there should be plenty of work in factories, though I would pretend to be mute, if I were you. Not many are willing to embrace the Germans, though you are embraceable enough." Michael gave me a smile. I knew he was trying to be kind and ease my fear. He added, "I am going to have to teach you English. Rickard can help."

I tried to smile, but I was homesick and worried both for my parents' welfare and for what I would do here. "If I don't witness to the fates of the children, I am spitting on their deaths. I need to do something to let people know what is happening."

"We are getting together later. We might be able to get your story into print, Erika. For now, try to rest." Michael's words soothed but failed to calm the restless energy gnawing at my mind.

Rickard rose from his chair, but as the two men made for the door, I protested, "Where are you going?"

"We will be back. I need to deliver these photos." Rickard took me gently by my shoulders. "You're safe now. Heidi is safe. Relax. We will come back." He kissed me, and I threw my arms around him to hold him close.

"I am being childish. Go, and I will see you in a few hours." I looked around the simple cottage. Rickard took my face in his hands and smiled.

"We will be right back. Don't worry."

The dishes were washed, and there was little to unpack. The image of Gregor as I last saw him on the dock made me shudder. Had it been self-defense? Gregor had already shown himself capable of murder, but had it been justifiable in the sight of God to shoot him? I rested on the bed and tried to force the scene from my mind. *Lord, I never wanted to hurt anyone.* We'd both done what we thought was right. Odd as it seemed, Gregor cared for Rickard, and we all sought the best for Germany. I hated that it had come down to this.

The sound of bells made me rise from the bed. I realized they must be church bells, and they reminded me of home. Outside, I could see a steeple not too far away, beyond a copse of trees. It was like a beacon calling me toward it.

A white cat jumped up onto the windowsill, startling me. A black spot along his ear gave him a familiar look, and when I noted the black mark under his nose, I gasped. The cat looked strangely like the Führer.

"I'm losing my mind. I have to get out of here," I said aloud. Once outside, I glanced at the cat once more. He stared at me with wise green eyes as I made my way to the beaten path. "Kitler," I mused.

After some exploring, I found the way to the small church. The cross was a beacon to come inside and worship during its daily service. I followed the stone path to the door, where a man held the door open for me.

"*Danke,*" I told him, and then made my way to the confessional, where I waited my turn to go into the small enclosed area to talk to a priest. There was a shuffling sound as I began speaking, and I heard the door close before I was told, in German, to continue. I thanked God for sending me someone who could understand what I said.

"Forgive me, Father, I have sinned. I shot a man." There was silence for a moment, and I was asked to continue. I told the priest about saving Heidi and shooting the SS officer who stood in the way of our bringing her to England. I explained I'd been trapped and felt I had no choice. I had not shot to kill, and I believed he might still be alive. There was silence for a moment, and I shuddered when I remembered Rickard telling me the Gestapo stood in the confessionals. This was England. There would be no Gestapo here, but what about sympathizers?

"Are you asking for sanctuary?" The screen hid his face, but the kind voice was like soothing ointment over my frazzled nerves.

"Yes. My name is Erika Lehmeier." I waited for my penance. The silence stretched forever, so I continued. "When I called a classmate a bad name, I had to say three Hail Marys and apologize. I imagine attempted murder would be more than that."

"I'm Father James. I will need to meet with you, Erika, and with the young man, as well. Can you come back tomorrow at six o'clock?"

"Yes, I think so. Thank you."

Going home to the cottage, my soul felt lighter. I could gain absolution for having hurt Gregor. Rickard turned as I walked in.

"Where were you?" He sounded more relieved than angry.

"I found the little church. I hadn't been to confession in months." I smiled as he folded me in his arms.

"You had me worried," he whispered, running a hand through my hair. He pressed his cheek to mine.

"He offered us sanctuary. We need to meet with him tomorrow night at six." I took comfort in the way he held me.

Rickard nodded agreement and whispered, "Love will be a rare commodity in the months to come. The English are very tense. There will be little joy to be found when the beast of war pounces."

I sighed and leaned into Rickard's touch. He trailed gentle kisses along my jaw before brushing his lips against mine. My heart pounded. The kiss deepened, and I parted my lips slightly. Warmth flooded my entire being, and I felt as though I floated. I pressed against him, wanting to merge myself into him. The stress and fear I'd had melted away.

Rickard brushed my hair away from my face and kissed me deeply, until he finally scooped me up into his arms and carried me across the room into the bedroom. He placed me on the bed as gently as he could, and I reached up and drew him closer to me.

I dismissed from my mind all worry over meetings, police, or the docks. I wanted to feel safe, warm, and loved before I dealt with what was ahead. I would have this time just for me, without the burden of the outside world.

Rickard held me closer, and his hands wandered lovingly along my sides, following the curve of my hip, and massaging along my thighs. The heat of his touch sent electricity along my skin, and I quivered. He paused, leaving a hand pressed against my thigh.

"I promised no demands," he whispered huskily.

I was heady, my heart pounding, my eyes focused only on his face as I took it into my hands.

"I want you, and I want this," I breathed, reaching for the buttons on his shirt. "Rick, you talk too much."

He seemed surprised at my response, but he smiled warmly, his blue eyes glowing. He sat up to unbutton his shirt as I pulled at the buttons on his trousers. Rickard took my hands and kissed them, brushing my fingers along his unshaven face. I found the slight roughness exciting.

"Patience." He raised a finger, asking me to wait a moment and slid away long enough to remove the shirt, exposing his beautifully muscular arms. I tried not to look any further and closed my eyes. Rickard took my hand and urged me to sit up. My breath hitched at the sight of the nude form before me. *He is the Aryan warrior*, I mused as heat rushed to my cheeks. Kneeling before me and disrobing me gently, he kissed every inch of flesh exposed as buttons were unfastened. Sliding the blouse from my shoulders, he caressed the bare skin beneath it, running his hands along my shoulders to lower the bra straps, then unfastening the back. I blushed as the unwanted garment was tossed aside. Soft lips trailed a path along my chest and between my breasts, before he tenderly nuzzled the modest buds. He took my hand, pulling me to my feet to stand before him as he cupped my face in his hands and whispered, "You are beautiful."

The simple sincerity of that statement brought tears to my eyes. He slid my skirt down my thighs until it lay in a puddle at my feet, leaving me in my garter belt and panties. Heat flooded my face as I hesitated to meet his gaze. Strong hands slid along my thighs, taking the cotton panties with them. Then, dropping to his knees once again, Rickard followed a path along the curve of my legs, kissing my inner thigh while at the same time removing the belt and hooks and sliding my panties to my ankles. "I want to leave no inch of you unloved."

I caught my breath at his words. He nuzzled my pubic curls as his tongue darted gently across the tender nub, sending a shockwave through my center and making me ache for more. Curling my fingers in his hair, I sighed in pleasure and lost myself to him. As if in a dream, I floated back onto the mattress. His gentle fingers replaced his tongue, stroking me to ecstasy. He eased himself on top of me, kissing me deeply, our tongues dueling and darting, and my legs parted in welcome to what I wanted most.

"I love you, my angel." His words sent my spirit soaring with the realization that I loved him, too.

Cradling him between my thighs, I felt him

move to enter me, slowly at first and then breaking my resistance with one thrust. I squealed, and he held me close, kissing me softly. The pain was over so quickly, and I became accustomed to the strange presence. My virginity surrendered gladly, and our marriage was consummated. "Are you all right?"

I nodded in response. He began to move within me, and the soreness gave way to pleasure. He rolled until I was on top of him, and he urged me to take control. I moaned aloud when his strong hands massaged my breasts, and my nipples stood at attention, pleading for more. Straddling his hips, the friction ignited new waves of pleasure, exploding from my heated core. In a crescendo of sensation, orgasm exploded.

"Yes! Rick!" One-syllable words were all I could manage. Bucking beneath me with his lovely eyes closed, I saw his expressive face in the throes of passion before he released into me and his arms came around me and held me close. Sated, I laid my head on his chest. The sound of his heartbeat lulled me into a state of bliss. The afterglow hadn't dimmed when he rose from the bed to get dressed.

"Where are you going?" My voice sounded dreamy to my own ears.

"I need to go to the docks. Some things were left in the boat. I want to be sure we meet our contact before I unload her."

Too sated to question, I only purred drowsy agreement. It was later, upon waking from a contented nap, that I began to worry. The light had faded at the window, and I realized I'd slept longer than intended. The emptiness of the cottage seemed foreboding. My skin prickled. I had to find Rickard.

The docks were clear; people must have returned home for supper. I followed the dusty lane to where the boat was berthed. There, shaking the disbelief from my eyes, I was just in time to watch as he was led to a police car. Pressing myself against the side of a building, I watched the car ease down the street. This was impossible. We had fled Germany only to be arrested when we got here? I couldn't ring Michael. I couldn't even ask where the police station was. *Oh, Lord, help me! Rickard has done so much. I can't be useless to him now.*

The church. Father James. We were asking for sanctuary. Surely, he could help us. I ran the whole way, ignoring brambles trying to snare my ankles as I fled through the woods toward the church. Would I be able to find a friend here like I had in Father Julian? I knocked on the rectory door, apprehension causing me to bounce on the balls of my feet.

"Erika?" A man in his late forties addressed me. I nodded vigorously and he let me in. The wingback chairs in his study offered no comfort for me. I paced back and forth as I told the priest what I had seen on the docks. Frustrated tears burned my eyes as I searched my mind. I only knew Michael and Constance by their first names, assuming those were their real names.

"Try to relax, *Fräulein*. Would you care for some tea?" His tone was kind, and the English accent bled through the German he spoke.

"No, thank you. I can't lose him. We have been through so much together, my husband and I." A stab of pain came with the realization we *were* legally married, both by the state and in the eyes of the Church. Rickard had risked everything to help me—and to help Heidi—and I couldn't help loving him. I had to do everything in my power to set him free.

"I assume they took him to the police station. Why don't we go now?" Father James' green eyes looked at me with compassion as he spoke.

Three stone steps led to the door of the police station, and a rounded ball sconce lit either side of the door. Father James spoke to the constable at the front desk. I wished heartily I spoke the language better. English seemed guttural and ugly to my ears. I searched the room for Rickard, but I found no sign. Finally, we were taken to an interrogation room. Rickard was in a holding cell. His eyes lit in surprise to see me run toward him. We laced our fingers together. I drew his hand through the bars and held them to my chest.

"It's all right, angel," he soothed. "I am being questioned. The boat was searched, and my SS uniform was found. I was driving Michael's car, and he is being summoned."

"What will happen? They have to know you aren't here to hurt anyone. We will just tell the truth."

Rickard stroked the hair that fell freely about my shoulders. To my relief, Michael strode into the room.

"Michael! Tell them Rickard is innocent!"

"They think I may be a sympathizer," Michael explained.

"We need to convince them you are not. I would rather not mention Heidi. If we are deported, at least she will be safe," Rickard said in German. He was willing to protect Heidi even now. My heart burned with love for him. Regardless of any other motive he may have had for coming, I knew he was putting Heidi's future at the top of the list.

"Tell them about the pictures," I protested.

We were interrupted by the sound of footsteps as a middle-aged man entered the room and joined Michael. He shook Rickard's hand through the bars.

"This is Michael's father, Harold Chadwick," Rickard explained to me. "He owns an import/export business, so he travels frequently. He will vouch for us."

"*Danke.*" I took hold of the older man's hand. "I

am Erika Lehmeier, sir, and it is a pleasure to meet you."

"Yes, likewise," he replied.

As the constable spoke with Michael's father, Rickard quickly translated for me what was being said.

"You will have to understand my position, Mr. Chadwick. A boat registered to your son was found. On this boat are two Germans, one an SS officer in possession of both a firearm and an SS uniform. There are two separate sets of identification papers, one saying he is married with a child, the other stating he is single. Which is he?"

Michael's father listened to all the man had to say. I could only hope we could prove our innocence. At this point, Father James must have insisted German be spoken, as I could now follow the conversation in my native tongue.

"Do you suppose," Mr. Chadwick spoke to the constable as a parent to a snarky child, "if the Nazis were to send a spy, they would send one who speaks no English? It would be difficult for the young lady to inform anyone of anything, if she can't understand what is being said."

The constable did not seem convinced. He leaned toward Rickard. "Let's start at the beginning. Who are you?"

"I am Rickard Sankt of Deaths Head Squadron SS. I met Michael Chadwick at the University of Munich, where we discussed non-violent protest of civil rights violations. He can verify all I have said."

"How did you get here?"

"I got here on a boat Michael and I, with help from two friends, put together. The engine is a new Italian model, designed to go thirty miles per hour."

The constable whistled. "What need have you of that type of speed?"

"We'd hoped to be able to outrun a pursuer if we

had to."

"What is your involvement with the SS?"

"I was recruited during my time at the university." Rickard told of the arrest of Hans' father and how, as a result, he was supposedly re-educated but carried the hidden hope of bringing knowledge of Reich activity to England in order to expose the Nazis.

"Are you a spy or a defector?"

"Neither, sir. I am a loyal German, but I am loyal to the Germany my father fought for. We fled the country to bring a child here, a child marked for termination at a treatment center. Our plan was discovered, and we left our homeland."

They took Rickard away for further questioning. I rose to protest, and Father James placed a reassuring hand on my shoulder. A lady officer resumed my questioning. I remembered what Rickard had said about the boys being separated so they could not corroborate their stories.

"Who is Rickard?"" she asked. The brown eyes searched mine. I almost smiled. Over the months, I had asked myself the same question.

"He is a Resistance operative who worked with a priest from my church. His position in the SS gave him a unique opportunity to help those who questioned the Reich, as he did."

"Were you forced to cooperate with him?"

Forced? This would be the time to say I had nothing to do with any of this, let the chips fall where they may, and let Rickard fend for himself. He had the uniform and the fake papers. *No.* I could never do that, but I thought this is what they expected me to do. "I was never forced. I begged him to help me take a child from Grafeneck Castle, and he did so at great personal risk."

"What is your involvement with the SS?"

"None. The SS seized Grafeneck while I worked

there with the children under my care. It was a monastery. It will be transformed into a killing center, although they like to call it a treatment center. The handicapped and retarded will be exterminated—death by gassing."

The constable and the priest exchanged a horrified glance.

"Will you tell us what you spoke with Father James about?"

"She will not!" The priest was off his chair so quickly it nearly fell over. "Confessions are privileged information, and I will not breach trust. Erika, say nothing."

"I shot a man who threatened us. I went to confession because I had not wanted to hurt him, and I needed absolution."

"Shot a man?" The constable leaned in. "Criminals are deported."

"If you deport her, it is tantamount to murder!" the priest roared in protest. "It was self-defense. They were fleeing the SS with a child in tow."

"Which brings us to the question of who are you?" She dropped two sets of papers on the table in front of me. Our phony documents stated we were Heidi's parents, and the actual marriage license had our real names on it.

"They are both me. We got married to procure a marriage loan. The money was used for this trip and for Resistance use. He is my husband. I am Erika Lehmeier-Sankt. My marriage bond is real, and I will not deny the marriage is valid."

"She has asked for sanctuary. I have extended this to her." Father James looked defiant.

The door opened. Rickard was sandwiched between two police officers. A man in uniform joined them, and he held the familiar envelope we'd brought from Hanover. The pictures were spread across the table. Airfields, youth practicing with rifles, factories and detainment centers were among the photos. It occurred to me that more than one person had taken these snapshots.

The officer who seemed to be in charge addressed me. "Will you agree to help the Kindertransport children adjust to their new homes? We need someone who speaks German fluently to help them acclimate."

I nodded an enthusiastic yes.

Rickard moved to sit next to me, taking my hand in his. His eyes looked into mine as he spoke. "I have given Michael my uniform. He is going to assume my fake identity and go to Germany. The information I gave them is enough to keep us from getting deported. What I need to know now is, do you want an annulment?"

An annulment would be a church ruling stating our marriage was invalid, as though it had never happened. I held fast to his hands. Through it all, he had been there, like a safe harbor, a rock to anchor my faith. "Rickard, I love you. I am your wife if you want me."

He leaned to kiss me. "After the war, Germany will need a healer."

"I will be there," I promised.

"I will always love you." His eye looked into mine, a kiss understood between us despite our surroundings. Our hearts were one. Whatever lay ahead, we would meet it together.

Epilogue

Christmas 1955
Frankfurt am Main, Germany

Nestled against Rickard's shoulder, watching our daughters play with their grandpa, I sit quietly, cementing the memory permanently in my mind. All of us together—our parents, our children— celebrating Christmas morning. Miraculously, we all survived Hitler's curse on our country. Our parents were interrogated but not brutalized before being released to live as normally as possible through the war years, while Rick and I served the cause of freedom in England.

We were able to see Father Julian once before his trip to Rome soon after the Allies' victory. The children who had crossed the border with him were settled in foster homes where their natural talents thrived, and Father Julian made sure I was able to keep in touch with them through the years.

Josef works in a toy factory now, putting parts on the toys. The repetition doesn't bother him like it might someone else, and he takes great pride in his work.

Wilhelm has started divinity school, where his talent for leadership will be well appreciated, while Lara, who is teaching art classes, sells her own paintings at steadily increasing prices.

The twins are working for Eisen Steel. They have the strength of a Sherman tank. Together they have cleared ruins and brought back tons of steel to be recycled at the factory. I wonder if Gregor realizes his best workers are the very ones who bested him at Grafeneck Castle.

I'll never know what Heidi saw when she stared into Gregor's face that day at the castle. She says she doesn't remember. Gregor blamed his grandfather's death on the Resistance, claiming his grandfather protected him and kept him from being killed on the docks. Rickard says he was saving his reputation, but I prefer to think a part of him still valued Rick's friendship, since he refused to admit recognizing anyone involved. It worked out for him. Since the injury kept him from serving further in the SS, the Allies didn't question him after the war. We don't keep in touch with him, although our paths cross occasionally. Heidi is a journalist and freelance photographer. She says the camera is an extension of the mind's eye, but it seems to me she sees into a person's soul and brings the hidden self out in the film.

Rick and I came back to Frankfurt after the war, and he has worked with his English friend to expand Michael's father's export business into a well-known international entity, while I joined the Free Democratic Party. I decided I needed to have a hand in the government of the country in which my girls would grow up.

Grafeneck Castle is becoming a tourist attraction, one we never visit.

About the author...

Jennifer Childers lives in North Carolina with her husband and son. She has been 25 years in the medical profession, as well as a volunteer guardian *ad litem*, and has worked in child abuse prevention classes. President Bush, Sr., wrote her a letter of appreciation for this work.

Visit her at www.candaceblack.net

Thank you for purchasing
this Wild Rose Press publication.
For other wonderful stories of romance,
please visit our on-line bookstore at
www.thewildrosepress.com.

For questions or more information,
contact us at info@thewildrosepress.com.

The Wild Rose Press
www.TheWildRosePress.com

Other Vintage titles to enjoy...

SHE'S ME by Mimi Barbour: A spoilt model pricks her finger on a rose thorn and is transported back to 1963 and into a chubby librarian's body. As "roomies" they learn a lot from each other and each finds the man of her dreams.
HE'S HER by Mimi Barbour: Same rosebush, different victims! WE'RE ONE, #3 of the series, is coming soon.
SCHERESADE by Ronit Lèvy: Erika's new life in America is full of promise. So why have nightmares returned? A passionate young neurologist and an embittered Holocaust survivor help her follow the clues to unravel the mystery of her past and discover true love.
DON'T CALL ME DARLIN' by F Cunningham: In Texas, 1957, Carole the librarian faces censorship. Will the County Judge who's dating her protect or accuse her?
THE TROUBLE WITH PLAYBOYS by Margaret Tanner: In 1939 a wealthy young Englishman travels to Australia to find his birth mother and falls in love only to discover a horrible secret. He meets his love again in Singapore for a few brief weeks, just as the Japanese invasion begins, but then in the chaos of war each believes the other is dead.
SOURDOUGH RED by Pinkie Paranya: At the end of the Klondike gold rush, Jen and her younger brother search for her twin, lost and threatened in Alaskan wilderness.
A DAUGHTER'S PROMISE by Christine Clemetson: Serene Moneto risks her family and her freedom to give shelter and aid to an injured American soldier. But as he recuperates, Miles finds himself fighting to liberate Serene from a life worse than any death.
BAD BETTIE by Layne Blacque: In 1948 Los Angeles, a handsome cop's world is rearranged when his squad raids a nightclub and he rescues the sultry blues singer.
SOLILOQUY by Janet Fogg: A special birthday present brings more than Erin could ever have asked for as she is swept back in time and into the intrigue of the French Resistance. Will her wishes save her and her lover, or will she lose him forever?
SOMEWHERE IN NORTH AFRICA by Lindsay Downs: In Algeria, a beautiful Army nurse and a handsome Navy officer are thrown together, then separated by the misfortunes of war. Will they have a life together?

CPSIA information can be obtained at www.ICGtesting.com
Printed in the USA
LVOW01s1933081013

356011LV00029B/1051/P